WE SHOULD NOT HAVE COME HERE

A Novel

Written by

J. D. Mills

Book Cover Design by J. D. Mills

Developmental Editing by Alysha Thornton.

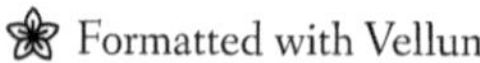 Formatted with Vellum

For Alyssa.
You would have loved this one, sister.

AUTHOR'S NOTE

There are few things I enjoy more than horror, though one of those is spending time with my loved ones. Earlier this year, in March of 2025, I lost my youngest sibling—my sister, Alyssa, to whom this book is dedicated. In fact, the loss hit right as I was working on the tail end of this novel.

As one can imagine, it was unimaginable to lose someone with whom I anticipated having decades more time with, who I envisioned taking part in my wedding one day, who had such a wonderful life ahead of her, and who was loved deeply and wholly. My family still hasn't recovered and, in many ways, I don't think we ever will.

Losing her had a profound effect on this story and the way that grief can change so much in such little time. I hope that she is proud of this story and that it's something she would have loved to read.

Thank you for giving We Should Not Have Come Here a chance, and for being part of this grief journey with me.We all have people and things that we lose throughout our lives, and the way in which we deal with that is incredibly personal. If you've endured such a loss yourself, you not only have my sympathies but also the knowledge that I am so proud of you for working to come out the other side of it. Grief is not something you overcome, but rather some you learn to live with. An impossible pain that sits atop your shoulders for eternity. Or, at least, that how it feels sometimes.

But, alas, it's the curse of humanity; to feel each loss like the gut punch it is.

Anyway, enough of my philosophizing.

Thanks again for diving into this book and for taking a chance to support an indie author. It means the world, and I am forever grateful.

Be afraid of what lurks in the dark...

CHAPTER ONE

A cool breeze scratched across the back of Ash's neck, as though the menacing fortress behind him had reached forward with its own pointed claws to taste his flesh.

"Are we rolling?" He asked, fidgeting with the last minute details of his outfit. The ends of his hair curled away from his face as it drifted down toward his shoulders, slightly covering his deep-set eyes. The two bright sapphires nestled against the rest of his dark features, casting chiseled shadows across the backdrop of his tanned complexion. The mix of Norwegian and Choctaw characteristics peppering his face was a puzzle, with each piece strategically placed and meticulously laser-cut.

Reddit threads and social media comment sections were full of users who fawned over the twenty-four-year-old's good looks and charisma. Despite the accuracy, no one on the team dared to feed into his ego by agreeing, as he was insufferable enough whenever the cameras came out. Now, in the midst of filming the opening shot for the newest episode of their ghost-hunting reality show, Ash wanted to ensure that everything would be *perfect*.

"Yeah, man, just go," Parker replied, annoyance tugging at his shoulders.

Parker was itching to move beyond Ash's incessant need to adjust his appearance for every take. They'd been up since the ass-crack of dawn, hauling their gear from the motel room into the van for the next location. After a crappy night's sleep—on one of the worst mattresses Parker had ever laid his head on—he was too tired to deal with his brother's dramatics. Especially not when they were in Hokisam, Oregon, surrounded by nothing but dense woodland and nary a shred of cell signal.

"That's what you said last time, and we completely missed the opening shot," Ash groaned. He was insistent that his attention to detail was what ensured they delivered a quality episode every time. "We botch the opening and there's no point in even—"

"For fuck's sake, Ash." Parker interrupted, rubbing the bridge of his nose with the length of his thumb. "If you don't start talking, I'm going to throw this camera. We're losing daylight here, not that you can really see it through those emo bangs."

Ash narrowed his eyes at Parker, shooting a dangerous glare that could've lit his brother on fire if he'd possessed pyrokinesis. Despite their nearly identical facial structure,

Parker's jet-black hair fell into two neat braids while his honey brown eyes warned Ash what would happen if he even dared to try. Yet, despite being the team perfectionist, Ash's jaw clenched. Despite all the years spent suffocating under their father's thumb, and growing up in a homophobic pressure-cooker, allowing anyone else to give him orders never went over well. The tail of his brow twinged as he made a mental note to soften the irritation coloring his features.

In most families, wishing spontaneous combustion upon your own sibling was probably considered a faux pas, but Ash didn't care. Parker had been screwing up his takes (at least, that's how Ash saw it) since they'd arrived at one of the country's most haunted relics: Crenshaw Castle. After spending a week in grimy clothes, enduring frigid showers with bad water pressure, and having to choke down coffee-flavored sludge every morning as he crammed into their van alongside his team, Ash was chomping at the bit to finish filming and grab a flight to the UK to be back in the arms of his boyfriend, Erick.

Ash's opposite in so many ways, Erick was kind and effortlessly stylish and smart—god, was he smart. They'd been forced to be long-distance while Erick worked on his PhD in Economics at the University of Manchester, much to Ash's chagrin. Currently on year two of their cross-continental relationship, it would be Ash's turn to visit once they were done shooting. That day couldn't come soon enough.

"Alright, then, cue the intro," Ash ordered, dreading

having to hear their incessant theme song through his monitor.

The entire *Phantom Files* team was on the ground, preparing for tonight's investigation: Ash (the lead investigator) and Parker Novak (secondary investigator, cameraman, and a slightly older, near-mirror image of Ash), Colt Pereira (secondary investigator and cameraman, alongside Parker), Embry Van Heerden (the video tech), and Rhett Broussard (the audio whiz). All of them, aside from Rhett, had been together since their show was created. Rhett's arrival was a network decision that followed the termination of their previous audio technician, who had pushed boundaries in the wrong direction.

After years of clawing their way out of the YouTube trenches, their ghost hunting reality show *Phantom Files* had finally earned them a seven-figure deal with the TerraX Network. And although they were about to film their first episode for their fifth season, Ash's heart just wasn't in it anymore. Filming had to go off without a hitch if they wanted to boost their viewership. They needed something to start this season off with a bang if they had any hope of holding onto their place as one of the channel's highest earners.

But as much as Ash wanted to quit, they only needed one more season to hit syndication—a milestone that would open doors to new revenue streams and give them the break Ash needed. All he had to do was get through this last season and he could walk away with his earnings and never look back.

"Count us down," Ash nodded, his pointed index finger making frustrated circular motions in the air.

Parker nodded and held up five fingers.

Then four... three... two...

As they stood in the courtyard of Crenshaw Castle, dark clouds in the sky began moving in quicker than the meteorologists on the local news channel had predicted. The dense forest stretched out behind Ash in a dozen shades of green, still and waiting. The wind blew through the leaves in a flurry, carrying with it a sharp chill and an ominous undercurrent. And their window to capture the opening monologue was shrinking. If they had any hope of getting their shot, they had to move fast.

Ash took a deep breath as his brother's finger pointed directly at him.

A signal.

Go time.

The fading light of golden hour glowing against his olive skin, Ash slowly stepped toward the camera and recited the lines he'd spent last night rehearsing. Every facial expression was carefully calculated, as was the intonation with which he spoke each word, to evoke the seriousness and solemnity required. Clearing his throat, he began.

"Nestled deep in the central Oregon wilderness is this

fifty-thousand square-foot structure, known colloquially as Crenshaw Castle."

Ash widened his arms to gesture behind himself at the looming complex, angling his chin to highlight the sharp jawline he was often complimented for. Parker and Colt panned their cameras to each capture a variation of their host's monologue, mitigating the chance that corrupt footage or malfunctioning camera equipment would derail their evening.

"We're here because we asked you, our dedicated fans, to tell us where we should go this season. We combed through thousands of social media posts and were shocked to find that Crenshaw Castle had evaded our radar all this time. For decades, visitors and groundskeepers have reported seeing strange apparitions and hearing unexplained footsteps in and around the premises of the institution. Now, they're inviting us—the very first paranormal team to be permitted to investigate this location —to step inside in hopes that we can provide answers. And tonight, *Phantom Files* is answering their call."

Taking a few steps, Ash glanced back at the campus' main structure before continuing.

"This hundred-and-fifty-year-old monstrous property, formally known as The Crenshaw Industrial Reformatory, sits on twenty-five acres of land and housed more than a thousand wards during the time of its operation," Ash continued. "The crimes committed here spanned decades, but the most gruesome period of its existence came at the hands of Archibald Elwood, one of Crenshaw's most menacing wardens. Acting as Headmaster to the hundreds of children who were sent here, Elwood had a reputation for the high rate of death and violence that occurred during his tenure. While we don't know exactly what happened to everyone who stepped through those doors from the time it opened in 1862 until its closure in 1989, what we do know is that this place is infamous for its acts of violence and abuse toward those who were in its care."

Ash lowered his voice and laced his fingers together.

Parker and Colt exchanged equally pained glances at Ash's melodrama.

As Ash's childhood-best-friend-slash-partner-in-crime, Colt was no stranger to his antics. In fact, it was precisely this flair for the dramatic that helped the two of them craft the initial idea for a ghost-hunting team in the first place. Growing up they spent their days playing in the same park, eating Brazilian food courtesy of Colt's mother, and watching episodes of *The Twilight Zone* together in Ash's basement.

The two of them had fallen into the world of the paranormal accidentally, nearly a decade ago. In high school, Ash and Colt had a YouTube channel, making up stupid skits and filming random acts of idiocy for views and subscribers. It became what they were known for. They ran around town with an air of earned popularity, even if what they were gaining acclaim for was what Ash's father called an 'embarrassment' and a 'colossal waste of time and energy.' It was their creative outlet, a place for themselves in the world. They'd created a safe haven where they could do something they loved without giving a damn about anyone else's criticisms.

One day, halfway through watching *The Blair Witch Project* in the shag-carpeted basement of the Novak family's house in North Falmouth, MA, an idea popped into teenaged Ash's head.

"We could do this," he'd said, pointing to the television screen.

"What do you mean?" Colt asked, leaning back on his hands.

"This," Ash jabbed toward the screen, twisting his body toward his best friend. "We could film a horror movie."

A burst of air forced its way through Colt's nostrils. "Yeah, okay," he said, eyes rolling up toward the ceiling.

"Look at the way they filmed this. There's no camera crew, no fancy lighting, no A-list celebrities."

Picking up the old school camcorder they'd pilfered from Colt's dad and hidden among the other curios on the cabinet shelf, Colt shook it at Ash as if it was pivotal to his argument. "No one believes this stuff is real when it's filmed on something like this."

"They absolutely do—*you* believed it was real!" Ash argued.

Colt shook his head. "I thought it was real 'cause it literally says it is in the opening credits!"

Ash waved him off. "You're getting off track. People believe in it because they *want* to believe it. It's about the story, the authenticity of it. They see randos walking around a forest with a camcorder and think *that could be me.* All we have to do is take some spooky old story that's been around a while and pretend we found evidence that the place is haunted or whatever."

Furrowed brows gave away Colt's hesitancy.

"Are you telling me you aren't capable of making something like this?" Ash pointed at the television.

"I didn't say *that*," Colt scoffed, hands raised in front of him.

"Okay, then I rest my case. We could do some spooky shit and make it seem like we found an *actually* haunted building. Bing, bang, boom, we're famous."

Colt had been there with him at the start of it all.

Back when they'd first filmed *The Spirits of Sheffield Farm*.

Their dinky hometown was a speck on a map, but it had plenty of its own creepy history ready to be exploited— starting with an old barn on the abandoned Sheffield farm where Trent Sheffield had brutally murdered his wife and two kids. It was notorious all across North Falmouth, and each of the three-thousand-some-odd residents were well-versed in the details. The farm was falling apart, left to rot for years and hardly visited aside from the occasional amateur ghost hunting team. In those rare cases, if one was paying attention, the faint shadows of people hauling cameras across the field at night could be seen under the moonlight.

The Sheffield Farm massacre was a few years after what had happened in Amityville, New York, and whispers among the God-fearing locals led many to believe that the

Sheffield tragedy had also been the work of the devil. That, somehow, whatever had possessed Ronald DeFeo Jr., had taken a bus across state lines and possessed the husband to wipe out his entire family. That event scarred the town and everyone in it like scorched earth.

That was back before *Phantom Files*, when they were known online as *The Ghost Gang*. It was just the two of them and a video camera from the nineties, but once they uploaded their first video to YouTube they became addicted to the dopamine hits from every like, comment, and subscriber notification. Not only had they exposed the world to their hometown horror, but they'd also revealed some hidden details to that local lore along the way. They'd spoken with a handful of people who'd known the family, people who had spent time in that house.

The deeper they dug, the more it seemed like Trenton Sheffield was not the man he seemed to be. There was a darkness in him. An unhinged anger lurking beneath the surface. Surprisingly, that's what their viewers were latching onto. Beyond the intrigue of demons and the occult, they found that people craved stories about the evil lurking within humanity. Well, that and the fact that they had an audience demographic that skewed heavily toward teenage girls who used the comment section to shoot their shot at Ash and Colt. Their 90s teen-heartthrob haircuts and thrifted outfits set them apart from their preppy, cookie-cutter classmates who would've rather died than not follow the latest trends. It gave them an edge—something to be known for.

And the world thought so, too.

That video went unbelievably viral—like, *thirteen million views in a week* viral.

Their overnight success turned into a consistent revenue stream that they monetized, pouring every cent back into their account's production value. Within a year, they'd amassed hundreds of thousands of subscribers and were travelling every weekend and school holiday to visit other haunted locations in the Northeast. With each video, they honed their skills and learned how to subvert their viewers' expectations. They also figured out that their ratings rose with the level of paranormal activity in each video. With a little ingenuity, Ash and Colt figured out how to use that to their advantage to fake the evidence they caught on camera with some post-production magic and special effects. They even invested some of their earnings into hiring an audio engineer to bring their vision to life.

With that success and a pair of high school diplomas under their belt, Ash was ready to get the hell out of his father's house and ready to build on their acclaim to turn it into something *real*. By the time Ash and Colt turned twenty-one, they'd surpassed a million subscribers online and even managed to bring an array of guests onto the show, from rapper Ivan Malcolm to social media icon Camille Lombard.

Not long after that, producers came knocking and the rest became history. Parker joined their team later on, after they'd made the move to join him out in Minnesota. Then Embry joined at the start of their first season, and finally

Rhett stepped in to round out their team. The show was dubbed *The Phantom Files* and it blew up overnight. It was the kind of instant career take-off that tended to happen the moment someone signed on the dotted line and sold their soul to the devil.

They'd become their own little motley crew of personalities that were all building toward the same shared dream of financial security. A dream that was within their grasp, so long as they continued to impress TerraX and their fans.

Now, at the site of a place where minors were sentenced for crimes and suffered beyond all belief, the pain they were sifting through wasn't their own—that memory felt a million miles away.

There was a stain blemishing this piece of yesteryear, a burn on the tapestry of history that torched the ground on which the sinister institution sat. It had been shuttered long ago, but the bodies of the wards who had lost their lives in untimely deaths on its premises still remained buried along the back side of the grounds.

"There's no doubt that this place is crawling with the tortured souls of those who have not yet been laid to rest," Ash continued. "And we won't leave until we have proof of the paranormal... here at Crenshaw Castle."

Ash held his position for a few moments, until Colt yelled, "Cut!" The red lights on the cameras blinked off.

"How was that?" He asked, with raised brows and an expectant curiosity. The only answers Ash would've accepted were *perfect, excellent,* or *pure genius.*

Instead, he got crickets.

After years of shooting these intros, they had it down to a science. Mostly because that's all it was—science. *Phantom Files* was formulaic in its approach, using strategy rather than relying on the existence (or lack thereof) of the supernatural. Ghosts and ghouls and spooky shadows were fodder for the kids at Halloween, as far as they were concerned. Sure, they played the game and bought into it for the sake of making sure their audience believed their antics to be reality, but at the heart of it the show was a farce. It was all smoke and mirrors, designed to appear real and keep the seams as imperceptible as possible. What mattered at the end of the day was the paycheck.

"Great, I think we're ready to move on to some interior shots," Colt concluded as he shut off his camera and lowered it to the side of his body. A hand raked through his chin-length, bleached blonde hair. "I'm going to grab a new memory card and I'll meet you guys inside." Turning on his heel, he headed for the tall, menacing front doors.

The grounds sprawled within the boundaries of the property, tucked between the edges of forest so dense that all light was lost within it. The institution's campus consisted of half a dozen buildings, each with their own purpose, but the largest was their investigation's primary target. Its combination of stone and brick had blackened over time, partially hidden by looping ivy and the roots of overgrown vegetation.

As Colt plowed toward the mouth of it, something inside Ash burned white-hot.

"The pause at the end was a beat too long, but we aren't reshooting it, so don't even ask," Parker added. "Luckily, it works real well with that broody look you got going on."

A quick glance at his phone put a sour look on Ash's face as he roughly shoved it deeper into his pocket. Cell reception was spotty at best, but his phone had been going off intermittently for the past two days, a mix of text messages and phone calls, but he'd refused to answer any of them.

Parker spotted the words 'LUTHER - IGNORE' flash across his brother's phone screen and understood why Ash seemed more on edge than usual. Tucking his camera under his arm, he pulled Ash aside.

"Are you going to answer that?" He asked.

"What happened to 'we're wasting daylight'?" Ash mocked with fingers bent into air quotations. He turned to walk past his brother, but Parker stopped him with a hand placed calmly at the center of Ash's chest.

"Dad's the one blowing up your phone, right?" Parker asked, though it came out in more of a matter-of-fact statement than a question.

Shrugging, Ash replied. "Doesn't matter. We've got more important things going on," he said, gesturing at the deteriorating fortress ahead of them.

"He told me he's been trying to get in touch with you for a while."

"Yeah, and?"

"*And,*" Parker emphasized. "Maybe he wants to apologize."

"That ship sailed a long ass time ago," Ash scoffed.

"That might be true, but people can change," Parker argued.

"Not him," Ash dismissed. "He's incapable of admitting fault in any aspect of his life. If he wanted a relationship with me that didn't revolve around treating me like I was the biggest mistake he ever made, then he should've thought about that twenty years ago."

"He's been asking me about you, y'know. Wants to know how you're doing, how the show's been going."

"Of course he wants to know. Now that we're successful, I'm sure he just wants to glom on."

"He's different. Truly. He even invited us to come visit him next time we're in Mass—"

"I'm never going back there," Ash interrupted with a simple shake of his head. "You're free to do whatever you want, but I have no interest in going home or seeing him."

"Hang on," Parker interjected.

"No, I'm done talking—" Ash argued, pushing past his brother, heading towards the entrance.

"Ash, hold up for a minute," Parker insisted, physically stopping Ash with a raised hand pressed against his chest.

But Ash didn't want to hear it. He'd faced enough heartache in his life to put up with any more. He'd only been eight years old when their mother, Yvette, had left in the middle of the night without warning. When their father's private investigator finally tracked her down, they found out she was living in a tiny town in Arkansas. She'd changed her name, dropped out of contact with everyone she'd ever known, and started over with a new family—complete with a shiny new man and a set of twins that looked like carbon copies of her. It wasn't that she hadn't wanted a family, it was that she hadn't wanted *their* family.

That was the first time Ash had ever felt unwanted in the depths of his bones.

"Clearly dad hasn't gotten the message that you don't want to have a relationship with him."

"You'd think he would figure it out, considering I haven't answered his calls, texts, emails, or carrier pigeons," Ash scoffed.

"I know this shit is hard, but you can't just keep bottling your feelings and pushing them further down."

"Easy for you to say, from up there on your heterosexual high horse. You never had dad chase your boyfriend away from the house with a baseball bat while loudly yelling slurs for all the neighbors to hear."

"No, I didn't. But living there wasn't a cakewalk for me either."

"Then why are you pushing this so hard?"

"I just know that you can't keep getting angry every time his name comes up on the screen. It's not healthy. So... go see a therapist, hash it out with dad, get a puppy you can dote on—do *something* other than getting angry every time his name comes up."

Forced into single fatherhood, Luther Novak failed to rise to the occasion. He was a cardiologist at Boston General Medical Center, and spent more time in the city for work and pleasure than he did at home with his kids. It wasn't all that surprising to those who knew him, though. He'd only had kids because it was expected of him; two-point-five kids, a three-bedroom house, and a white picket fence. What he'd ended up with were two 'ungrateful' children, an ex-wife who couldn't be bothered to send a birthday card, and a house he hated spending time in because it reminded him of all the ways in which his life wasn't what he wanted it to be. Time spent at home started to require a spiked BAC. He stopped noticing when Parker wasn't around, and emotionally detached from Ash entirely.

Ash just stared at Parker, fiery eyes narrowing as his despondency melted into fury. "Fuck all the way off," he spat through clenched teeth, shoulder-checking Parker and heading straight for the doors of the institution.

Parker reached out for his little brother and grabbed his arm as he moved past. "Ash, wait—"

Grabbing Parker's hand as it landed on his arm, Ash pulled it off of him like a tick.

"No, I'm sick of you acting like I don't have a right to be pissed off!" Ash barked. "You know exactly how he treated me in that house. You got to leave and never look back. Why can't I do the same? I don't owe that man a goddamned thing." He wanted to add, *or you,* to that statement, but even Ash knew that part wouldn't have been true. With that, he yanked his arm out of Parker's grip and headed across the courtyard.

CHAPTER TWO

R hett Broussard had joined *Phantom Files* at the start of season four, on a referral from their production company following the departure of their previous sound engineer. Having freelanced on other projects, she was familiar with this style of docu-tainment. There would always be industry problems that rolled over onto the production of the show—budget limitations on replacing equipment, strict filming schedules, and non-negotiable appearances in mind-numbing meetings —but those were secondary to the issues that came up when working with a close-knit cast.

Or, at least, what she *assumed* was a close-knit cast.

The rapport amongst the other cast members left her feeling singled out from their first meeting. Even now, a season with them under her belt, Rhett was still the newbie on the outside looking in. There were times when Rhett could do nothing else but keep her mouth shut, flying under the radar in order to keep her job. Those feelings were exacerbated when it came to personal ethical conflicts. The rest of the team was perfectly content to make jokes about spirits of the deceased, and even to use aggressive tactics in the name of entertainment, but how far was too far?

Rhett sighed, pulling off her headphones entirely and setting them on the desk beside her. She'd kept her past to herself for a long time, for fear that she'd somehow reopen those old scars and that *Phantom Files* would be cursed just like her family had been. Little good it would do to dig up the skeletons of the past and parade them around, taunting the universe into doubling down on its fury. Instead, her silence was a desperate plea for protection.

Having grown up in an area that revered and respected history and those who had passed on, Rhett believed the team's approach to be reckless. Prioritizing a means to an end that didn't involve respect for the dead, but rather an exploitation of them, was Rhett's biggest complaint when it came to how *Phantom Files* approached the paranormal. They all needed their paychecks to survive, but this was a line they shouldn't be crossing.

Rather than voicing her concerns, though, she kept silent. While Rhett was no stranger to speaking up and making sure her voice was heard, she couldn't reconcile the idea of standing up against these industry darlings and risking her paycheck. That definitely wasn't in her best interest. Not when she was holding out for bigger and better projects. Her secret hope was that once the executives at TerraX Network decided they were done pandering to the masses with ridiculous ghost hunting shows, they'd transfer her to another production.

She often wondered how the *Phantom Files* crew could just waltz into a place and balk at a belief in the paranormal, acting as though those who believed were childish or silly. Growing up within throwing distance of the French Quarter, Rhett was no stranger to spooky sightings and the spirit realm. There was a part of her that took this job to maintain a connection to that part of her life, the part that longed to uncover the mysteries of the unknown.

Once she was in, though, it was clear that *Phantom Files* was anything but legitimate. They'd made their name hocking fake experiences in the name of 'reality' without any intention of taking it seriously. A mockery, that's what it was to Rhett. But she needed the money and the name recognition from this production. It was a means to an end that would get her far away from *Phantom Files* and on to productions that mattered.

Fast forwarding to the present day, the team was trying to keep up with the increasing demands as their careers snowballed. With four seasons of a hit reality show, merch, a subreddit dedicated to them, and millions of followers on their social media accounts, success was a never ending fountain of opportunities and cash money. Licensing agreements, talk show circuits, book deals—anything they could ever want was presented to them on a silver platter. That is, until new ghost-hunting shows cropped up and started to take over the lime light. Now the team had to prove that season five could make up for the heavy dip in ratings seen from season four.

But if it had been up to Rhett, they would've packed it in and called it quits.

The only thing keeping her there anymore was the paycheck.

If the rest of the team wanted to continue playing with fire, taunting things they didn't understand, she'd have no problem letting karma do its job.

The end of autumn had brought with it the cold and the rain, drowning the sole, lonely road into or out of Hokisam. It created a natural isolation in the area, as though the landscape was closing in on itself to keep outsiders from crossing its threshold. Luckily, it had been dry the past two days, so their rental van had been able to make the journey out to Crenshaw without getting stuck in muddy trenches. Where they expected to see warm, earth-toned leaves adorning the trees, but everything just looked *dead*. As far as the eye could see, once-thriving foliage lay mangled and decomposing. The few remaining leaves had turned black, like the greenery was rotting in real time.

Still in the midst of setting up her station, Rhett's eyes scanned her computer screen as she booted up all of the audio software. Each active microphone connected to the system via a transmitter, and they appeared on her screen with their specific labels to identify which team member they belonged to.

Strangely, Ash's mic wasn't on her radar.

Grabbing her Walkie-Talkie, she pressed the large side button to open the channel.

"Ash," he confirmed. "What's up?"

"Your mic isn't connecting to the system," Rhett replied. "Did you shut it off after you filmed the intro?"

"No? It must've just died," he sighed, his tone then shifting to an accusatory one. "Why didn't you swap the batteries in my mic pack?"

"I just put fresh ones in before we started filmin' the intro," Rhett argued, the Creole intonation of her Louisiana accent weaving through her words. "Ain't no way those should'a been drained already."

"The lights won't come back on." Ash sighed, rapping his knuckles against the device a few times while his finger held down the button to keep the line open.

"There could be a short somewhere in the cord," she offered, despite thinking it was unlikely.

Irritated that he'd have to unclip the lavalier microphone hidden at the neck of his shirt to double check that the cord was still fully connected to the USB-powered transmitter in his back pocket, Ash sighed.

"Come on, Rhett. Just admit you didn't do the pre-production prep," he fired back through the Walkie-Talkie.

Her blood was boiling at his accusation.

As if *she* wasn't going to do her job properly? *Bullshit.*

Now, with their future resting on the shoulders of season five, the pressure was worse than ever before.

"Excuse me? You—" Rhett cut herself off and sighed forcefully into the open channel.

Rhett knew that Ash's biggest pet peeve was feeling unprepared, or rather that his team wasn't ready for the tasks of the day. As if he thought that the quality of their work, regardless of the subject matter, was something the rest of them weren't taking seriously. Sure, she knew that he was a skeptic, but she did appreciate his belief in the power of producing the best content they could and earning the paychecks that afforded them their livelihoods. It was clear to her that Ash was fighting for the show's future. What she *didn't* appreciate, though, was his attitude.

Especially after shooting their last season had almost disbanded them entirely.

CHAPTER THREE

WELCOME TO

HAUNTCAST

WELCOME TO HAUNTCAST

The premier forum for discussions on hauntings, possessions, demonic symbolism, and more.

Posted *6 months ago* by *phantomfan97*

HAS ANYONE ELSE NOTICED THE WEIRD TENSION BETWEEN THE CREW IN RECENT EPISODES?

NIGHTWALKER:
Oh yeah, it was bad. I
remember seeing some videos
posted online during filming,
supposedly by a former crew
member (who later got fired, I
think). Heard they almost
didn't get a renewal for a
fifth season 😬

COUNTERSTRIKEROPS:
Yeah but they did, it's gonna
start filming soon

ASSISTANTTOTHEVAMPIRE:
Source?

COUNTERSTRIKEROPS
www.kctv7.com/news/phantom-
files-earns-new-season-
despite-controversial-fourth-
season-and-lead-investigator-
threatening-to-quit

XO_MSHORROR_XO:
The magic of PF is gone ngl

TARTARBINKS:
I SWEAR I thought Ash was
gonna bean Colt with his radio
in 04x07!

CYGNUSWOLFOWL:

Seems like the team is falling
apart, so I doubt it'll keep
going the way it has been. The
brothers will probably stay
together, but I bet we'll see
a shake-up in the crew.

THE-GENERAL-MUSTARD:

Idk tbh I think they're done.
Doesn't seem like they enjoy
it anymore?

MOTHER_RASCAL:

WHAT A JOKE 😂 I'm done
watching this trash

VICTORLAMBDARHO:

Did you check out any of their
social media lately? Ash
posted about the team being
'kidnapped' to some middle-of-
nowhere cabin and that they'd
be off grid for a week. Could
be some kind of reality check
from their management.

JILLIANMCPHERS4:

Sounds like some forced family
fun lol

COTT-THE-ANGLER:

More like a hellscape lmao

CAPTAINPOTATOHEAD:

He updated again! They're back
online. If you check the
TerraX socials, they posted a
teaser for season five!

NOTSOCREEPYXX:

Wow, everybody's so cynical! Yeah they seem a little off lately, but I think it's just growing pains. Every show has their off seasons, and it's gotta be rough spending so much time living and working with your coworkers. Cut them a break!

CHAPTER FOUR

"Bring it back and I'll swap 'em out before you start the interview," she conceded through gritted teeth.

"Copy," Ash grumbled.

Then the line went silent.

On the lower level of the sinister gothic structure, the team had secured an old administrative office as their control center and equipment locker. The frigid interior was oddly colder inside than it was outside. Rhett could hear Ash's footsteps as they echoed through the thick air, bouncing off the walls and tall ceilings until he stepped through the open doorway of their command center.

Folding tables had been set up as workspaces side-by-side for Rhett and Embry. Each of them had a dedicated computer with monitors for the camera feeds and audio software to monitor sound levels and mic statuses. Wires and cables zig-zagged around the room, converging along the back wall to slither out a cracked window and connect to the generator outside. The room was warm thanks to the piles of electronics that were buzzing like cicadas, filling the room with an oscillating thrum.

Behind her computer, Rhett was seated in a folding chair, focused on connecting all of her power cords and setting up her station in precisely the way she preferred. Ash leaned against the door jamb with a crooked grin tugging at the corner of his mouth, observing her.

"Hey Rhett, catch!" He interrupted.

She looked up just in time to catch the device, mere seconds before it smashed into her keyboard, eyes wide and fiery.

"What the fuck, Ash?" She spat. "Do you have any idea how much these are worth?" Her dark eyes glowered at him. The back of her throat burned as the anger seethed. White-hot tension in her shoulders screamed. Squeezing the Walkie-Talkie tightly in her grasp, Rhett took a deep breath to reassess and walk back her initial anger. "Break shit on your own time, when we don't have to justify every cent spent on equipment procurement forms."

It was always a mistake to cross Rhett, especially when she was clearly stressed out.

A mistake Ash had made not once but thrice already that week.

Not for want of driving her up a wall, he'd tried to explain, but because she was so easily riled up in the first place.

Ash laughed and threw his hands up in surrender. "My

bad, just trying to keep you on your toes. Real fast reflexes though, Broussard. Color me impressed."

Before they'd been on TerraX's payroll, back when they were the only ones calling the shots, it didn't matter how many mic packs they went through. The repercussions were nil. Now, with their production company breathing down their neck about the budget, they had to be careful. If they didn't come in under-budget, there would be cuts elsewhere —like fewer episodes in the season or shittier hotels booked at other locations.

"Watch it, Novak," Rhett grumbled, taking out the batteries and putting them into the tester to double check them.

Dead. Dead. Dead.

Eyebrows furrowed, a mumbled "weird" escaped her and she leaned back in her chair to reach for a bag of spare double-As. If she'd speculated about the cause, she kept those thoughts to herself.

Rhett's fingers nimbly swapped out the batteries like she was on a miniature NASCAR pit team. The muscle memory kicked in as she worked, tossing the spent batteries into an open plastic bag at her feet.

The sun would fall beneath the horizon in just a few hours, according to the digital LED clock on one of the tables, and that would completely screw up their schedule. They were running out of time. Soon they'd have to suffer through the setup of this behemoth location with just flashlights, a few worklamps, and the night vision mode on their cameras that would give everything a grey overlay.

Doable, yes, but a definite pain in the ass. Working at night was standard procedure in their line of work, sure, but it came with its own complications. There were higher risks for injury, the greater chance of losing something and it never being found again, and even the slim possibility of being caught off guard by squatters (again).

"Ash!" Parker yelled from out of sight, his voice carrying from the foyer where he and Colt were getting the rest of the equipment ready to begin the interview portion of the episode. "We need to start if we want to get the walk-through done before dusk! Move your ass!"

"Shit," Ash hissed. "Coming!"

"Here. Go." She tossed the mic pack back to Ash and returned her focus to the monitor without another word.

"Great talk," he teased. "Thanks, Rhett, you saved me once again." Cheekily grinning at her before taking off, Ash patted the door frame firmly and then took out of the room at a slow jog toward the main entryway.

Part of her hoped his arrogant skepticism would be a magnet for the underworld and that that the ground would split apart and swallow him whole.

"Dumbass," Rhett whispered under her breath.

Embry laughed, catching only the last word as she rounded the corner and through the door. Her strawberry blonde hair coiffed into a messy mullet that fell past her shoulders. Freckles sprinkled across her face in unique constellations. Eyes glinting in the light as her gaze met Rhett's, she folded one leg over the other as she took her seat.

"Which one, Colt or Ash?" she asked.

"Ash," Rhett grumbled.

"Don't let him get under your skin," Embry advised. "He's got a lot of shit pent-up, but he means well."

Huffing in disbelief, Rhett rested her chin on her palm and returned her attention to the computer screen.

Pulling out her phone, Embry typed out a text to her girlfriend to update her on the trip and the fact that she wasn't entirely sure they weren't going to kill each other by the end of it.

"Delivery failed? Ugh," Embry's eyes threatened to roll into the back of her head in frustration. "Great, this dump has shotty cell signal. Love that for me." Pocketing her phone, she sighed and ran her tongue along the ridges of her teeth. "Sorry, Devi, you'll have to wait to see if I make it out of here alive," she muttered to herself.

In the simplest of terms, Devi was a worrier.

In more elaborate terms, she was the type to call a dozen embassies across Europe when her girlfriend failed to let her know that she was safe and sound after an excursion to a remote island off the coast of Spain.

Embry loved Devi more than anyone else in her world, but Embry was a historically—and chronically—bad communicator. Not because she didn't care, but rather because she hyper-focused on what was in front of her. This often led to disagreements between the two of them, as well as between Embry and her coworkers on *Phantom Files*. She'd walk off without so much as a word to anyone, not giving a second of thought to how that might impact the others. In some ways, she wished she could be more like Devi and think about others before she did things. Then again, it relieved her of the burden of constant worry and overthinking.

A double-edged sword primed for swallowing.

CHAPTER FIVE

The key to a successful episode was setting up the background information so that the frights would land. Letting viewers in on the secrets buried beneath the location, and the history of those who once walked its halls, was key. That was the nail in the coffin, convincing them that what they were about to see was real.

Stomping footsteps rang out as Ash jogged over to where Parker and Colt were waiting. The stationary camera was already set up for the main interview, and two portable cameras were ready for the walk-through. The building was damp and drafty, the remaining daylight only streaking in through crusty, high windows and the open front doors. It was as if the premises had a moratorium on everything bright and airy, blocking out as much light as possible with brick and stone.

Even the furnishings and leftover decor from decades

past were more or less untouched, aside from bits of graffiti and water damage. Soggy pillows covered in a layer of god-knows-what were flopped against each other on a tattered, floral sofa. Velvet paintings still clung to the wall, shades of white and green crawling in from the corners like moldy spiders. Broken lamps littered the floor, their bases shattered while the shades twisted and contorted into ungodly shapes. An old sideboard sat against a far wall, slumped in the center as though a mysterious weight had overstressed the wood to the point of no return. The room—the entire place—was a shrine to a world long since lost to time.

The red light on Colt's camera glowed angrily as he turned on the LED light panel mounted atop it.

"Who's got the Spirit Box?" Ash asked, hand raised to block as much of the panel's light as he could. "We should film some EVP sessions around the place and then Rhett can splice those in later to fill any activity gaps."

Parker flipped the camera around and centered himself in the frame.

"For those of you who are new to *Phantom Files*," he began. "An EVP is an electronic voice phenomenon or, in other words, spirit voices communicating on frequencies that we can't hear with our own ears."

There was a mathematical aspect to their production that accompanied the science. In order to retain their audience, and build it at a steady incline, they relied on an algorithm to determine when activity bursts had to happen between the more informative moments. Those were key, at least from the TerraX Network's point of view, but it also wouldn't be nearly as entertaining for viewers if there wasn't enough of the spooky shit.

Faking electronic voice phenomenon was one of the easiest parts of their post-production process. Some mics, a script, and sound modulation software were all it took to convince four seasons worth of an audience that they actually heard disembodied voices in the places they visited. It didn't take much to fake the 'proof' that *Phantom Files* gathered from the haunted locations they visited.

There were a few times that they'd been criticized online for scripting their show, or for inserting special effects noises in lieu of actual paranormal evidence. Of course, they never responded outright to these claims. There was no upside to that. Instead, they waited for their loyal fanbase to go rabid in their defense.

It was truly a win-win.

Ironically, Crenshaw Castle had been highly requested by their fans for years. But it wasn't until recently that someone at the Schuyler Foundation—the deep-pocketed organization in charge of maintaining the property and controlling its funds and future—had contacted their manager, Camden, about having *Phantom Files* film an episode there. The details, as they had been relayed to the team, were fuzzy. Cam had been vague about exactly *why* the folks at Schuyler wanted them there, or whether it was a payoff or something equally shady, but somehow they'd gotten the scoop that no one else had.

Phantom Files was about to make history.

The folks at Schuyler played it close to the vest when it came to their financial ventures, and there was little to be found online when Parker had done his initial search. It was clear that they'd been around for quite a while, but that was it. However, as they dug into the board members, there were family names that traced back to the origins of the institution. Descendants of every former headmaster, previous staff members, and even a several-great grandchild of the original landowner who had sold the property to develop the reformatory in the first place. The connections felt important, but what they couldn't piece together was the relevance of it all. Even stranger was the fact that a caretaker was on the board, but that they weren't able to track down a crumb of verifiable information about her identity outside of being named in Foundation documents.

Their search left each of the *Phantom Files* team members with one question in their minds: *who is Maura Barton?*

Fortunately, they were planning to find out.

Parker reached into his back pocket and pulled out a Spirit Box SB7 Pro, extending its antenna before handing it off to Ash. The black plastic was no worse for wear despite having endured years of abuse in the form of ankle-deep puddles, two-story drops, and accidental spaghetti sauce submersions (that one was Colt's fault). Its job was to sweep various FM radio frequencies at a high speed and provide a source of energy for spirits to communicate with the living. At least, that was what it was *supposed* to do. For *Phantom Files*, it was just an expensive white noise machine that could easily be mistaken for a walkie talkie if someone wasn't paying attention to what they were grabbing off of the equipment table.

The red backlit screen fired up, and Ash's slender fingers moved to the volume knob to silence it. Part of their process involved opening equipment-heavy shots with a brief explanation of what they were doing for the audience.

"Ready?" he asked.

Colt and Parker nodded in sync, eyes flicking between their camera screens and him.

Ash took a beat then launched into his spiel.

"We're now standing in the lobby of Crenshaw Castle, where even the remnants of furniture and discarded pieces of its history are symbols of the decades of decay this place has experienced." His solemn expression was an excellent smokeshield, concealing the fact that he didn't have a crumb of concern for those that had once lived and died on this property. "In an effort to connect with those who have not yet crossed over, we'll be using this," he continued, holding up the Spirit Box for the camera to focus on, "to communicate with the spirits who remain here."

Buzzing and hissing whined out of the device's small speaker as it came alive, reverberating off of everything in its path like a bouncy rubber Super Ball that had been thrown by a major league pitcher. It continued to whir in his hand, a slew of nonsensical sounds blasting out of it as it quickly scanned through radio channels.

After a few seconds, Ash threw on a shocked face and reacted as though he'd just heard something. "Oh my god!"

he exclaimed, panic shredding his voice in just the way he'd rehearsed. Despite the years spent doing this professionally, his perfectionist streak required him to nail down every angle of his facial expression and body language. "Did you hear that?" Swiveling toward his fellow ghosthunters, it was their cue to jump in.

"Whoa! What the hell was that?" Colt shrieked, his own shock and awe adding a layer of believability. "That sounded like a little kid!"

Parker's camera twitched from Ash to Colt, the latter man's camera then moving to point back at him.

"Did the voice say 'help me'?" Parker asked, as Colt's frame momentarily zoomed into his face.

This was the way their little ruse worked.

They'd feed in little tidbits of things they'd learned through their research, and then Rhett and Embry would work their magic and make it seem like they'd truly heard voices coming through the Spirit Box. They'd do this for a litany of things that couldn't be reproduced in the moment, unlike footsteps or other sounds that could ring out from hidden speakers or lights strategically placed to mimic spirit activity. By the end, they'd have what looked—to the untrained eye, at least—like proof of paranormal activity. It was foolproof.

"That's a Grade A EVP," Ash explained. "We've never captured something that clear from a Spirit Box session before. It seems like the spirits here really want to communicate with us, that's a great sign."

Reaching into his pocket, Parker pulled out a small

remote control and pressed the large circular button on its face. The silent detonator for their next trick. Above them, three distinct knocks came from nowhere. Well, *almost* nowhere.

The three of them jumped back, shoulders jerking as they pretended to hear a disembodied voice sail down the hallway. The cameras zoomed and panned to capture each of their faces in some way or another. Bright lights from atop the cameras reflected in every direction, glinting off of the metal zippers of their jackets and the rings adorning half of Ash's fingers.

A mixture of horror and actual fear was what usually sold their reactions, though sometimes it was harder to connect to those primal feelings of abject terror.

That's where rehearsals came in handy.

Although Ash's dreams of fame were focused on the dollar signs rather than a star on the Hollywood walk of Fame, Colt had always wanted to be an actor. When he and Ash were kids, Colt would memorize the lines from his favorite movies and recite them as they watched, doing his best to match the cadence and emotion of the actors on the screen. In high school, he became entranced with theater and was in nearly every play—even when Ash teased him relentlessly for it. He'd even played Willy Lowman in the spring production of *Death of a Salesman* in their junior year. Colt was a powerhouse, but Ash had always been secretly embarrassed by his friend's affiliation with what he considered to be the biggest dork club on campus.

Yet, they'd both ended up here, on national television.

After twenty minutes of their charade, they called their footage of the lobby sufficient. It wasn't one of the most-haunted rooms in the fortress, and there were other areas they wanted to spend ample time in. Based on their research, they'd compiled a list of rooms to check out, including a few that Parker had noted as being the setting for some especially gruesome acts, and some that were purely points of interest (like the atrium and the infirmary). Hangings, stabbings, drownings, and defenestration had all occurred on the property. Colt, specifically, had a thing for morgues, but the lack of one mentioned in the blueprints meant he wouldn't be investigating one on this property. The rest of the high-activity rooms, however, were all pretty standard *Phantom Files* fodder. With a bit of expert lighting, any room could be made to appear as creepy as a tomb.

This place just needed a little less help.

CHAPTER SIX

Fans of *Phantom Files*, most of whom would never get a chance to explore these places themselves, were always interested in seeing locations as up close and personal as possible. A cohort of their most dedicated die-hard fans were known to get into a little light trespassing to visit the destinations from their most popular episodes—for whatever reason, the rusty door hinges and moldy wallpaper really did it for them—but they were few in numbers. However, for the majority of their audience, the interviews and backstory were what drew them in the most.

The real life encounters and the storytelling were what kept fans watching, awake at all hours of the night in the comment sections of their favorite social media platforms. Interviews were what connected the fans to the history of the tormented spirits and made it all feel real. And at the end of the day, if you want to fake a haunting, you have to draw on the experiences of real people—even if they've imagined those ghosts to begin with.

Once they'd reset from filming their EVP session, the three of them returned to the foyer to meet up with their guest for the episode: Maura Barton, herself.

"Test, one, two, testing Interview Lav Two," Parker said into the secondary lavalier microphone, before speaking into his radio. "You got that, Rhett?"

"Good to go," she signaled over the radio.

With a nod, Parker clipped his radio to his back pocket and pinned the mic onto their interviewee.

"Alright, Barton's all set," he confirmed into his radio.

While the episode was intended to create buzz around the property as a tourist attraction, the Schuyler Foundation had established limitations around where the team was allowed to film. Initially they had wanted to close off the entire fourth floor, but that was a no-go. TerraX had done backflips to ensure that *Phantom Files* had unadulterated access to the entire property for the lockdown.

Ironically, despite their difficulty in identifying who *exactly* Maura Barton was, getting in contact with her directly was the easiest part of the entire process. Maura had agreed to be interviewed under one condition, though: no personal questions. Given that the interview was only about Crenshaw Castle itself, none of them had batted an eye at her request to keep her personal life private.

As Ash sauntered over to them and flashed a winning smile that looked like it was made of luminous ceramic. "It's Maura, right?"

The thin woman nodded meekly, her hands gingerly clasped together as the billowy sleeves of her navy blue cardigan hung off of her like drapery.

It was most likely the first time the elderly woman had been in front of a camera, given the nervous energy that surrounded her. Her knit cardigan, buttoned only once at the top, sat carefully over a pressed salmon blouse. It's lace collar peeked out at her neck, highlighting an antique golden locket that rested against her chest. Pressed trousers hung down to meet glossy, patent-leather loafers that had been carefully shined. Her presence was quiet, but the way she was so put-together yielded a calm confidence surging beneath her turbulent exterior.

"Great to meet you." He reached out a hand to grasp hers, and the clamminess led to instant regret. "I'm Ash Novak, I'll be interviewing you today. Thanks so much for agreeing to be part of the episode."

The wrinkles at the corners of her eyes softened as she shook his hand.

As subtly as possible, Ash slid the damp palm of his hand along the thigh of his pants.

"Oh, yes, of course." Maura smiled quietly, her voice a squeak above a librarian's scolding. "I've actually seen the show, and I'm quite the fan of your work. You know, I'm surprised it's taken so long for you to visit this property, you see we've..."

Her words trailed off as Ash studied her face, features almost blurring together against the soft creases in the landscape of her skin. Maura reminded him of his grandmother, in a way. The one whose house had always smelled like fresh-baked gingersnaps and who never left home without a bottle of hand sanitizer in her purse. Kind eyes behind round-rimmed glasses with thin frames perched gently on her nose. The mother of his wretch of a father—god, why couldn't his father have been more like her instead of a raging asshole?

Before he knew it, his gaze had wandered past their interaction and he was absently staring at the rest of the room behind her.

"It really is a beautiful property, isn't it?" Maura asked, catching Ash's wandering eyes and assuming he was admiring all of the old artwork and furniture that dotted the first floor.

"Yeah, it's very..." The words caught as his gaze landed on a haunting portrait of Headmaster Elwood, barely hanging on to the stained, wallpaper-covered wall. Standing tall, and wearing what looked like military regalia, he held one arm in front of himself while the other was bent behind his back. Two cold eyes stared back through the layers of dust and grime, piercing through time in an ornate brass frame. Ash swallowed hard before turning back to Maura, putting on his best face and a thousand dollar smile. "It's lovely."

"Ready, Ash?" Parker asked with a raised brow.

Taking a few seconds to quickly fix his hair and ensure that nothing was out of place, Ash nodded. His vanity was never the cause for a scene's reshoot, despite the never ending amount of jokes at his expense.

"Rolling!" Colt shouted—the one word that would keep any one of them from making a sound. Eyes glued to the flipped-out LCD screen on the side of his camera, he adjusted the zoom, perfectly framing the two of them in front of the once-grand front room.

"We're here with Maura Barton, the acting caretaker for the Crenshaw Industrial Reformatory's grounds and board member for the Schuyler Foundation." Ash started, turning toward their guest. "So, tell us, how long have you been working here, Maura?"

"Well, I believe it's been... oh, just about thirty-three years now." Her hands hung at her sides, an odd aura of comfort surrounding her as she spoke, as if this place was home.

"Can you clarify for us why you choose to work here? In most cases, we find that board members don't tend to have boots on the ground, so to speak."

Maura's eyes continued to scan the room, looking everywhere but at Ash.

"This place has felt like home for as long as I can remember," she hummed. "I grew up in town and my father worked here, his father before him. I always knew I'd end up here, too."

"And what is it that you do here in your capacity as caretaker?"

"I oversee the groundskeepers to ensure that the property is taken care of, and I'm on the Board of Trustees that manages the property as part of the Schuyler Foundation." Maura cleared her throat into a balled up tissue. "And, of course, I take on additional responsibilities as needed."

Ash couldn't help but figure that this interview was one of her *additional responsibilities.*

Forty-some-odd years ago, they'd started doing tours there; at some point during her tenure with Crenshaw, Maura had taken over responsibility for coordinating them. They'd allowed anyone to buy a ticket and explore the place at their own discretion—the first three floors, anyway. The fourth floor, including the Headmaster's quarters, was always blocked off to keep visitors out. It was said that there were structural issues on the top floor, that it wasn't safe to walk around up there. Parker's research, however, never uncovered any documentation to prove it. And with no paper trail to keep them out, *Phantom Files* had pushed their way through to ensure that the fourth floor was fair game for filming.

Ash nodded. "In your thirty-three years of looking after the Castle, has there been a history of unexplained activity?" His hands clasped together, fingers interlocking pensively. "Any instances of staff being harmed or experiencing anything strange?"

"Oh... unfortunately, yes," Maura answered with a solemn nod, as if she's been dreading this question. "We've had complaints of cold spots in areas of the estate that are historically well-insulated, unexplained scratches and bruises, and strange sounds like footsteps and knocking that don't appear to have a rational cause."

Ash waited a beat, gave a hand signal to let Parker and

Colt know to cut the cameras, and then turned back to Maura.

"Okay, so that's a great start," he complimented, before diving into a coaching moment. "But we're going to need something... *more*. Is there anything beyond sounds or things that could be easily attributed to the weather? We want to really dig deep into the underbelly here, but what we were able to uncover in our research was fairly... *limited*."

"Underbelly?" Maura questioned, almost pointedly.

"Yeah, we need something to really grip the audience. Has there been anything especially creepy or weird since the reformatory shut down?" He asked, met with a look of confusion on her face. Tilting his head the way he did when frustration bubbled at the back of his throat, he took a deep breath. "We want to highlight the things about this property that make it *uniquely* haunted, does that make sense?"

If Maura had picked up on it, she'd have realized how condescending he was being.

"Well, there have also been incidents of hair pulling, but it only seems to affect female staff," she said after a beat.

"That's perfect, make sure to talk that up, okay? And anything else you can think of as we go along in the interview. Feel free to be a little vague with your answers or mention some of what happened to visitors in the past—it's all fair game." Ash grinned. "And if you want to embellish a bit, that's totally fine. We want to really sell the fear factor."

Nodding, the pair readied for the cameras again.

"Reset!" Counting down on his fingers, Colt yelled, "Ready... three, two, one, action!"

"So, Maura, is there anything else about the grounds that we should know about before we lock down tonight?"

Her lips pursed slightly and she offered a soft, delicate smile.

"I assume you've heard about what happened to Archibald Elwood, correct?" She asked.

Within their research, Parker had found the headline from the day that Elwood's body was found. It read 'HEADMASTER OF TROUBLED BOYS SCHOOL FOUND DEAD, KILLER UNKNOWN' in two lines of sizable lettering above a photo of Elwood's draped body on the floor in his quarters. Not much else ever happened in this town to earn such salacious headlines, let alone to someone in such a high profile position, so it was no wonder that this attack had made the front page.

"Yes," Ash replied, remembering the extra-large printed copy of the article that had been strewn across the coffee table. "I believe that was sometime in the mid 1930s?"

"Thereabouts," Maura nodded. "This area... it's always had a violent history. When the Headmaster perished, there was a lot of talk about how strange the case had been. How impossible it had seemed, at the time. No one could figure out how a person could've been capable of that kind of *inhumanly* gruesome act."

"Sure, but what makes you think it was paranormal?" Ash asked. Partly for show, and partly because that had been his exact point when they'd first dived into the story's details.

Her nose crinkled and her lips drew into a tight line.

While the *Phantom Files* crew weren't shy to use the term 'paranormal' while they were filming, Ash noticed that Maura seemed almost put-off by it. Her distaste for what they were doing was palpable.

"Unfortunately, this is America and there's no shortage of murders or criminals to commit them," Ash continued. "The United States is ranked first in the number of incarcerated citizens per capita, after all. Murders happened a lot back then, usually at an exponentially higher rate in rural areas like this."

Maura's expression remained stoic.

"My dear," she began, reaching out a hand to touch his arm gently. "When you've lived as long as I have, you see more cruelty dealt than you would think possible. You learn to recognize the signs of true evil."

Raising his hands and tilting his head, Ash decided to give her the benefit of the doubt.

"It's not outside the realm of possibility, that's all I'm saying," he added. "But I do believe in overturning every stone, so I'm incredibly curious what you mean by *true evil* here."

As if that was the answer Maura was waiting for, an unsettling smile slid across her face.

"Would you like a tour?" She asked.

CHAPTER SEVEN

Ash's arm was still vibrating from where Maura had touched him during the interview, but he hardly had time to focus on that. Maura had begun to lead the three of them on a walk-through of the institution, stopping at some of the areas that the team had already identified in the research as being home to unexplained activity or violent stories. She was able to provide additional perspective to the history of the place, helping to bring it off of the microfiche and into an active dialogue that would suck in their viewers.

The first stop was a washroom where a boy had drowned in a half-full bathtub.

"Arthur Crowley drowned here in 1927," Maura explained. "He'd only been at the institution for six months, the poor dear. He was around nine when he was brought to the Castle, I believe it was for delinquency. One night, he was found floating face-down in one of these tubs."

"Did they ever find the assailant?" Ash asked.

"No." Maura shook her head. "And no one ever confessed."

Then, they wandered toward a bedroom where a member of the staff had once been strangled by a ward less than half his size. Maura's feet shuffled down the creaking corridors, the tips of her fingers touching the walls as she passed by. Her familiarity with the building was intriguing, and Ash made sure to nudge Parker and silently direct him to hone in on her.

"Tell me about the staff member that died here," Ash guided. "I believe her name was Sofia Weber?"

Maura hummed. "Yes, Sofia was beloved. She was the youngest faculty member at Crenshaw during her tenure here, and was only twenty-six at the time of her death."

"The boy that killed her," Ash began. "Did he ever explain why he went after her?"

"He claimed to be possessed," she uttered, matter-of-factly, her eyes lingering on various spots in the room before moving onto the next. "He said that a darkness overcame him, drawing him to her and forcing him to end her life. Of course, there's no way to prove something like that in the legal sense, so the authorities took him away. But many of us have long wondered how much truth there was to his claim."

There didn't seem to be any shortage of gruesome deaths and sordid histories at Crenshaw, but that was a far cry from anything paranormal. People died everywhere, after all.

Ash nodded along thoughtfully. "Is it true that Sofia is buried in the cemetery out back?"

Pausing, Maura's hand gently caressed the knob of the door as she stood beside it.

"It is," she answered. "Her family was from Nebraska and unable to afford to come retrieve her body. The headmaster here at the time decided that she should be buried here, out of respect."

A recreational room where a boy was stabbed to death came next. Walking into the large space, Maura's face dropped just enough for Ash to notice.

"Amos Pinckney," Maura murmured.

"What was that?" Colt swiveled centering Maura in view with the room behind her.

The team had already found an article from the *Hokisam Tribune* talking about Amos' death the day the story broke. But they were dying to hear how Maura was going to explain it.

"Amos, a little runt of a thing who had to have been no more than eleven, was cornered by a group of older boys in this room," she added. "He was bullied relentlessly for months, and one day his tormentors cornered him right over there." A bony, wrinkled finger pointed to the far corner, as far away from the windows as one could get in there.

"He was stabbed twenty times, was he not?" Ash asked, double-checking her story with what he'd read himself.

"Twenty-three," Maura corrected, eyes piercing through Ash's. "With sharpened pencils."

The pencils bit hadn't been in the informational packet,

but at a place like this it wasn't surprising. They were already locked down, with limited access to anything sharp or stabby, so the fact that pencils were the weapon of choice seemed appropriate.

"It's speculated that he had been the witness in the crime committed by one of the other boys, right? Isn't that what resulted in their incarceration at Crenshaw?"

Maura dipped her head toward one shoulder. "That's the story. No one really knows for sure, as those records have long since been lost."

Ash's eyelids closed halfway, pinching his field of vision into a warped rectangle of blurry lines and blobs. One of the things that intrigued him the most was the various stories that had developed over time. It wasn't entirely clear which story was *the right one,* or at least *the true one,* but they were going to find out. Their job was to bend the truth to reveal what they wanted to show, and that's exactly what they were going to do.

Finally, they arrived at the Headmaster's quarters—on their list for obvious reasons.

"No one goes in there, anymore," Maura remarked, stopping just outside the doorway of the old Headmaster's Quarters on the fourth floor. After a moment, the age in her voice revealed itself as she stuttered out that, "it's been c-closed... for renovations." Her hands fidgeted in the pockets of her cardigan, as though she was searching for something that should've been there but wasn't.

Based on Parker's research, this was the area with the highest concentration of activity in the entirety of

Crenshaw Castle—but he'd found nothing indicating that there were any renovations occurring in this room. Thinking she was waiting for them to enter first, Ash stepped over the threshold and an intense draft swept across the back of his neck as he strode toward the center of the room. Shoulders arching in response, he tilted his neck and took a few long blinks as it cracked and released the pressure that had been building at the base of his skull. But Maura didn't move from the doorway, as if her feet were cemented in place where she stood.

"The energy in here is wild," Colt piped up from behind his camera. "What's the temp?"

Parker pulled out a digital infrared thermometer and pointed his camera's lens at the reader. "Forty-three degrees fahrenheit."

Ash's eyes widened. "That's almost twenty degrees cooler than it is outside right now."

"At least," Parker added.

There must've been a wicked draft coming up from the basement, circulating that frigid stagnant air into the rest of the building. Or maybe the wall wasn't as insulated as it was claimed to be. It was over a hundred years old, so there were bound to be loose stones and crumbling brick with ancient mortar. The windows were just as old, so that was also a likely culprit to explain the chill. There was no telling what had happened to this place in the years it had sat abandoned, the elements causing further decay and deterioration.

Ash turned his attention back to Maura.

"Maura, you said this room is being renovated? We didn't find anything about that in our research." That's right, Ash, play dumb. "We know this area has some of the highest activity on the grounds. But what makes this the worst room in the Castle?" he asked, eyes darting to both Parker and Colt to ensure that they were still rolling.

Of course they were.

Maura's eyes shifted from one corner of the room to another, hands writhing over one another and twisting nervously. "Well..." she started. "This is where the most violent murder took place." Her eyes locked onto Ash's. "Archibald Elwood, one of Crenshaw Industrial Reformatory's most well-known headmasters—and most vitriolized, if we take into account what those awful articles wrote about him—was brutally killed." Maura swallowed hard, lips pulled tight into a pitying pout. "There was also significant damage done to more... well, *sensitive* regions of his body."

"He was stabbed thirteen times, if I'm not mistaken," Parker chirped. "And his body was completely exsanguinated. He was found several days after his death, with a smile carved into his face and his own intestines tied around his neck."

The look on Maura's face was clear; she was sickened.

Ash almost thought he saw sympathy in her eyes, but he convinced himself that it couldn't have been. That there was no way this woman could feel sorry for such a loathsome man who had both committed and sanctioned unspeakable, spine-chilling acts that were still being uncovered decades later. For someone who treated the children under his care with such gruesome hatred, it was a wonder that Elwood had been named Headmaster in the first place.

Studying her, Ash wondered if Maura had seen the crime scene photos from the discovery of Elwood's body, or if she'd merely imagined what his mangled corpse must've looked like. Visualized the broken and bloody flesh, twisted and slashed and pulled apart until his insides were on the outside. Her palpable discomfort made it clear that this was likely not the kind of information they freely exchanged with the public, but that this was something she, personally, wanted them to know. Perhaps she hadn't been interested in being part of their investigation but had been *volun-told.*

Colt zoomed in on Maura, enveloping the frame with her face. Almost as if he could see the cogs whirring inside her skull. Thick, stagnant air hung around them as the silence buzzed with tension. Where he expected to see a pensive expression, instead it appeared that there was an almost nostalgic glint in her eye. Almost like she was recalling a fond memory.

Until her eyes darted to Colt and sent a cold shiver down his spine.

"Okay, that's a wrap," Colt said, clearing his throat as both he and Parker shut off their cameras.

Ash turned to Maura, holding a hand out to shake hers. "That was great, Maura. Thank you so much for your time and for playing along with our interview process."

Maura smiled as she shook his hand, but something

about the smile was unsettling to Ash. Her lips were pursed like she was holding in a secret, keeping it locked away before it blurted out unintentionally.

Her grip was tighter than he expected, her nails digging into his flesh like pincers, and Ash winced as she drew him closer. Her Hulk-like strength was unexpected, catching him entirely off-guard.

"Friendly advice," she warned, voice dropping to a sinister volume. "I'd be careful what you play around with here. Some doors don't like to be opened."

"Excuse me?" He asked.

Maura backed off and her smile eased, once again, into a caricature of the quintessential grandmother.

"Nothing, dear. I hope you find what you're looking for," she cooed.

Usually the interviewees that participated in *Phantom Files* productions were more forthcoming with the gruesome details and gave the team what they were looking for, or at least gave the impression that they were firmly on one side or the other of the skeptic-believer fenceline. With Maura, though, it didn't feel like she'd been telling them a story that she'd memorized.

It felt like she was telling *the truth*.

As Maura walked over to Parker to remove the lapel microphone, Ash cradled his crushed hand and stretched his mouth wide until his jaw popped. Thoughts of what Maura had meant with that odd comment were swirling in his head. Most of what she'd said in their interview was historical and validated by their research, or at least prompted by his advice to go wild with her interpretations of the crimes that had happened there. While she might have meant that the premises were old and dangerous, and thus they should be careful horsing around inside of it without paying attention, there was something sinister hidden in her words. And what had she meant by *finding what he was looking for*?

Something was off and Ash felt it.

Especially given how she'd talked around the topic of Headmaster Elwood's demise and the way in which his body had been found.

Luckily, they'd been prepared and had a stack of documentation to shed light on what really happened to Elwood before he became ground beef.

There were endless opportunities present for someone else in town to have committed any number of the crimes in Crenshaw's history, even if no one was willing to admit to having committed the crime. And the deaths were public record, after all. Information like that could make anyone feel like there was something spooky clinging to the dark corners. The imagination could easily play tricks if it was motivated enough.

Standing in the room where it had actually *happened* was an entirely different thing to talking about it around a coffee table over an old newspaper article. The walls there were steeped in secrets and it was unlikely that this had been an outside job. If anyone had it out for Elwood, it was undoubtedly a member of Crenshaw Castle's inner community, if for no other reason than that those within its walls tended not to leave.

The murder of the institution's Headmaster was just one of several scandals that eventually led to its downfall. That, and the turning tide of public opinion regarding reformatories and the children who were often mistreated within them.

Whatever the reason, someone wanted Elwood out of the picture.

CHAPTER EIGHT

Finally, they were setting up their stationary cameras to capture as much of the building as they could from Embry's computer screen. Starting in the bathroom, it was both more disgusting and exactly as disgusting as they expected it to be.

Green-hued tile bled across the floor and three-quarters of the way up the putrescent walls, enveloping the room in a pool of faded emerald. Once white grout was now a dingy grey, mottled with shades of mold and decades old ooze. Shower heads lined a far wall, half of them broken and exposing rusted pipes and shattered ceramic. It wasn't hard to see this room and envision what it might've looked like in its prime. Damp, stagnant air flooded the bathroom with air too thick to choke down. It was viscous and slimy, like the ancient bathwater collected at the bottom of the tub that sat in the corner of the room.

"So, who do you think did it?" Colt asked, setting up a tripod for one of the second-floor stationary cameras.

This room was a staph infection waiting to happen, and both of them were careful not to touch anything with their bare skin for fear of catching a strain of bacteria that had been mutating unsupervised for years.

"Did what?" Ash asked, leaning cautiously against a peeling window sill.

"Put Old Man Elwood out of his misery," Colt replied, locking the camera onto the tripod with the twist of a silver screw.

Ash shrugged, thumbing through some of the research saved on his phone.

Parker, ever the history fanatic, had put his microfiche skills to good use and dug up a ton of old newspaper articles and documents related to both Archibald Elwood and the Crenshaw Industrial Reformatory. Having poured through library resources, hours of archived film on the microfiche, and everything available online, he'd ended up with a pretty decent stack of records for the three of them to peruse. There were birth and death certificates, an announcement in the *Hokisam Tribune* about Elwood's appointment as Headmaster, and even a barrage of stories about Crenshaw through the years.

As one of the first reformatories to be established on the West Coast, there were stories dating all the way back to the early 19th Century. At the time, these facilities were emerging as the premier way to deal with delinquent youth. Instead of sending youth to prisons, they were put into the care of wardens and headmasters. These wards of the state were expected to be re-educated while atoning for their crimes at these industrial schools, using a mix of military discipline and vocational instruction.

While this sounded like a good idea on the surface, there was a darkness hiding in plain sight. Many wards were mistreated, starved, abused, and even killed at these reform schools under the guise of 'curing the wayward youth problem.'

"The fan favorite theory seems to be that it was the spirit of his late wife," Ash said, pensively gnawing at the inside of his lip. "Apparently Elwood's wife went crazy and he institutionalized her." Swiping further, Ash's brows raised. "He was also suspected to have poisoned her, causing the psychotic break."

Colt slowly nodded and sucked air through his teeth. "Sounds like a real stand-up guy."

"They had a kid, too," Ash added, digging through the notes in his email. "But it looks like most of their family records were lost in a house fire in 1926—one year after the wife lost it."

"You think the wife died in the blaze?"

Sometimes Ash wished his own father would've died in a fire.

They had a turbulent relationship, at the best of times. At the worst... Well, Ash got out of there as soon as he could. The day he turned eighteen, he was on the highway driving from North Falmouth, Massachusetts, all the way to St. Cloud, Minnesota. Parker had an apartment near St. Cloud

State and he moved in with him, toting a pair of duffel bags and a future that didn't involve his narcissistic father's abuse. As far as Ash was concerned, he had written his father off entirely and blocked his number. There was nothing left to say to someone who cared so little yet couldn't pass up any opportunity to lash out as his own spawn.

Closing out of the research files, Ash locked his phone and then tapped the screen. He stared longingly at the wallpaper; a photo of him and Erick, his longtime boyfriend. They'd been together for years, the definition of 'college sweethearts', and some days Ash still couldn't believe how he'd scored with that man.

"Ash?"

Colt's voice pulled Ash back from the memory of his father's constant disappointment.

"It's possible," he shrugged, remembering what Colt had originally asked. "Most of the info on Elwood is from his time here at Crenshaw, so there's not much out there about his personal life. There's a birth record for his son, record of his marriage, but other than that... nothing. No record of his wife's death or what happened to the kid. Maybe we can find something in storage here somewhere, though." Ash gestured out the hallway, knowing that there had to be remaining documents that were left behind after the building had been shuttered.

"Maybe he killed the wife and she came back to kill his ass from the great beyond," Colt joked, dragging his thumb against his throat in a slicing manner.

"Or maybe she killed him and then went on the lamb," Ash offered. "I thought I read somewhere that she was institutionalized for, like, consumption or something, but when I tried to find that same article it was gone."

"If the wife really *did* die and come back from the dead to kill him, this might be our first chance to actually catch some real ghost shit on film," Colt laughed, ignoring Ash's alternative theory. "Then maybe Rhett won't have to work her special effects magic this time around."

"Pfft," Ash snorted. "Don't tell me you're actually becoming a believer in all this mystical woo-woo bullshit, Colt."

"Of course not," he rejected. "All I'm saying is it would be cool to actually catch something for real." Colt stood up, cracking the knuckles of both hands before gesturing at the camera setup. "This one's good, I think we're ready to rock and roll."

Just then, both of their radios went off and Parker's voice rang out across the tiled room, overlapping like the voices in a crowded elevator.

"Is Barton still on the property?" He asked, his voice catching in just the right way that Ash knew something was wrong.

He reached for his own radio and pressed the talk button before speaking. "Uh, no, she left about..." Ash looked to Colt, who glanced down at his watch and mouthed 'ten' emphatically. "About ten minutes ago. Why?"

"Which floor are you guys on?" Parker's voice echoed again.

Ash and Colt exchanged bewildered looks. "Second," they replied in unison.

Colt's brows dug into his eye sockets. "The hell is he on about?"

Shrugging exasperatedly, Ash radioed again. "Everything okay?"

"It's nothing, I think," he answered shortly. "Could've sworn someone was walking around upstairs in the Headmaster's quarters, though."

CHAPTER NINE

Colt gulped one breath, then two, then began to fidget with the ring on his middle finger. The pause after Parker's last message stretched on for a minute too long before finally Ash brought the radio up to his mouth again.

"Did something happen?" He asked.

"The stationary camera up there in the rec room turned off, and Rhett caught footsteps. Must've been Embry, she walked off somewhere and hasn't come back yet."

"You let her walk off by herself?" Colt practically shouted in disbelief.

"I didn't *let* her do anything. She's a big girl, she'll be just fine."

"I went to the *bathroom*, freaks. Quit talking about me," Embry chimed in.

Clearing his throat, Parker course corrected. "Anyway,

get your asses going, we gotta finish setting up the rest of the cameras. Over and out."

A second of static ended their conversation and Ash clipped the radio back onto his belt.

"Your brother is gonna catch some heat, isn't he?" Colt laughed, turning on his heel to head back out into the hallway.

"One can only hope," Ash retorted, looking forward to Embry tearing Parker a new asshole.

He followed behind Colt, picking up the bag of additional tripods for the rest of the cameras on the second floor. They had three left to place, and then they would need to double back to the fourth floor to investigate the one that had turned off mysteriously. If they hurried, they could be finished before they missed the smackdown that was sure to come.

"You know, I think Cam was right. We really oughta do something a little more *out there* this season," said Colt, winding down the hall toward the creepy bedroom with the supposedly high levels of poltergeist activity. "More intense visual effects, eerier sound effects, maybe even add some CGI? I know Embry could do it, she's got some skills in the editing department."

"Nah, man, that's cheesy. You saw what happened to the *Spirit Seekers*, they went way over the top and it ruined the whole vibe of the show. Ratings tanked and they didn't get renewed, then there went the whole franchise." Ash made an explosive sound with his mouth, one hand gesturing outward as if he was visualizing their futures going up in flames. "I think we need to steer a little more into the history, really make it more about *why* spirits would be stuck in this place. So much fucked up shit has happened here... we could make it believable."

Someone had to keep their eyes focused on the money.

"Yeah, yeah, whatever you say, buzzkill." Colt waved Ash off, stopping at the doorway. "I'll take this one," he said, gesturing to the bedroom. "And you head upstairs to three to put one in the other bedroom. Deal?"

"Deal," Ash agreed.

The hallway turned a corner up ahead, forking into a stairwell and another corridor. Everything about this place gave Ash the creeps, like he was being watched. One creaking step at a time, Ash ascended the stairs toward the third floor with only the beam of his flashlight to guide the way.

A gust of frigid wind swept across his neck, turning his skin to gooseflesh and prickling his scalp. Every hair on his arms raised, nail beds went purple, and even his lips felt dry as a bone.

Taking the steps a few at a time, the creaking wood reminded him of the place's age. He made a mental note to step close to the edges of the treads, not wanting to step through the rotting wood. About halfway up, the unexpected sound of metal dragging had Ash stopping in his tracks, listening for it to happen again.

"Colt?" he asked.

Before he could think, a wooden chair collided into the side of the staircase, smashing the banister into splinters.

Crouching down, Ash covered his head until the flurry of wood chunks stopped falling. Pieces skittered across his exposed skin, catching it and pulling until beads of crimson rose to the surface. As he hunkered there, his lungs burned as the stale air within them exhaled abruptly. Ears pounding with the sounds of his quickened heart rate and rushing blood, Ash's head tilted up and his eyes flicked back toward the upper floor. Carefully standing, his flashlight spun with him and swept down the stairwell, finding nothing but bits of dust floating through the air like specks of toxic, mildewed snow. The railing was still in place, untouched. There was no wood littering the stairwell. No sign of the chair that had been hurled in his direction.He forced down heavy gulps of air when he could no longer hold his breath, looking for an open window or some other explanation.

"Jesus..." he whispered to himself, emitting a soft chuckle at his own expense. "Quit freaking out, it's just an old building," he reminded himself, taking another step upward.

Another low creak rattled the wooden staircase.

If he didn't know better, he might've thought it was the weight of another body.

But he did know.

There was no way anyone else was nearby, waiting in the wings to spook him. It was just his imagination getting the best of him, messing with his perception of his surroundings.

Once again, Ash's flashlight was powerless to uncover

any monsters hidden within the darkness. There was no boogeyman out to get him, or sinister force waiting in the wings—it was just him, alone in the darkness, letting his imagination run away with him.

"Colt?" Ash called down. After a few unanswered moments, Ash pulled out his radio. "Hey, Colt, you there?"

The other man's voice barely broke through a barrage of static. "Yeah, w—t's up?"

"Piece of shit radio," Ash muttered, smacking it against the palm of his other hand. "Where are you at?" He asked, peering over the railing down at the desolate second floor.

"Still i—edroom. Literally just unzi—amera bag. You okay?"

"Copy. All good." Ash ran a hand through his hair, shaking the fear from his mind and taking the remaining stairs two-at-a-time. "You just imagined it because you're hungry," he whispered to himself, lugging the camera equipment toward one of the bedrooms where ghostly hair pulling was known to be a common occurrence. "Old buildings are creepy, that's just how it is. Ghosts aren't real, and if they were it wouldn't take five fucking seasons to catch one on camera."

Ash kneeled on the floor to set up the camera in record time, and a loud *thwack-bang-kshhhhck* exploded on one of the lower levels. It reverberated up through the empty, echoing walls and stopped him in his tracks. But the shrill scream that followed chilled his blood until it was ice.

"For fuck's sake!" Embry groaned, her head tilted backward as if she was cursing the sky.

"The hell happened down here?" Colt asked.

Rhett, eyes darting to the floor, grimaced as Colt and Ash stepped out of the shadow of the halfway and into their makeshift control center.

Everyone's eyes immediately fell to Embry's second monitor, laying face-down on the floor like a dead body floating in a pool.

Ash dropped the empty camera bags onto the ground in a haphazard pile. They'd set up a total of nine stationary cameras across Crenshaw Castle's four floors and Embry had each camera's feed pulled up on the surviving monitor.

"We lost one," Embry grumbled, bending down and kneeling beneath the plastic table to pick up the monitor before flipping it around to reveal the screen.

It had been shattered into a spiderweb, the backlight flickering and distorting. There were even tiny shards of plastic missing, littered on the floor and in the crevices of the authentically distressed wooden flooring where the corner of the monitor had made contact with the floor.

"Shit, you really did a number on this one." Parker leaned down, poking at the broken screen with his index finger. "How'd it happen?"

"It probably got caught on one of those cables," Ash

pointed out. "Looks like no one gaffed them down like they were supposed to." His eyes narrowed as the corners of his mouth tightened into a frown, elbow jabbing into Rhett's side gently.

"Hey!" She swatted at his arm before giving Parker a solid shove that took him a few steps to recover from. "Those cables were nowhere near the monitor, we had it all buttoned up over here."

"Maybe it was the ghosts," Colt teased, a wicked smirk on his face. He stuck his fingers out in front of himself, wiggling them wildly.

"He's convinced there's *actual* ghosts here," Ash teased.

"No, I'm not," Colt tried to interject.

"Really?" Rhett asked in response to Ash.

"I wasn't saying I thought the shit was *real*," Colt backpedaled. "I was just saying that *if it was real* it would be badass if we actually captured something on film."

Rhett arched one eyebrow with piqued curiosity—a reaction that Ash quietly assumed was because she'd been the only true believer in their ranks.

Until now, if Colt was changing his tune.

"And that's different *how* exactly?" Parker prodded. Wrapping an arm around Colt's neck, he aggressively pulled him in close, knocking off the backwards hat he was rarely caught without. "The closest thing to a ghost you've ever captured was an old coat in a closet."

A frustrated growl escaped Colt as he fought Parker's grip, fingers digging into the other man's forearm until he released. He smoothed back his hair and repositioned the ballcap. Yet another Novak-ism that Colt had been forced to become accustomed to after two decades of friendship. Hell, after all of the time spent glued to Ash as they grew up side-by-side, by now he was an honorary brother, anyway.

"Hey, that thing was moving around all by itself! It ain't my fault I didn't see the broken window," Colt defended.

"No, but it *is* your fault that you let yourself believe in that crap for even a split second," Embry added. "I will forever remember the high-pitched way you screamed for Ash in a panic." She grimaced. "Thought I was going to have tinnitus for a week after that."

Ash, happy to see Colt given a little guff, glanced over at the clock to check the time. "Hey, Park, we should probably start testing some of the effects. You and Rhett wanna take the top two floors and Colt and I will take the bottom two?"

It would've saved time to do it all at the same time as the stationary camera set-up, but the bulkiness of the equipment limited how much they were able to transport from one floor to the next. Especially in this location, where the lack of elevators meant everything had to be hoofed up the rickety stairs.

"Sure," Parker agreed, before looking at Rhett who nodded in confirmation.

Ash turned his head toward Embry. "Are you all good down here by yourself for a minute?"

She scoffed. "More than good, I'll be celebrating a minute of peace," Embry smiled, waving for them to get out of the room so that she could continue prepping all of the camera feeds on her laptop and the one remaining working monitor that she had. Her fingers tucked a few flyaway hairs behind her ears, her shock of pink hair tied up into a messy bun. "Get outta my hair before I find something for you to do in here."

Grabbing all of the special effects equipment, the four of them headed out of the room.

"Feisty," Colt murmured within earshot of Ash, who looked over just in time to see the other man's eyebrows wagging up and down like a cartoon character.

Shaking his head, Ash's hand found a home at the back of Colt's neck and squeezed. "Trust me, she doesn't want you," he laughed breathlessly.

There was an art to positioning the effects for maximum output while remaining minimally conspicuous. Crenshaw Castle, while not entirely dissimilar to other locations *Phantom Files* had investigated, had its own unique challenges. For one thing, everything they used had to be battery powered and small enough to conceal in the dark corners of doorways and stairwells. It was nothing short of a mystery that they were even able to find a spot in the first room to secure a speaker they planned to use to play sounds on electromagnetic frequencies.

"Can you hand me the gaf—" Colt started to ask, when he was interrupted by Embry's voice powering through the radios.

"Saw lights go off on the fourth floor northwest bedroom camera. Was that a strobe test?"

Fourth floor? Ash wondered. *Wasn't that the same floor that Parker asked about earlier?*

It was dead silence for at least half a minute until…

"Rhett and I are on three, no strobe tests from us," Parker stated through the radio. "Was it the puck lights going off?"

"Hard to say, caught it in the reflection of a mirror. I'll play it back and see if I can debunk before you guys get back."

Ash put his radio away, thinking that was the end of the conversation, but Colt's voice crooned out from his hip in a *Twilight Zone* sing-song.

"Keep your eyes open," she warned. "Never know what you'll find in the dark."

CHAPTER TEN

"Speaking of the dark," Embry chirped. "There's something wrong with camera seven." Her finger rapid-fire clicked the mouse to enlarge that piece of the grid. "Colt, you must've screwed up the install. The feed is completely black."

As she finished her sentence, the feed glitched again. Waves of static rolled across the picture as it warped the input. It almost looked like the camera was recording underwater, gurgling and bubbling as it slowly died. It was video failure unlike anything she'd ever seen.

"Weird..." Embry mumbled, furtively clicking her mouse.

"I didn't screw up anything," Colt interjected, his words steeped in denial. "I used the good tape this time."

"Well something's up with it," Embry insisted. "Do me a favor and double check it when you're done?"

"Ugh, fine," Colt grumbled. "But you owe me a cheese danish."

Embry was quick to shut him down.

"I owe you nothing. You spilled your coffee all over my Noah Kahan t-shirt yesterday," she replied sternly. That shirt was her favorite one, and she'd gotten it at a show in her hometown: Strafford, Vermont. "Just fix the camera, it's not gonna kill you to do your damn job." Tossing the radio onto the table, a deep sigh escaped her lips and her two fingers rubbed at the space between her brows. There were days when she regretted joining their wild goose chase of a fame dream and this was one of them.

This season was supposed to be different.

Instead, it was all turning into a joke. Again.

As camera seven rebooted, Colt's face enlarged on screen and Embry was looking directly up his nose as he readjusted and admired his work.

"See?" Colt scoffed, glancing over his shoulder at Ash. "Embry's so full of shit, I didn't fuck up the install."

Raising her radio, Embry cleared her throat into the live microphone. "Then why wasn't it working until just now, smartass?"

Colt's face dropped into a frustratedly contorted frown, eyes locked onto the lens of the camera as though he could see Embry's smug expression in its reflective exterior.

"The lens was covered," he reasoned, eyes boring into hers through the computer screen.

"Uh huh," she replied, her voice flat. "Well you two

were the only ones on that floor, so if it wasn't your fault then it obviously had to be your fearless leader's doing."

"Hey!" Ash chimed in with downturned eyebrows and pursed lips.

"Sorry, I don't make the rules, I just enforce them." Embry shrugged, despite the fact that they couldn't see her. She looked up to find that Parker and Rhett were strolling into the control room, ready to move on to shooting the next scene. "If you two are done fooling around, we're all waiting down here for you."

Once all of the cameras were back in working order, it was time to start their investigation. The sun had dipped low enough that it was fighting through the forest for visibility. Enormous trees with slender branches outstretched toward the sky like fingers grasping at a gradient canopy, desperately trying to graze the atmosphere.

"It's a quarter past seven o'clock and we've just begun our lockdown here at Crenshaw Castle," Ash said solemnly into the camera, his vocal cadence shifting lower and slowing to give the impression that something ominous was going to happen.

It wasn't, of course.

All of that would be added in editing.

"We've also set up Radiating Electro Magneticity Pods, also known as REM Pods near each of our stationary cameras. They'll alert us of changes in ambient temperature. We've also got several strategically placed here along the first floor, as well." Ash held one up of the radiating electromagneticity devices as he explained to the audience. "These babies will light up when they detect high levels of electromagnetic energy, using a similar technology to our EMF detectors but utilizing lights to visually communicate those energy spikes—"

The REM pod in Ash's hand lit up for a split second before he could finish his sentence.

"Damn it," he swore, smacking the device with his palm.

Parker raised his radio. "Hey, Em, we're gonna have to start again. The REM pod malfunctioned. Resetting now."

"Copy," Embry confirmed.

It wasn't unusual for the devices to go off unintentionally. Anything could set it off, and it was likely that someone had gotten a text or some other notification. The REM pods were so sensitive that it made their jobs a tad harder at times.

"Ready when you are," Colt said to Ash, directing him to start from the top.

Ash nodded and cleared his throat, shaking his hair out of his eyes to get himself camera-ready. "It's half past seven o'clock and we've just begun our lockdown here at Crenshaw Castle," he repeated, with a slight tweak. "Using this," he held up the EMF detector, "we'll measure our location's electromagnetic field to get a baseline before we—"

Interrupted by an intense vibration, the floor beneath Ash's feet was shaking rapidly. Almost as though someone had taken a chainsaw to it and the reverberations were lashing out in all directions. And as quickly as it had started, it stopped.

Ash sighed, entirely irritated with the interruptions. "What the fuck was that?"

Eyes shifting to her left, Embry surveyed Rhett's studious expression. Brow furrowed, headphones locked into place over her ears, eyes glued to her screen as she clicked through waveforms and replayed the sound for herself. Their gaze met and Rhett's features melted into concern as she slid one side of her headphones off of her right ear.

"What?" Embry asked, sensing hesitation.

"I don't know." Rhett gnawed at the inside corner of her mouth. "It sounded like something being dragged, but I can't quite identify it."

"What, like a dead body dragged down a hallway?" Embry joked.

Rhett simply blinked.

"Oh, come on," Embry rolled her eyes. "We're in old buildings all the time, those creaks and thumps are nothing to write home about."

Speaking into her radio, Rhett sighed.

"Not sure, there's nothing on the cameras. Just keep going," she said.

Head thrown back as a guttural groan escaped him, Colt's camera feed perfectly captured Ash's irritation. It was an accurate representation of Ash's view of this place, too, considering that he'd initially fought the decision to visit Crenshaw Castle this season. He thought the ghost stories were overblown and unbelievable, that it was clearly a hoax set up to make this remote, abandoned property relevant again. That it was nothing more than an opportunity to give the foundation that ran the place a reason to open up to tours again and rake in the dough.

Production hadn't agreed with him.

"Alright," Parker acknowledged. "Let's get one more take and then we can splice the clips together with some close-ups of the equipment."

"Copy," Rhett chimed in. "Grab some B-roll while you're up there, too."

"You got it."

After a few deep breaths, Ash was ready for another take.

"Hang on," Colt interjected. "I've gotta swap batteries."

He flipped the LCD screen and a drained battery icon flashed repeatedly until the screen went completely black. Pulling a fresh one from the cargo pocket of his dark olive pants, Colt swiftly replaced the old ones and pocketed them. The camera powered on, the screen illuminating Colt's face in the darkness, and he looked up to Ash and Parker with a contented smile. "Let's get this party started."

Once the red light was illuminated on both cameras, Ash put on his solemn *Phantom Files* voice and got into character.

"Let's check our baseline reading on our EMF detector," he repeated, looking down at the device's screen and tilting it so that Parker's camera could zoom in on it for the audience. "The needle remains consistently around 10 milli Gauss, which is within the normal range for ambient EMF readings in remote locations like this one," he added. "Any time this needle shoots up, it's indicating high levels of electromagnetism. In other words, spirit activity."

"If anyone is here, please communicate with us!" Ash's raised voice boomed around them, reverberating off of the walls and echoing down the hallway.

The three of them looked around in the silence, appearing as though they were waiting for an answer from The Great Beyond (or whatever).

"We're here to understand what's keeping your spirit trapped here." He had to contain himself at the cringey dialogue, mentally cursing Parker for writing the crappiest script known to man. "If anyone is here with us, tell us your name!"

As the echoes dissipated, silence cradled the three of them like straightjackets. They never expected a response— nor did they ever receive one—but the way their voices echoed through the cavernous corridors gave Crenshaw an especially ccric vibe. Every ounce of light was swallowed up by the building's dark corners as soon as a flashlight was shone in any one direction.

With a nod from Ash, it was time for them to review what was captured on the digital voice recorder held out in Parker's free hand. He pressed play and they heard Ash's voice reiterating the very first thing he'd said to whatever ghosts were probably (not) haunting the place.

"If anyone is here with us, tell us your name!" Ash's voice played through the device, sounding a little bit staticky and like he'd spoken through a tin can.

The static grew louder, and louder, until a high pitched, guttural scream whined out.

CHAPTER ELEVEN

P arker's eyes darted between Colt and Parker. "You guys heard that, right?"

They nodded, the three of them equally unsure of what they were hearing. Colt grimaced and Ash frowned, while Parker stared at the recorder with concern.

"Is that thing broken already?" Ash groaned into his hands. "For fuck's sake."

At the mention of broken equipment, Rhett's ears perked up beneath her headphones and she grimaced into her radio from behind her makeshift desk.

"You'd better not be breaking shit up there!" she warned. "If y'all broke it, then we're down to two, and I doubt any of the shops in Hokisam carry 'em."

They'd started out with four, but one had been damaged and was apart in pieces on the table beside Rhett's workstation (where she was attempting to repair it after it had gotten smashed at the bottom of Colt's gear bag), and another had fallen into a muddy puddle the size of a fourth grader.

"We're not," Ash argued.

Rhett's exasperated breath puffed through the radio, intentionally.

If there was one thing that could be counted on, it was that Ash and Colt never listened. That was the lesson Rhett had learned after working with them for all of last season. There was nothing she could say that would tear them away from whatever was at the forefront of their one-track minds, even if it was to steer them away from disaster. Hell, Ash had nearly shattered his knee, and all she'd gotten in response to saving him was *why were you distracting me?*

Talk about adding insult to injury.

Sometimes, seeing Ash and Parker together made Rhett wish she had siblings she was close with. Families were inherently messy, and she couldn't imagine what it was like to spend every day with people who knew the most painful pieces of your past. As someone who spent *maybe* two weeks a year in the presence of her own family, working on *Phantom Files* proved to her that she'd made the right call getting out of New Orleans when she did.

Ash's voice ripped through the silence of Rhett's thoughts and vibrated her Walkie where it had been left on the table.

"Let's meet up in the control room and assign rooms for the individual walk-through," he instructed over the radio waves. "I want to get this show on the road."

"Copy," she answered, adding in her reply along with Colt and Embry's.

Parker's voice never came through, but ten minutes later he was standing in the doorway, arms crossed over his chest, listening as the plans for what they'd long ago dubbed the 'Lore Walk' were hashed out.

It was a simple task, really.

Cameras in hand, the three guys headed off to separate rooms, armed with digital recorders and the background information on what travesty had occurred within the walls of their assigned room. It was more or less designed to build tension and escalate their viewers' fear, while simultaneously building the world that this location had once belonged to. It connected the past to the present in a vivid way—along with the photos, videos, and visual graphic effects overlaid during the post-production process.

Coincidentally, this was Rhett's least favorite part of every episode, because it required her to pay explicit attention to what each of them were doing at the same time. With lighting equipment fairly ineffective in Crenshaw's oddly dense darkness, and her computer's brightness already maxed out, Rhett would be left to squint at her screen for a while.

"Colt, you're going to take the second floor bathroom," Ash stated.

Despite their general sense of democracy, Ash was usually the one that made the final calls. At some point during the second season, he'd become the de facto leader of the *Phantom Files* team. Parker didn't seem to mind, but

Colt took it kind of personally at first. Yes, the show had been Ash's idea in the first place, but Colt was the one who'd always wanted to be a star. Letting someone else, even if that someone else was his best friend, take the prime spot in the limelight crushed his ego like an aluminum can. Eventually, though, he got over it and took his place as Ash's sidekick alongside Parker.

Colt groaned, head tilting up toward the bug infested ceiling joists. "Seriously? I already had to set up the cameras in there and it creeped me the hell out." Whipping out an index finger, he pointed it at Parker with an outstretched arm. "Send Parker, he hasn't had to be in there at all."

Ash ignored him.

"Parker, head to the dormitory wing on three and hit those two bedrooms that Maura said had a lot of activity. I'll take the classroom on two and then we'll meet up and the three of us can tackle the Headmaster's quarters and the infirmary together. Cool?"

Parker nodded as Colt grumbled his disapproval, both of which Ash took as affirmatives.

"Alright, then. Let's get what we need and—"

A set of piercing scratches, like nails on a chalkboard, echoed through the hall. It was one of their usual sound effects, but the timing was off. Nothing should have been triggered until they were ready, and with all of their remotes still in a bag at the command center, there was no way they could've been set off by anyone on the team.

Simultaneously, all of them looked upward and froze.

"Who the fuck set that off?" Embry huffed. "I didn't even pass out the remotes yet!"

Rhett's eyes drifted to the open bag of remotes on Embry's side of the table, waiting to be taken upstairs later in the night. Some quick mental math revealed that they were all accounted for. A pull at the back of her mind, like an itch she couldn't scratch, festered there. Her head flooded with thoughts of ghost stories she'd heard growing up in the Crescent City, of buildings haunted by the shattered souls of those destined to cling to the places they'd spent their final violent moments.

"Come on, guys, we agreed not to set off the sound effects until *after* the Lore Walk," Ash complained. "Who timed it to go off early?" His gaze stopped on each of them, waiting for someone to confess to the crime.

Colt raised two hands and a breathless laugh came out. "Don't look at me."

"It wasn't us," Parker said. "The remotes are still downstairs."

"He's right," Rhett chimed in over the radio. "They're all down here and accounted for." It was standard procedure that everything *Phantom Files* did to fake their haunts had to be controlled by someone on their team at the exact moment that they wanted it to go off. But rarely did they experience equipment malfunctions where their devices went off without explanation.

The quick scuttling of little feet echoed across the floor above them.

Disembodied giggling wafted down toward them.

Picking up one of the heavy-duty Maglites, Colt tightly wrapped both hands around it like it was a baseball bat he could wield in case someone ran up on them.

"What the hell is that?" He whispered.

"SHHH," Ash instructed, stifling the other man with a wave before speaking into his radio. "Parker, was that you two?"

"Was what us?" Parker responded.

"Come on, you know what."

"I really don't want to play this game. What are you talking about?"

"The footsteps and the giggling," Ash sighed. "That shit stopped being scary when we were in grade school, man. Cut it out."

"Ash, I don't know what you think you heard, but it wasn't us."

"Well, he was no help," Ash complained, as he parked the radio and turned to face Colt. Raising an eyebrow at the other man's choice of weapon, he nodded toward it. "And you're going to, what, illuminate them to death? You dropped out of tee-ball when you were six, so I don't know if using that thing as a bat is the greatest plan."

With a raised middle finger aimed at Ash, Colt strode out of the room and toward the sounds of movement above them.

As he headed down the hall toward the back stairwell, Colt glanced into every open door along the way. All he was able to discern in the dark were the shapes of battered furniture and pieces of decor. The beam of his flashlight revealed a desk here, a bed there, a lamp with a shade torn almost entirely off its frame, and a snowstorm of dust flakes floating through the air. He was almost at the stairs when the ceiling above him creaked with the weight of something shuffling across the floorboards right above his head.

"Gotcha," Colt muttered, the corner of his mouth creeping upward into a menacing grin as he quickened his pace and ascended the stairs two at a time.

Once he was on the second floor, the sounds had dissipated and been replaced with an otherworldly silence. The bone-chilling quiet raised the hair on his arms as he slowly crept forward, as though his body was warning him to turn back.

"Hello?" His voice ricocheted and carried itself down the long hall. Five long seconds passed as he stood there, flashlight panning around, waiting for the intruder to make another sound. "Whoever's up here, you've gotta leave! This is a closed set and you're not allowed to be here!"

No one answered.

"Look, if you leave now, we won't call the cops, alright?" he shouted, taking a few slow steps forward. "But if you wait for us to find you, it's not going to go your way!" Passing the first open doorway on his left, Colt shined the flashlight across the room's contents.

Empty.

As Colt approached another room on the right, the floor creaked behind him.

Whipping around, knuckles white as his grip tightened

around the flashlight, his heartbeat pounded in his ears. What if whoever was up there had a weapon? Sure, he had a ten pound flashlight he could swing, but that would be no match for a knife or a gun. And if there was more than one of them, he'd be doubly screwed.

Nostrils flaring as Colt took in deep breaths to steady himself, a burst of ear-splitting static came through the radio he'd clipped to his shirt pocket

"Fuck!" He swore, scrambling to grab the device and lower its volume.

A sound slid out between the static, barely as audible as a whisper and incredibly choppy.

"Ash?" He tried to reply, but the device let out a few warbled beeps and then went dark. "Ugh, damnit." Of course the batteries died right when he needed them.

Stuffing it back into his pocket, Colt continued to inch along his path.

Room after room came up empty, looking just as untouched as they had earlier that day.

"Where are you hiding?" Colt whispered.

Another stampede of footsteps echoed across the hall ahead of him. The flurry of footsteps were so loud it drove a horde of Deathwatch beetles and Silverfish from their hiding places, where they'd been nestled beneath the edge of where the rotting baseboards met the floor.

Once again, a sweep of the flashlight's beam revealed nothing.

"I know you're up here!" His voice barked, trying to fake his confidence until the nerve could be worked up enough to stand on its own. Jaw clenched, awaiting whatever might be hiding in the shadows, he stalked forward toward the direction of the footsteps. "I'm armed!" he lied, grip tightening on the Maglite. "This is a closed set! You have five seconds to come out and vacate the premises, or else!"

CHAPTER TWELVE

The rotting floors screeched beneath Colt's feet as his body weight shifted.

Three footsteps on the stairs had him whipping around on his heel, the wood flooring grating and groaning with each of his movements. He raised his flashlight, illuminating a silhouette at the top of the stairs. Their face was immediately blocked from view by a raised hand, preventing the bright stream of light from beaming directly into their eyes.

"Jesus, Colt!" a voice bellowed.

One that he immediately recognized as Parker's.

"Lower the flashlight, would you?"

Sighing with relief that it wasn't an axe murderer ready to slice through him, Colt lowered the beam of light to keep from further blinding the other man.

"You scared the shit out of me," Ash croaked, feeling a cool dampness clinging to his forehead. The irritation he felt earlier climbed back up and the bite in his throat returned. "I'm up here hunting trespassers."

"You're a lot of things, but intimidating isn't one of them," Parker said, moving down the hall with his own, smaller, flashlight in hand. "Did you find anything down there, Sherlock?"

Ash caught up to them at the stairwell just in time to jump into their conversation.

"No," Colt admitted defeatedly, continuing to peek into each room as they investigated the rest of the floor for hidden assailants.

"I'm beginning to think there's an open window or a door we don't know about," Ash interjected. "How else could anyone have snuck past us?"

"There are no other operable entrances or windows," Parker said, shaking his head. "They've all been boarded up, except for the front entrance and the back service door. The backdoor is chained up and padlocked, I checked during the exterior sweep."

"They could've been here way before we arrived," Colt countered. "Who knows how long a squatter could make this place home before anyone noticed."

Ash tilted his head, acknowledging the man's fair point.

Standing side-by-side-by-side, the three of them waited with bated breath. If something was still in there, they'd hear it move if they were still and silent for long enough.

As they stood there, intently listening for any sign of life other than themselves, even the sound of their own breathing became loud.

"Maybe I scared them off," Colt mused, chest puffed with unearned bravado.

"Or maybe they're lying in wait, ready to hack you to pieces when we start the Lore Walk," Ash teased, earning himself a furrowed scowl from his brother.

Rolling his eyes, Parker let out a small laugh. "Relax, it's probably just a raccoon or something."

"A *raccoon* made the sound of human footsteps?" Colt asked, incredulously.

Parker shrugged. "It had to be something, why not a raccoon? Those little bastards are troublemakers." His mind wandered to a time when a raccoon had gotten stuck in their garage and wreaked havoc. A nostalgic half-smile across his face, he turned to Ash. "Remember that time one of them knocked the storage bins onto dad's car and he lost it over a couple of dents in the roof?"

Chuckling to himself, Ash nodded. "Yeah, dad went ballistic and tried to shoot him with a pellet gun. Poor guy barely made it out of there alive." A moment of reminiscing was all he needed before he pulled himself back.

"It sounded way too big to be a raccoon," Colt chimed in, bringing them back to the topic at hand.

"Well, then let's keep checking all the rooms so we can go back downstairs with clear heads," Parker suggested, in an effort to get the team back on track.

Nodding in agreement, the three of them set off down the hall and began to check each room, letting the others know each was clear as they went along.

Ash was just about to stick his head into one of the final

empty rooms—perhaps used by staff as a bedroom—when the door slammed shut right in front of his face. The burst of air blew his hair into his eyes, sending his head rearing backward out of sheer shock. The smacking sound of the wood rang inside his mind, splitting into rolling waves, and his hands instinctively reached up to cover them as if the sound was coming from somewhere other than the inside of his head.

Raising his flashlight to illuminate his brother, Parker stood firmly a few feet away.

"You good?" He asked.

"Yeah," Ash mumbled, shaking the dust from his face and wiping at his eyes. "The door must've gotten caught by a draft."

"No one was in there, right?" Colt chirped, warily.

"I didn't get a good look," Ash replied, gripping the doorknob again and turning it—only to find that it was now locked. "What the hell?" he mumbled, in disbelief. Tightening his chokehold on the brass knob, he wrenched it to the left with all of his might.

Nothing.

Pushing and pulling and twisting the doorknob in every direction with all of his strength, it still wouldn't budge. With both hands tightly wrapped around it, the knob abruptly dislodged and separated from the door. It sent him stumbling backward into the wall behind, where he made contact with it at a high enough speed to send him tumbling to the floor with the doorknob still grasped in his palm.

Head ringing and now throbbing, Ash sat there for a beat while Parker and Colt approached.

"Are you okay?" Parker asked, extending a hand to help him up. "Hell of a draft."

"Yeah, I think so," Ash groaned sharply, rising to his feet carefully. "That really fucking hurt." Fingers massaged the back of his head, trying to circulate blood flow and reduce the chance of a bruise forming. "Do I look okay?"

Parker's eyes threatened to roll into the back of his head like loose marbles.

"Clearly he's fine," he deadpanned to Colt.

"Guess I'm stronger than I thought," Ash mused, turning over the chunk of brass in his hand.

"Or that shit is old and it didn't take much to break it," Colt countered. "Can I see that?"

With a shrug, Ash passed it to him.

Despite his apprehension, Colt walked it back to its door and inserted it into the slot to which it belonged. Gently twisting it, he was able to push the door open to reveal a windowless room that was far smaller than the other bedrooms they'd come across on this floor. Perhaps it wasn't a bedroom at all, but a small office. There wasn't any furniture or decor to reveal what the room had once been used for.

Something about its cold, windowless interior gave Colt the creeps.

He started to back away, but Parker and Ash were suddenly right behind him and pushing further into the room.

"I'm gonna go ahead and say that it probably wasn't a draft," Parker quipped, his flashlight sweeping across each corner as he looked for a crack in the wall. "Guess there goes that theory."

"Guys," Colt began, attempting to mask his nervousness. "I think this floor is good, let's just–let's go back downstairs."

Frigid air whipped around them, like an unseen doorway had opened to a snowy tundra, yet it was completely still.

Colt's breath caught in his throat and he swallowed hard. The eerie feeling had crept further into the pit of his stomach, sinking its claws into him. Looking down at the gooseflesh covering his arms, he crossed them to insulate his body heat.

Ash's head swiveled as he shined his flashlight all around them. "Maybe we should head back downstairs," he agreed, looking forward to getting back on track with the night's investigation. away from whatever cold spot was stuck in this part of the building. "Obviously no one's up here. Might as well get back to the others."

As he headed out of the room, Colt followed closely behind him.

"Yeah, okay..." Parker agreed, looking around slowly and retreating after the two of them and back toward the stairwell.

CHAPTER THIRTEEN

Eyes were on them the moment they walked back into the control room. Embry's were full of concern, but Rhett's were masking fear.

"You okay, Ash?" Embry asked, wincing. "It looked like you fell *hard*."

Embry had kept an eye on the cameras when Ash, Colt, and Parker had disappeared to look for the intruders, and she'd clearly seen what had happened with the door and his clumsiness. In the heat of the moment, the fact that they had set up a stationary camera on that floor had been completely forgotten.

"All good," Ash managed. Eyes slightly dry as he fought the delirium, he flashed a brief smile. His arched lips revealed perfectly arranged and artfully bleached teeth that appeared even more unnatural in the dim light of the room.

"We saw the whole thing and it looked pretty painful," Rhett added. "How's your head?"

Ash waved her off. "I'm fine."

"I think y'all should see what we saw…" she pointed to her computer monitor and took the headphones off from around her neck.

The five of them crowded around Rhett's monitor. There was a segment of audio queued up in the software, waveforms enlarged to show every detail beneath a series of timestamps.

"This segment is from when you three were upstairs," Rhett explained. "At first I thought it was just reverb—and maybe it is, I haven't spent enough time on it yet—but it sounds like somethin' very specific to me and I can't tell if it's just my mind playing tricks on me or—"

"Rhett," Embry interrupted, a hand gently touching the other woman's arm. "You're rambling, take a breath."

Shaking her head, Rhett refocused. "I need you to listen to this and tell me if I'm onto somethin'…"

Unplugging her headphones from the auxiliary jack, Rhett glanced at each of her teammates and then turned back to the computer and pressed the spacebar to play the audio snippet.

As the clip played, the boys' muffled voices could barely be heard from where they stood. They had to have been almost thirty feet from where the camera was set up on its tripod. Their voices grew louder as they continued down the hallway toward the stationary camera, words getting clearer in the stillness of the second floor air.

Ash leaned as far as he could toward the monitor

speakers, straining to figure out where they were in the scheme of his memory.

The sound of the door slamming played through the speakers, followed by their back-and-forth at the door. Ash reached up to rub at the back of his bruised skull, searing heat rising to meet his fingertips.

"Right there," Rhett commented, pausing the video. "Did y'all hear it?"

"Hear the door slam and then Ash fall on his ass? Yeah," Colt teased.

Ash jabbed him in the side and Colt let out a breathless *oof*.

"No, listen carefully," Rhett said, backing the video up to just eight seconds before the door slammed shut.

The volume was already cranked as high as it could go, but none of them heard anything but static coming through the speakers.

"Okay, wait…" Reaching down for her headphones, she plugged them back in and handed them to Ash first. "Listen with these, that's how I heard it the first time. It's faint, but I swear it's there."

He doubted that there was anything to hear, but Ash decided to humor Rhett by gingerly placing the headphones over his ears and adjusting them until they were comfortably blocking out everything but the computer's audio as the clip began to play again.

"Play it again," he instructed Rhett, pushing the headphones against his ears to hold them in place. His eyes strained as he followed the path of the waveform, listening for every flicker in the static. "But slow it down to half speed." Eyes closed, Ash waited for the clip to play again so that he could dissect the sound.

The door slamming echoed between his ears like a game of Tug of War, but it was the background sound he was most interested in.

The hissing was almost a whisper, yet different somehow.

"Can we isolate that any further?" Ash asked.

Rhett shook her head. "Not any further than I already have. Not without better equipment, anyway. All I got is this laptop."

All of her best hardware was back home. She wouldn't dare risk damaging any of her favorite gadgetry by bringing it along on location. Especially after seeing how Ash treated the mic packs.

Ash pulled the headphones down, a pensive look swallowing his features.

"I can't put my finger on it, but it's almost like whispering or something," he said.

"That's what I thought, too!" Rhett nodded, pointing emphatically at Ash. "I heard something specific, but I don't want to influence what any of y'all might've heard, so I want to wait to say what I heard until each of y'all have a chance to listen."

Each of them took their turn with the headphones, popping them onto their heads and listening intently to the audio clip Rhett played. Each turn lasted a little over a minute, but those few minutes stretched on for what felt like forever.

By the end, the only thing they could all agree on was that it was melodic, like a euphonic whistle.

"Olive?" Embry asked as she pulled off the headphones.

The rest of them were confused, but not Rhett.

"That's exactly what I heard," she nodded. "In a small, childlike voice."

What she *didn't* say was that the voices of children were often masks for the demonic. She also wasn't ready to cop to the fact that she believed in the spirit world, because she knew she'd been laughed off the team faster than her daddy used to down a po'boy.

"There must be something wrong with the equipment if we're getting weird feedback like that," Ash said. "Was everything calibrated properly?"

Rhett shot him a pointed stare, her voice defiant. "Wanna ask that again?"

In other words: *you think I didn't do my job?*

Ash sighed. "There's an explanation here, we just have to figure out what it is."

"It's obviously a ghost asking for an olive," Colt teased. "Maybe they're making martinis in the afterlife and missing an ingredient."

Parker somehow managed to refrain from calling Colt an idiot, despite the corners of his own mouth pulling into a grin. "There's definitely something going on, but I think we may have to consider that the answer could be something we're not going to like."

Rhett eyed him cautiously, wondering where he was going with this.

"This place might *actually* be haunted," Parker admitted.

"Jesus, not you, too," Ash groaned.

Looking over to find that his brother was mid-eyeroll, Parker sucked air through his front teeth and ignored him. "I know it sounds unhinged, but it's one of the only explanations left. So, it's either that or someone is playing a very fucking elaborate prank on us."

The prank was honestly more likely, but their remote location—and distance from anyone who actually knew who they were—practically guaranteed that this was anything but a joke.

"Hauntings aren't real!" Ash countered, in utter disbelief over what he was hearing.

Since their start, they'd all been in silent agreement that there was no such thing as ghosts. No ghouls. No shadow monsters. Nothing hiding under the bed or in the back of a closet.

It was all fake; they knew that.

But now Parker was going to stand there and pull a one-eighty?

Unbelievable.

"Calm down," Parker chided. "It's not a personal attack, it's an observation based on evidence."

Irritation clouded Ash's judgment and a terse, "fuck you, Columbo," spilled out of his mouth.

There were few times when Parker's eyes grew dark, but this was one of them.

"I'd shut up if I were you," he suggested, unblinking. "Before you make me say something you'll regret."

The downside to living and working with your sibling is that they know where all the bodies are buried—figurative and otherwise. They might be your deepest confidant, but at the end of the day the potential for betrayal still lurks beneath the surface. Even if you know they'd never pull that trigger, the barrel of the gun stays rested at the nape of your neck, cold and metallic and unwieldy.

You never know when it might go off and ruin everything.

Parker's words dared Ash to cross the line he'd now drawn in the sand, but his self-preservation didn't allow him to utter another word. There were too many things that his brother could say to tarnish his position in this group and give the rest of their crew a reason not to trust his leadership.

Unfortunately, Parker was right.

It was better if he shut up.

"Fine," he muttered through clenched teeth, throwing his hands in the air. "Then explain this fucking evidence-based bullshit you've cooked up." With a sigh, Ash allowed the wall beside him to take his body weight as he slouched into it.

Not another second was wasted on their interaction as Parker moved on, straining to remember his original train of thought.

The two of them looked at each other as if to ask *should we say it out loud* before answering him. Embry raised her brow in deferment to Rhett, who shifted focus to Parker. She'd heard it first, so it was only fair that she be the one to respond.

"I heard a word. Or a name, maybe." Rhett said. "*Olive.*"

CHAPTER FOURTEEN

"Any luck?" Colt asked from his place on the floor, voice semi drowned-out by the pattering of rain against the propped-open window.

"Not yet," Parker answered, thumbing through a barrage of printouts and swiping through scans he'd taken of old newspaper articles and hundred-year-old documents he'd found in the library's archives. "I haven't found a single mention of anyone named Olive in relation to Crenshaw."

Ash was leaning back in an old armchair he'd dragged in from the lobby, fidgeting with a sliding pair of magnetic ace of spades cards.

"Maybe the lead paint in here is decomposing into the air and we're all being poisoned by it," he stated flatly, the tone of his voice doubling down on the fact that he didn't believe for a second that there was actually a ghost on the premises. "Let's get real, here," he added, looking from Embry to Rhett. "There's a higher probability that we're mass hallucinating than that there are actual ghosts hovering down the hallways."

If looks could kill, Rhett's glare would've shattered Ash into a million tiny shards.

In an effort to manage her emotions, though, she simply flipped him off and kept her eyes glued to the screen in front of her.

Parker, ignoring Ash's bait, spoke up again while scrolling through the documents on the property's history that he'd saved to his cloud drive. "It looks like there was only ever a handful of female staff on the premises..." He rested his chin on his fist, a low *hmmm* vibrating out from his lips. "All of the wards were boys, too. Maybe the voice meant *Oliver*?"

"That's going to be impossible to track down," Colt piped up.

"Hard, but not impossible," Parker corrected. "I'm going to look for Olivers in the list of wards and see what I can find..."

"I'm gonna need more time, though," he added.

"How much time do you think you've got before this ghost, or whatever, tries to kill us all?" Ash asked, the metal cards sliding between his fingers, a teasing smirk crawling up the side of his face.

Before Parker had a chance to respond, Rhett slipped her shoe off her foot and heaved it overhand at Ash's head. It connected with the side of his face, smashing into his ear before it crashed to the floor and fell into a pile of equipment cases.

"Ow, fuck!" Ash cried out in pain, grabbing at his throbbing ear.

Embry and Colt broke out into a burst of laughter the moment the shoe made contact.

"Maybe that'll teach you to shut the fuck up," Rhett muttered under her breath, growing increasingly impatient with Ash's visceral disrespect toward things he didn't understand. It was one thing if he was unwilling to believe in the paranormal, but to outwardly challenge the universe to smite you with its spiritual prowess? That was just plain reckless.

"Would you two knock it off?" Parker asked, exasperatedly waving an angry hand at them as he broke his attention away from the computer screen. "You're like toddlers, my god."

"He started it," Rhett replied, just as Ash exclaimed, "She started it!"

Parker sighed. "Incorrigible, the both of you."

Knowing better than to throw Rhett's shoe back at her and risk damaging their equipment even further, Ash picked it up and threw it out into the hallway. The smug look plastered across his face was goading, begging her to pick a fight with him.

Not even a second later, Embry was wrestling Rhett's other shoe from her hands to keep her from launching it across the room even harder than she'd thrown the first one.

"He's not worth it!" Embry whispered, using her height to her advantage to overpower the shoeless sound engineer.

Rhett muttered something inaudible and clicked

around on her computer so loudly that Ash watched with certainty, waiting for the mouse to collapse into warped plastic shrapnel under the pressure of her death grip.

"Okay," Parker said, raising a hand to direct everyone's attention toward himself. "There are eleven documented Olivers in the history of the Crenshaw Industrial Reformatory, going back all the way to the institution's inception in 1862." His eyes scanned the notes he'd compiled. "Three of those were staff while the other eight were wards. The downside is that we don't have any of the files they kept on the wards. Most of them never made their way off the premises after the doors were closed for good."

"What do you mean?" Colt asked, leaning back on his hands. "Like they were destroyed or just left here to rot?"

Parker shrugged. "Could be either one."

"What about the last names?" Embry asked, wondering if there's some other avenue they hadn't considered. "Are there any red flags there?"

Pulling up the list, Parker chewed at the inside of his cheek and then shook his head.

"Nothing that sticks out, but here's the list," he said, moving toward the door of the room with a black expo marker in hand. The top half of the door was inset with a rippled pane of antique glass, on which Parker began to scrawl the list of names.

.   .   .

*Oliver Andrews **
Oliver Bardot
Oliver Beckett
Oliver Cassady
Oliver Grint **
Oliver Klein
Oliver Langley
Oliver McCowen
Oliver Preston
Oliver York **
Oliver Zabarowski*

"The ones with the asterisks are the faculty members," Parker clarified.

"So, what, you think the ghost might've been trying to say Oliver?" Rhett asked, reaching a finger up to scratch behind her ear. Could the ghost have been trying to say Oliver? Everything in her wanted to believe it had been *Olive* that she'd heard, but now she was second-guessing herself.

"Maybe the ghost's name is Oliver, or that's who they're trying to contact," Parker mused.

Ash scoffed, amazed at how ridiculous they were being.

"You can't be serious," he said, words piercing incredulously. "There is no ghost!" He rose to his feet defiantly, hoping they'd realize they were locking themselves in a wild goose chase by focusing on something that didn't exist. "The longer you keep up this charade, the more time we waste while we're supposed to be filming this fucking episode. You all realize that, right?" Glancing around the room, it was clear that everyone was starting to buy this ghost nonsense but him.

What. The. *Actual*. Fuck.

Ash sighed and flicked his head back to shake the hair out of his eyes. "Can we at least table this until we get the footage we need?" He pleaded, hoping that this final bargain might be his lucky chance to pull their focus back onto getting the episode done.

Three seconds of dead silence dragged on like minutes.

"Fine," Parker conceded. "Everyone in favor of solving this mystery *after* we finish filming the episode?" He looked around at the others, gauging their reaction. "Or at least until something in the episode ties back to this?"

Embry, Colt, and Rhett nodded in agreement.

"Fucking finally," Ash groaned, dragging his hands down his face.

CHAPTER FIFTEEN

Colt nudged Ash with the messenger bag at his side as they climbed the stairs side-by-side.

"You good?" Colt jabbed a thumb over his shoulder. "You kinda lost it back there."

"No, I didn't," Ash defended, far too quickly.

Looking at his friend with a smug grin on his face, Colt's self-approving nature shined like a glow stick in the dead of night at an abandoned rave site.

"Piss off," Ash grumbled.

The only thing worse than that look of satisfaction on Colt's face was having to see it in the dark by flashlight, the shadows dancing along his features and playing tricks with Ash's eyes.

"Why does it get you going so badly? You've been on edge ever since we got here."

Colt wasn't wrong, but Ash hated admitting it—even to himself.

"He's just... I don't know, man," Ash sighed. "Parker's just on my last nerve. Suddenly he's believing in fucking *ghosts*?" He asked incredulously, the question rhetorical. "And trying to get me to answer Luther's texts and shit? I'm over it."

Face dropping, Colt nodded slowly. "It doesn't sound like you're over it, but I get it. Your dad..." He mused, then quickly corrected himself. "*Luther* did a number on you, and if you don't want to talk to him then don't. It's that simple. Whether Parker agrees with it or not, he had a totally different experience than you did—for obvious reasons—and that's on him."

Sometimes Ash forgot how insightful Colt could be when he was in a serious frame of mind. It was like seeing him in a different light, with the perceptiveness and profound thoughtfulness that he was capable of showing on full display. He contained multitudes and Ash often wondered why he chose to turn it on and off at will, but deep down he was jealous. To be able to control that so easily was a foreign concept to Ash, who had always been quick to emotional responses out of anger or frustration.

"This is you," Ash said, pausing at the top of the landing on the second floor. He had learned long ago that the best way to end a conversation was to deflect to something else. In this case, it was Colt's intense focus on their conversation as they'd climbed the stairs.

Nodding with a heavy exhale, Colt began to walk away, turning back after a few steps.

"It doesn't hurt to be vulnerable, Ash."

"Saying shit like that is exactly how I know you're not a Novak!" Ash called back without turning around, already halfway down the long hallway.

The soles of his boots dropped heavily onto the corroding floorboards with each step, reverberating so much that they hummed in the darkness and enveloped him in a hypnotic swarm of incessant tinnitus.

Ash turned on his camera and turned it around so that it faced him. Switching off his flashlight, and enabling the night vision feature, the LCD screen glowed viridescent.

"Parker, Colt, and I have split up across the four floors of Crenshaw Castle, taking some time to explore the dark recesses of this location and communicate with the spirits one-on-one," he explained, his voice low so as not to taint Colt's footage. "This," he panned around the room, showcasing the wall-mounted chalkboards and scattered, decaying books, "is one of the classrooms where the wards of the estate would continue their educational lessons so that they could leave this place with the same level of education they would've had if they'd remained in the public school system."

There were a dozen child-sized wooden desks in the room, all facing a much larger desk. All of them had a thick coating of dust atop them, but one of them caught Ash's eye. At the back of the room, near a boarded-up window, the dust had been disturbed. In the center of the attached table top, the filth had cleared in the shape of a handprint.

Weird, Ash thought. *Bet that was Parker trying to get a rise out of me.*

It wasn't going to work, though.

Ash was all business tonight, and he wouldn't be giving Colt the satisfaction.

"According to the local news story from 1904," he continued. "Amos Pinckney was thirteen years old when his life was brutally taken from him in this very room." Ash made his way over to the teacher's desk and perched on its edge. "Not only was he stabbed more than twenty times, but his face was mutilated and he was found with a bright yellow pencil sticking haphazardly out of his neck. A gruesome death, indeed, but not the worst one to happen on the Crenshaw grounds. Not by a mile. You see, Amos's death was one of dozens during Crenshaw Industrial Reformatory's sordid history, and it has marked this spot forever."

A little over the top? Maybe. Good television? Absolutely.

"With that in mind, I want to try to reach out to Amos's spirit and see if his soul is still haunting the place of his violent end."

Ash rested a REM pod on the desk beside himself, and then pulled out a digital recorder. He turned it on with a *beep* and held it in his hand as he spoke.

"Amos," he called out, as loud as he could without yelling. He had to make his performance believable for the camera, even though his anti-ghost argument with the team was still at the front of his mind. "I want to hear your story." Eyes darted in the dark, not seeing anything in the shadows but feeling the chill of the Oregon air sneaking past the warped plywood that covered the windows. "Can you tell me who murdered you?"

Silence, aside from the distant mumbles and movement of his teammates on the floors above and below him.

"Do you know why you were attacked?"

Silence.

"Is anyone else here with us?"

Silence.

"Can you tell me—"

A sharp crack split through the air, so loud that Ash sat up straighter than an arrow in response. It sounded like it had grazed past him, but what it had been was a mystery.

"The hell was that?" Grabbing the camera, Ash stood to find the culprit. "I'm not sure if you all heard that," he added, guiding his steps with the screen on the camera and faint light drifting in through cracks in the wood-covered window. "But it was super loud."

As he made his way to the doorway and peered out into the hallway with his flashlight in hand, he kept his camera rolling. The beam shined through the murk of the second floor. The hallway twisted halfway down, so Ash couldn't see anything beyond that. Add in the echoey way the sound had traveled, and it was impossible to figure out where the sound had originated.

Static ruptured the silence and Ash's hand felt for the radio on his hip.

"Colt?" Embry's voice rang out. "Your video is glitching really badly."

"And all I hear is static, it sounds like running water," Rhett said.

Silence.

"Now we've lost your sound entirely, Colt. Can you radio back?" Rhett added.

No response.

Embry's voice piped back up. "Ash, Parker, can one of you find him? I think his camera is broken, it's completely wigging out."

"I'm on the same floor, so I'll go check on him," Ash answered, clipping the radio back onto his belt.

"Copy. Thanks, Ash."

Re-entering the hallway felt different this time. Colder, the temperature likely dropping from the rain that had just begun to pour outside. Surprisingly it hadn't started leaking too badly inside, which was a sign that the Schuyler Foundation had at least been maintaining the building's roof. Clunking along the hallway, the depth of the quietness grew.

Why can't I hear Colt? He wondered.

Even if Colt kept his voice low, he should've been able to hear him as he grew closer to the second floor bathroom. Especially since they usually left the doors open on their Lore Walks. It didn't make—

Except that the door was shut.

Ash's face dropped. Not only was the door closed, but he couldn't hear Colt at all. Not a word or a sound or the flash of a light from beneath the door. His guts bubbled and broiled as he reached for the door's knob.

Locked.

Pressing his ear to the rotting wood, all he could hear were the sounds of distant water splashing.

"Colt!" Ash called out, banging on the door with the side of his closed fist.

When he didn't answer, Ash's thuds against the door grew louder to no avail.

"The door to the bathroom is locked and he's not answering," Ash announced over the radio. "I don't know if he's still in there or not."

"His camera feed froze and then went black," Embry replied. "I can't see anything."

A blood curdling shriek screamed out from behind the door.

"COLT!" Ash roared, grip tightening on the doorknob as he willed it to turn.

When it didn't budge, Ash tried to shoulder the door open but ended up sending a shockwave of pain up through his left arm and down his leg through to his bad knee. Groaning, he clutched the part of his arm that had made contact with the door and radioed again.

"Parker, I need you down here now!"

CHAPTER SIXTEEN

"Already on my way," Parker answered, materializing not even a minute later.

"It's stuck!" Ash yelled, gesturing at the door. His eyes locked with Parker's and they were full of fear. "I heard a scream, I heard *Colt* scream."

Parker's brows dug into the bridge of his nose and his fingers wrapped around the doorknob. The moment he turned it, it unlatched with a rusty *clitch* and squealed open.

"Guess it's not locked anymore," he mused, a hesitant hand subtly shaking as he placed his palm against the door and slowly pushed it open.

As it swung open, a foul odor swept out toward them, its noxious gas capturing them in its grasp.

The hallway echoed with the creaking of the door's hinges as the two brothers entered the bathroom, fighting for their lives against the smell. Colt's flashlight was left on, shining a beam of light across the tile floor. It looked as though it had fallen and rolled to rest against the far wall. The malachite-hued tiles were far more menacing now, their reflective surfaces highlighting every eldritch aspect of the room with what little illumination the flashlight provided. The hard pattering of the storm outside had eaten away at the remaining daylight, swallowing the sunset and drowning Crenshaw in a sea of grey.

The room was empty, but where the hell was Colt?

"Colt?" Parker called out, the two of them rushing into the room with erratic heartbeats. "It's not like it's big enough for him to get lost in here."

Ash began to scour the room. "He was screaming bloody murder from the other side of a locked door, Parker. I know what I heard."

"Could've been stuck, not locked," Parker offered, playing the part of the Devil's Advocate.

"Trust me," Ash insisted. "It was locked."

In the corner of the room was the familiar bathtub from earlier, when he and Colt had been in here setting up the stationary cameras.

"The camera!" Ash shouted, swiveling his head in both directions.

The camera was gone.

"Where the fuck is the camera?" He questioned, searching the floor and every surface it could've been set upon.

Parker raised his radio. "Hey, Em, can you see the feed from the second floor bathroom?"

There was a pause, and then Embry's voice rang out.

"Doesn't look like we have a camera in there..." she said. "The only feed blacked out is Colt's, though."

Face twisted in confusion, Ash shook his head. "Not possible. We set a camera up in here, Parker, I swear to god."

"I believe you," Parker assured from the other side of the room, nearest the decrepit clawfoot tub. "You might wanna come look at this, though..."

Swallowing hard, Ash prepared himself for what he would find within the tub. Parker hadn't been able to take his eyes off of whatever lay within it, and that wasn't a good sign.

"What—" Ash started.

Then his eyes landed on the contents of the tub.

Murky, green-black water filled the bathtub nearly to the brim, so dark that the bottom was indistinguishable. The putrid smell wafted up from the surface, a stench of rotting pumpkin, spoiled milk, and boiled death. It made Ash want to vomit, stinging his eyes and nose until he lifted his shirt over his nostrils in an effort to block some of the stench.

"Oh, god, what died in there?" Ash asked, pointing his camera down into the tub.

Whatever it was, it definitely would definitely be the *wow factor* that Cam was looking for to make this season soar.

"It reeks," he coughed.

Parker spotted blood slicked along the side of the tub, its bright red color an indicator of its freshness.

"This doesn't give me a good feeling," Parker said, pointing at the maroon mess, his eyes sunken with worry.

Ash's stomach was in his throat, gatekeeping all words from finding a way out. His concern for Colt had doubled in a matter of nanoseconds, and seeing the blood only led him to one conclusion: he was dead.

Parker held the flashlight closer to the blood and noticed that it was part of a larger trail. Smeared droplets dragged along the tile floor and up the wall, bleeding into the cracks of several broken tiles.

As his breathing grew heavier, Parker cleared his throat.

"We need to find Colt," he said, turning to Ash, the flashlight's beam held steady on the spot where it looked like someone's head had been bashed in. "*Right now.*"

CHAPTER SEVENTEEN

Ash's throat began to constrict as though two muscular hands had wrapped around his neck and tightened until all of the air had squeezed out.

"Embry, do you see Colt on any of the cameras?" Parker urgently asked over the radio.

Quietly thankful for his brother's take-charge attitude in the face of danger, Ash struggled to see straight. Mind racing with a million horrible scenarios after seeing the aftermath of an obvious altercation, everything in his field of vision was vibrating erratically. Acid churned in his stomach as his anxiety rose. He couldn't help but tremble at the thought of what might've happened to his best friend. That blood belonged to *someone*, and if it was Colt's then there was no telling what kind of trouble he could be in. Heart pounding in his ears, Ash's clammy hands reached up and intertwined behind his neck, pulling downward with the weight of his concern.

Finally, Embry's voice broke through the damning silence.

"I can't–he's not on any of the cameras," she frantically responded. Her mouse clicked rapidly in the background. "*Fuck*," she swore. "None of the mics are picking up anything useful, either."

"Goddamnit," Parker muttered, willing his brain to process faster. "Well, he's got to be somewhere, we just have to—" His words dropped off mid-sentence and he froze.

"Have to what?" Ash asked, not following his brother's train of thought.

"Colt," Parker whispered, voice cracking.

Ash followed his brother's gaze back down into the bathtub—where a ghastly pale hand had floated up from the depths of the caliginous liquid. Eyes as wide as saucers, his body couldn't decide whether to jump out of its skin or melt into the grout. Ash wanted this to be another Schrödinger's Cat, where he could never know if Colt was gone or just playing a deeply-psychotic prank.

"Is that...?" Ash began, unable to finish his trailing thought.

"I'm going to regret doing this, I just know it," Parker uttered, swallowing his disgust.

Rolling up his sleeve until it was well above his elbow, Parker reached into the tub until he felt the soggy fabric of Colt's flannel shirt and pulled. The water sloshed with the shifting of the weight, rolling like hostile waves against the sides of the tub. It splashed against Parker and left foul spots along the front of his shirt.

"*Ugh,*" Parker groaned, the revolting scent making him want to recoil and scratch through his skin. "Even if I burn this shirt, I'm never getting this smell out of my brain."

As he lifted, vaguely familiar features appeared.

Sopping wet curls, flattened by the putrid bathwater, were like a mop atop a mannequin's head. Only, it wasn't a mannequin.

It was Colt.

So long, Schrödinger—the cat's out of the bag, now.

Ash stepped back, eyes wide, utterly unable to breathe.

Colt's water-logged body surged out of the tub, sloshing the foul water until it splashed out onto the tile flooring and soaked everything in its path. His mouth gaped open, revealing a blanched tongue and icy lips. Glassy eyes looked everywhere and nowhere all at once. Revolted, Parker jerked backward and his grip unintentionally released on Colt's shirt, sending his body submerging back down into the tub, sending waves of disgusting ancient bathwater flying everywhere again.

"Jesus Christ," Ash managed, bent over with his hands on his knees.

His heart breaking in real time, Parker stared down into the murky water the last of his body finally sank beneath its surface. The boy was like his second little brother, and had caused just as much trouble as Ash in their younger days. But now, he'd give anything to undo what was happening here. This was a searing pain that would scar them forever.

Ash's head was spinning with thoughts of how he'd break the news to Colt's family, the incredibly suspicious circumstances they were in, the nausea he was fighting as he looked at the dripping shell of his best friend. Who was going to believe that they'd found him like this, when there were clearly signs of some sort of struggle? The barrage of irrational grief thoughts were hitting him like a freight train speeding down a cliff face.

Parker took a deep breath and grabbed his radio. "Embry, Rhett... we found him."

"Thank god," Embry sighed with relief, just as Rhett asked, "is he okay?"

"He's gone," Parker answered, deflated. He looked at Ash, whose face was whiter than a sheet. "We're going to need a minute here, but then we'll meet back up with you two and figure out what to do next."

There were only so many things they could do about all of this. But, undoubtedly, calling 9-1-1 was probably at the top of one of his crewmate's heads. It was the logical thing to do, of course. Ash knew that. But it would ruin everything.

Ash couldn't let that happen.

"We can't call the paramedics," he insisted to Parker, eyes focused and jaw set. "We can't call anyone."

Parker raised a brow, flabbergasted beyond belief. "Why the fuck not?" He tilted his head. "You don't think we should call the police to address the literal *dead body* of your *best fucking friend* that we just found in a goddamn bathtub? Did *your* head get slammed into a tile wall, too?"

"We have to finish filming," came Ash's reply, slithering past the guilty lump nestled deep in his throat. "Colt would've wanted us to keep going, to make his death mean something. I know what you're going to say, but–"

"I don't think you fucking do," Parker interrupted. "'Cause if you did, you wouldn't have said that insensitive ass shit about not calling the cops." Parker looked at him like he'd grown a second head before his eyes, and then exploded with angry disbelief as he pointed at Colt. "We can't just leave his body here, Ash!"

"If we call the cops, they'll make us pack up—plus we'll be suspects—and his death will be for nothing!" Ash argued. In his mind, they were going to lose their shot at keeping *Phantom Files* alive if they stopped now. Not only would their season be ruined, but they'd be insulting Colt's memory by allowing this to derail their best season yet. "We could use this!"

"Wow," Parker scoffed, fury boiling within him. "I knew you could be a selfish prick, but this? This has to be the most tactless, egotistical bullshit you've ever said in your life. And you've had some stupid fucking shit snake outta your mouth." An exasperated laugh exited his body, taking with it every bit of understanding and patience.

"He'd want us to keep going," Ash doubled-down.

"Shut up, Ash!" Parker commanded.

"But–"

Parker's horror twisted into rage as his hand wrapped around his brother's throat and thrusted him against the tile wall. "You're done speaking. Got it? I don't want you uttering a single fucking word about continuing on with this cursed ass episode until the rest of us decide what we're doing about all of this."

As pain radiated from the back of his head down through his neck, Ash coughed.

"Do you understand?" Parker asked, squeezing tighter.

"Yeah, yeah, got it," Ash squeaked, hands reaching up to peel away the other man's fingers.

Shaking his head, Parker let go and backed off, still in disbelief that his brother could be so callous toward someone he'd grown up with his entire life. Refusing to look at Ash while his blood was still molten hot, his gaze drifted toward the far corner, where a small red dot glowed in the shadows. Curiosity got the better of him and he got up to go retrieve what ended up being Colt's camera.

And it was still recording.

CHAPTER EIGHTEEN

"What?" Ash wheezed, rubbing his neck as he watched Parker pick something up. "What is it?"

"Colt's camera," Parker answered curtly, turning it over to inspect it.

"Did it capture what happened?"

"Jesus, give me a second to find out, would ya?" Parker spat back, still irritated with Ash.

He turned off the recording and navigated to the stored files to find the most recent one. Using his thumb to press play on the screen, the video started to play. As Parker watched, Colt began to speak to the camera with his place of death looming in the frame behind him. Seeing him alive again was a startling contrast, but one that he welcomed with a hint of a melancholic smile.

"Okay, Colt Pereira here," he said, pupils dilated in the dark.

Night vision mode made everything a glowing shade of green, including the whites of his eyes. His brown irises blended into black pupils and he looked positively possessed.

"I'm in the second floor washroom of the Crenshaw Industrial Reformatory." Colt gestures around the room, paying special attention to the tub. "In this bathtub, a nine-year-old boy drowned in 1927. Arthur Crowley, who'd only been at the institution for six months, was found floating face-down in what I can only assume was this very tub."

Parker took a shuddering breath.

"According to our sources, there is no arrest record or indication of whoever was responsible for Arthur's murder," Colt continued. "In fact, Headmaster Elwood went so far as to double-down on Crenshaw's innocence in the matter, claiming that 'while those responsible may reside inside the walls of Crenshaw, there is no proof left behind to identify the assailant' and thus the mystery was never solved."

No matter how many times he heard the story, Parker always felt so utterly betrayed for Arthur Crowley. He'd been left to the hands of the state at a young age, and then cruelly killed, without so much as a slap on the wrist for his killer. It had resonated with him ever since he'd first heard the story, because he saw young Crowley in Ash. Parker knew the kind of man their father was—the way he'd take his anger out on those around him, especially Ash—yet he'd abandoned his brother there to go off to college multiple states away.

As the video kept going, Colt started to say something else when the right side of the frame grew dark.

"What is that?" Parker asked, pushing his face closer to the small screen to see better.

"What's what?" Ash piped up.

"Shhh," he hushed, holding out a finger.

Behind Colt was a shifting shadow, misaligned with his own body movements. Just then, the video glitched and bands of black, white, and bright neon green dragged across the screen and jumped around from top to bottom. Colt's voice was there at first, but it contorted and morphed into animalistic growls and then faded entirely. Grainy static filled the screen and then the video turned black.

"Nonono, come back!" In an attempt to get the video back, Parker furiously prodded and poked the screen—all to no avail. "Shit," he groaned. "It's gone."

And so went their shot at seeing what, exactly, had happened to Colt.

"What's gone?" Ash took the camera from Parker and tried to work his own magic, but it was hopeless.

Without warning, the low battery symbol began to flash erratically and the entire camera shut off. Now a brick in his hand, their last-ditch effort was to salvage the memory card and hope that Embry could retrieve and restore the files. Gingerly, he pulled out the card and pocketed it.

"We can't leave him in there," Parker said, staring at Colt's bloated corpse. "At the very least we need to pull him out and lay him on the floor."

"Because the floor is so much better?" Ash asked.

"No, because he deserves better than to swell up and be so unrecognizable that his mother can't identify him," Parker snapped, rising to his full height. "Help me get him out," he demanded, stepping toward the tub. "You grab his legs."

Groaning, Ash stood and begrudgingly followed instructions. Grasping Colt's legs as best he could, the jellied skin was ice cold to the touch. Each angular lift had rotting water running down his arms and soaking into his clothes. His stomach churned as the sour smell of fermented orange juice mixed with fecal matter danced into his nostrils. Ash focused on keeping the vomit from rising further up his throat, but it was a losing battle. Seven awkward, sideways movements were enough to clear the side of the basin and they gently put Colt's body down on the floor. Not a moment later, Ash was bent over in the corner of the room, emptying his stomach of its contents.

He was practically unidentifiable already.

A swollen face, bruised and stained with blood. Chest bruised and swollen to three times its size, as if something had crawled under his skin and made his chest cavity its home. All of his features were blown out of proportion like he'd been left submerged for days or weeks.

As Ash racked his brain, he couldn't imagine how that could be.

Decay took longer than a few minutes, or even hours.

"It's weird, right?" Parker asked, noting the way his brother was looking at Colt's body. "The decay... it doesn't make sense. It looks more like he's been dead for weeks, but that's impossible."

"Yeah, maybe," Ash considered, chewing on the inside of his lower lip. "Do you remember that movie we watched, about that haunted house that turned out to be, like, a time-warp portal or something?"

Parker nodded. "Yeah, time moved differently inside the house."

"This kinda reminds me of that."

"So believing in ghosts is too far, but believing a building can affect the flow of time isn't?" Parker asked, incredulously.

"I don't know, I'm just spitballing here."

"According to the theory of relativity, that would require an immense change in gravity and relative motion. I'm not saying it's not possible, but it's theoretical at best."

From the moment they'd parted in the hallway, to the moment they'd found him, Colt had only been left alone for a maximum of thirty minutes. Yet, if that were the case, why was his body so distorted and rancid?

Something strange is happening here.

CHAPTER NINETEEN

Ash stood nervously behind Embry, once in a while breaking out into a bout of pacing.

"Any luck?" he asked again, for the third time in twenty minutes.

Embry glanced over her shoulder, eyes red and cheeks tear-stained.

"No, and your hot breath in my ear isn't helping," she hissed. "Give me some space to figure it out."

Immediately Ash leaned back. "Alright, alright, I'll back off." He stepped past Embry and Rhett's pair of makeshift work areas, over to where Parker was standing.

Pulling out his phone for a quick stolen glance at his wallpaper, seeing Erick's smiling face tugged at Ash's heartstrings. It wasn't enough to make what had happened to Colt okay, but it helped a smidge.

Until it made him think about Teddy.

Ash had only ever fallen in love with one person: Theodore Park.

He was the kindest, gentlest boy that Ash had ever known, and from the moment they met Ash worried he would ruin him—like the way that little kids want to squeeze the ever-loving crap out of cute puppies. He knew that Teddy was too good, too pure, too *perfect*. There was nothing Ash could bring to the table to make it an even exchange between the two of them. So, in typical Ash fashion, he avoided the problem.

That is, until the problem became his physics partner.

As Ash and Teddy grew closer, feelings became undeniable and everything changed.

From then on, they were inseparable.

Right up until Teddy took his last breath.

From the moment that Ash brought his new boyfriend home, his father was unbearable. Luther made it clear that he expected better from him, that this sort of behavior was unacceptable, and that he wouldn't have it tarnishing their family's reputation. That first dinner, his father launched a plate across the dining room and howled profanities until Teddy became so uncomfortable that he left. The screaming match between Luther and Ash that followed that almost-meal was world-shattering.

That's when Ash learned that his father's love was conditional.

"Dad again?" Parker asked, nodding toward the phone in his brother's hand.

"What?" Ash asked, attention shifting. "Oh, no, it's

nothing." He pocketed the device and cleared his throat. "Embry is still working on the memory card." Even as the words came out of his mouth, all he could think about was Colt's bulging and waterlogged body that had burned into his brain.

"You okay?" Parker asked, before taking a deep breath. "Look, I'm sorry for losing my temper earlier, I just..." He sighed, glancing up toward the ceiling to process his words carefully. "I shouldn't have gotten physical like that, it was out of line. Not that what you said wasn't also out of line, but still."

With a slow nod, Ash scratched at his ear. "I know... I just wanted to do one last thing for him, y'know? Make sure his death wasn't in vain, that it would *mean something*. He always wanted a legacy, y'know?"

It was more than a lot—it was the end of an era.

Phantom Files would never be the same again.

Hell, life would never be the same without Colt.

"I know you think Colt would want us to keep going, but we really oughta call the cops, Ash," Parker said softly. "The longer we wait, the more it'll look like we were trying to cover up his death."

Ash sighed, working his bottom lip between his teeth. "Okay," he relinquished, despite how badly he didn't want to give up on the investigation. "Crenshaw doesn't have to be the season opener, we can shoot somewhere else and pass on this episode."

"It's the right call," Parker said, dropping a hand on Ash's shoulder and squeezing gently. "I'll take care of it."

Pulling out his phone, he pressed a few buttons and then his face fell. "No signal," he groaned, lifting his phone above his head and waving it around to see if he could catch a bar.

The foreboding grey sky had opened up and rain was drilling hard against the windows now, streaming down the glass and trickling in through the opening where the cables snaked out to the generator. They'd secured a rolled-up towel in the open space to reduce the amount of water flowing through, but even that was drenched. Whatever storm had hit them tonight was only getting worse, like a menacing omen for what was to come.

A nearby tree branch smacked against the glass and both Ash and Parker flicked their wide eyes toward it, their nerves still on edge.

"I'm guessing the weather is playing a part in that," Parker's jaw tensed. "I'm going to step out to the van and see if I can get a better signal. If I'm not back in ten minutes, come get me."

"Alright, be careful out there," Ash advised, pointing to the jacket he'd left on one of the wall hooks. "Take my jacket, it's waterproof."

Nodding, Parker announced, "I'll be right back," before lifting the hood over his head and disappearing out of the room back toward the entrance.

The large front doors were heavy, but Parker managed to muscle them open as he headed for the Ford Transit parked twenty-five feet from the fortresses' entrance. The wind blew into him as he followed the dirt path toward the van, the mud sloshing beneath his feet as his boots slid with every step. By the time he got to the vehicle, Parker was soaked and fumbling for the keys deep in his pocket.

"For fuck's sake," Parker grunted as they fell from his grasp, tumbling into a puddle of mucky rainwater. He looped his finger through the keyring and shook them off, flicking bits of sludge across Ash's jacket and the door of the van. "Come on, come on..." he muttered, pressing buttons repeatedly until the door unlocked. "Oh, thank god," he sighed in relief, sliding into the driver's seat.

He pulled out his phone—no signal.

Then he remembered: you could still make emergency calls even if you had no bars.

Wet fingers tapped open the keypad and dialed nine, then one, then...

The device vibrated in his hand.

A notification on the screen flashed 'Low Battery!' and then promptly faded as it died in his hand. In a matter of minutes, he'd lost his ability to call the police or drive to the nearest service station. The cherry on top of a terrible fucking day.

His last ditch effort was to see if he could get the car started to plug in the phone to charge, even if just for a few minutes.

The engine roared to life, but as the radio buzzed alive

there was nothing but static. Every station was a different flavor of white noise, a cacophony of noise that lasted just a few seconds before the engine sputtered and seized then shut off entirely.

"No, no, don't do this to me," Parker pleaded, twisting the key in the ignition in hopes of getting it to start again.

No luck.

"Fuck!"

Hands slammed into the steering wheel.

Head fell back against the headrest, eyes closing in frustration.

Climbing back out of the van, Parker slammed the door shut. The wind was stronger now, and it had shifted directions so that he was now walking back into it. It was taking a lot more effort to trudge against it now than it had when he first headed out, as though the wind was playing games to torment the already-frustrated man.

As he reached the front doors, they refused to open. He yanked on the large brass handles, even going so far as to press the soles of his boots against the other door to add leverage. Yet, they didn't budge. Eventually, he succumbed to banging on them in hopes of getting the attention of someone inside.

"Ash!" he called out, fists slamming into the wood. "Rhett! Embry!"

God, was it getting colder? It must've been, because Parker's teeth were chattering and he couldn't make them stop.

"Someone open the—!"

One of the doors began to open and Parker's eyes fell onto Ash, whose face was sporting a look of bewilderment.

"You okay?" he asked gingerly, as though his brother was a bomb waiting to go off.

Arms wrapped around himself with fingers digging into his sleeves, Parker shivered as he walked across the threshold and into the foyer.

"Just peachy," Parker spat, now a human popsicle that was slowly defrosting. "The Transit's dead and so's my phone." He wanted to peel off the jacket and get warm, but his arms weren't moving from where they'd taken hold. "Have you gotten a signal?"

Ash shook his head. "Not since dad tried calling and texting earlier. I don't even have a single bar now," he said, pulling the phone back out again to double check. The battery icon in the corner was blinking now, which was odd. When he'd checked before, it had been at eighty percent.

A high-pitched beeping emanated from the device as it flashed an angry 'Low Battery!' message across the screen.

Three seconds later it was dead.

"Aaaand now it's dead." Ash grimaced, stuffing the phone back into the front pocket of his jeans. "Fantastic."

Does it make me an asshole if I'm glad he can't call the cops? Ash wondered.

There was still a chance that they could finish the episode.

"So, what now?" Ash asked the other man, his voice low in an attempt to keep their conversation relatively private. "I'm devastated about what happened to Colt, but does it tarnish his memory if we let his death mean nothing? We have to wait for someone to come jump the van, anyway, so maybe it's a sign that we should keep going."

"I distinctly remember telling you to stop bringing that up." Parker had already warned Ash to quit talking about this, and his little brother's disinterest in listening was wearing on him. Shucking the jacket as he entered the room, Parker hung the head of damp fabric back onto the hook and collapsed into a folding chair. "Since you can't seem to keep your mouth shut when I tell you to—let me make something clear. Colt is *dead*, Ash," he emphasized, eyes locked onto his little brother as he tried to forcibly infuse common sense into him. "In what world does finishing an episode make that okay?"

"It doesn't," Ash agreed. "But it gives closure to his death. If you're right about this place being haunted, which I still don't totally buy, then something here killed Colt." His skepticism had been challenged by what they'd encountered in the bathroom, though it was a far cry to claim something paranormal was slithering within the walls of Crenshaw Castle. Regardless, he had a mission, now: convince the others to move forward. "What better way to honor his death than to figure out what it was that took his life?"

Parker's eyes narrowed at Ash as he thought it over, jaw tensing pensively. His gaze wafted to Embry and Rhett, both of whom had their headphones half-on-half-off as they subtly eavesdropped on the conversation.

"What do you two think?" Parker asked, craning his neck.

Embry was barely holding it together as she fiddled with her computer.

"It's bad enough we lost Colt." The words were sticking in her throat. "I don't want to risk anyone else getting hurt. Can't we just leave?"

"No," Parker stated, with a shake of his head. "It's more dangerous to try to leave on foot in this storm."

With a sigh, she shrugged her shoulders. "Then I guess we don't have a choice."

All of their eyes fell onto Rhett, the final vote to be won.

"I don't think it's a good idea," she warned. "If you fuck with the darkness, sometimes you let something loose that you can't lock away again. Whatever it was that killed Colt, it could come after us, too." Her eyes traveled the length of the ceiling. "We could end up letting something loose."

Silence befell the room, like an itchy wool blanket that couldn't be peeled off.

"What do you mean?" Embry asked.

Perhaps this was a sign that it was time for Rhett to speak her truth; to arm them against the unseen evils of the world with which she was all too familiar.

"I know this is going to sound ridiculous to y'all," Rhett said, her eyes landing on Ash with a glimmer of annoyance. "But I believe in the spiritual world, whole-heartedly. There's a darkness that lives alongside us, and I've seen it firsthand." She took a deep breath and then let it back out in a slow, deliberate sigh.

If she wanted them to understand, she was going to have to start at the beginning.

"Years ago, when I was about fifteen, I lost my entire family in a house fire," she started. "It was late one night, 'bout two o'clock, and I smelled smoke coming up through the crack at the bottom of my bedroom door. Our house was real old, passed down through the generations, and I used to sleep in a back room on the first floor. It was small but I didn't mind, mostly 'cause I was right next to the back door so I could sneak back in late at night with my parents none the wiser. I wasn't the most trustworthy teenager—who is, you know—but I did a good job hiding that from my folks up until the very end."

Rhett smiled at the memory, before it could be soured by the rest of the story.

Embry and Parker were enthralled in the story, while Ash sat curiously and studied Rhett.

"See, what I didn't know was that there'd been activity in the house. It was real bad toward the end, and that's what led to the fire. " Her thumbnail picked at the cuticle of her middle finger. "Anyway, they kept hoping it would go away, but it didn't. The day of the fire, my mama had called my aunt and told her about some wild shit that my aunt didn't believe. Later, when she told me all this, she said mama was a fool and that there wasn't nothin' in that house except for faulty wiring and rats."

Rhett never did believe her aunt's musings.

She knew her parents never would've lied about something like that. They were self-professed Good

Catholics that never watched horror movies or uttered the word 'devil' for fear that the earth would open and swallow them into the depths of hell for their misdeeds.

"I think it was angry spirits that burned the house down," she admitted. "Something got stirred up in those walls, and I don't mean the rats." Her cuticle was shredded now, bright red blood raised to the surface and saturating the surrounding flesh. "I remember the way the flames licked up the stairs while thick, black smoke billowed everywhere. I could hear their screams piercing through the clouds of soot, but I couldn't get to them. The neighbor's boy, Peter, pulled me out, but it was too late for everyone else. By the time the fire department arrived, the fire had burnt everything to a crisp."

Placing a careful hand on Rhett's shoulder, Embry's lips have tightly pressed against her teeth and formed a sorrowful line across her mouth. Her eyes, still glassy from crying, were beginning to well up with tears, again.

"I'm so sorry, Rhett," she offered quietly, to which Rhett attempted a meek smile of acceptance.

"What makes you think it was angry spirits?" Ash asked.

"When we were going through the remains of the house, I found a bunch of bird bones and feathers stuffed into my sister's pillowcase. My parents never allowed that sort of thing in the house—in fact, they forbade it. The strangest thing, though, was that she had no idea where they had come from. No one was ever allowed into her bedroom, nor did she have any particular grievances against anyone in town. We could never explain it, and now I'll never know how those got there. But I think someone wanted to cause her harm, and it was only the tip of the iceberg."

Another moment of tense silence passed between them.

"I think whoever placed those bones used their ill will to open a portal and allow something to come through. Something that has been following me ever since," Rhett added.

"Why do you think that?" Parker asked.

"Because I was the only one that lived, and I don't think I was supposed to."

CHAPTER TWENTY

Ash never brought Teddy home again—until prom night.

Dressed to the nines in their rental tuxedos, Ash in emerald green and Teddy in a crisp navy blue, they spent the night lavishing affection on one another and dancing the night away. As the party dimmed to a close, the couple didn't want to let the night end. So they did what any other sexually-charged pair of teenagers with absentee parents would do: they ended up at Ash's house.

In his defense, his father wasn't supposed to be home.

There was some charity dinner that a bunch of the hotshot doctors and surgeons from the hospital were highly encouraged to attend (in order to rub elbows and sweet-talk donors into giving them more of their money). Ash hadn't expected his father to return home until well after one in the morning, if he even came home at all.

Unfortunately, he did come home.

And he walked right into their after party.

Clothes were balled-up all over Ash's bedroom floor, beside two pairs of dress shoes and color-coordinated ties. The two of them laid beside one another between the cotton sheets, interrupting the taupe, block plaid pattern. Teddy's hands traced every childhood scar on their way down Ash's body, while Ash intertwined their legs. At that moment, everything was right with the world. Their bubble of love had not yet been popped by the hatred of those who couldn't understand it.

Then three succinct knocks at the door ended their shared bliss.

"Ash!" his father's voice bellowed from behind the solid oak door.

The two of them scrambled as quietly as they could, Teddy clambering out from atop the bed and grabbing his clothes as quickly as he could.

He wasn't fast enough, though.

The door swung open and Ash threw a sheet across himself while Teddy attempted to crouch behind the bed's sturdy frame. It didn't quite hide his body in its entirety, but it was large enough to cover himself while he shimmied on his boxers and undershirt.

"Dad! What the hell?" Ash complained, following his father's gaze as he clocked Teddy's presence in the room.

Luther's face twisted up into a gritty snarl, an angry fire lighting the whites of his eyes.

"What did I say about this!" He snapped, fists clenched so tight at his side that his knuckles were a ghostly white.

"I–I should go…" Teddy murmured, trying to slip out unscathed.

"You're not going anywhere," Ash said, holding out a hand at Teddy.

While this wasn't the best time to challenge his father's authority, with nothing but a sheet covering himself, he wasn't going to let his father's homophobia control his life. One week from his eighteenth birthday and one month away from graduation—there was nothing his father could do to keep him under his thumb any longer. It was time to shut this whole thing down for good.

"Teddy and I are together," Ash said matter-of-factly, staring back into his father's cold green eyes. He'd been afraid of those eyes his entire childhood, afraid of what they might see if they stared at him a little too long. But now, with someone as wonderful as Teddy at his side, Ash couldn't feel the fear gnawing away at him anymore. "I don't know what your weird hang-up is, but you need to get over it. Soon enough I'll be out of here, and there's nothing you can do to keep me from leaving and never speaking to you again."

Expecting his father to fly off the handle like he usually did, Ash was surprised when his father turned around and stalked out of the room. His footsteps quieted as they drew further and further away, a sense of relief washing over the two teens.

Exhaling a stale breath, Teddy picked up his pants off the floor and pulled them on.

"What are you doing?" Ash asked, brow creasing at the

center of his face as he pointed toward the door. "We won, he walked off. You don't have to go anywhere."

Teddy glanced at Ash cautiously. "Nothing about that interaction felt like a win," he retorted, buttoning the waistband of his trousers and reaching for the dress shirt draped over the bedpost. "I get that you think there's something entertaining about pissing off your dad, but..." Teddy sighed, pulling his arms through the shirt's sleeves. "One of these days he's going to fuckin lose it, because that's what loose cannons do, Ash."

He had a point, but Ash wasn't willing to give his father an inch when it came to this.

"What do you want me to do?" Ash asked harshly. "Let him run you off because of his fucking bigotry? How is that fair?"

Teddy shook his head. "I'm not saying it's fair, babe. All I'm saying is that maybe it's best we keep a low profile around your dad, at least for now." His fingers nimbly fed each button through its hole, moving from the hem of his shirt toward the collar.

"Is that what you want?" Ash asked, hurt stinging his eyes.

"It's not what I want," Teddy clarified, stepping toward Ash and bending down to cup his face between his soft palms. "But I think it's what we need to do for now."

Smiling, he leaned down and kissed Ash tenderly, a final act of love.

"I'm going to head home, okay?" Teddy said. "But I'll see you tomorrow, yeah? My turn to bring the coffees," he smiled, fingers combing through Ash's hair. Saturdays were their standing thrift-stores-and-plant-shop-date days.

"Deal," Ash reluctantly agreed. "Caramel macchiatos at ten it is."

With a smile, Teddy slipped on his shoes and left.

Ash drifted to sleep without another interruption by his father, dreaming of seeing his love's face the following morning.

Except that Teddy never showed up.

CHAPTER TWENTY-ONE

"I don't get it," Ash said, abruptly. "I mean, it's a heart-wrenching story, don't get me wrong. I feel for you and it's super shitty that all that happened. But it also kinda seems like you're talking out of your ass?"

"Ash!" Parker shouted.

"What don't you get, exactly?" Embry sharply defended.

"No offense," Ash offered. "But there's no logical reason why finding a bunch of random bird bones would mean that there was a demonic..." Ash struggled to find the world, his hand motioning in the air as his mind blanked.

"Entity," Parker chimed in.

"*Entity*—thank you—attached to you. It just doesn't make sense."

"I can see how a story like that might rattle the precarious hold you have on reality, Ash," Rhett said with a nod. "But your lack of belief doesn't make it any less true."

Ash crossed his arms over his chest as Parker glared daggers at him, daring him to utter one more word as the devil's favorite advocate.

"Anyway," Rhett continued. "The reason I took this gig with *Phantom Files* is because I thought maybe it would help me deal with what I've been carrying around all these years. Help me figure out what happened to my family, and whether what hurt them is still out there."

If Rhett had known at the time that this was all bullshit, she would've taken that other offer to work on *Deadliest Diving*. It wouldn't have paid as well, but at least then she could've bragged about working in the Red Sea. The only reason she stayed now was for the paycheck, because she was earning herself consistent bonuses that were being funneled into paying off her Toyota RAV4. She kept her distance from everyone, avoiding developing their co-working relationships into *actual* friendships for fear of getting attached.

When she grew attached to people, bad things tended to happen to them.

"But now... I think I'm the reason Colt is dead," she said, head dropping into her hands as they rubbed at her eyes. "Whether or not you think this is real, we lost someone tonight. And the rest of us aren't safe until we find out how to stop it."

"*If* there's even something to stop," Ash mumbled, at a volume only he could hear.

"I think we oughta find a blanket, or a sheet or something, and cover Colt's body," Parker said, hands on his knees. His attention turned to Ash. "If for no other reason than out of respect."

Ash nodded. "Yeah, okay. I think there's a moving blanket in one of those bags," he said, pointing at the pile behind Parker. "It was wrapped around the tripods, I think." They used an assortment of random blankets to protect their equipment from damage during transport, especially since Rhett had joined their team and insisted upon it.

Parker dug through several duffels until he found what he was looking for, tucking the folded navy-blue blanket under his arm as he turned back to Ash. "Got it."

"Alright," Ash said, clearing his throat. "Parker and I will go check on Colt and cover his body. I think it's too risky to try to carry him down the stairs."

Raising his brows, Parker nodded in agreement.

"I'm going to bring the camera, just in case, to see if we can salvage what we can from this investigation," Ash added, digging his fingernails into the palm of his hand. "Including the footage we have from finding Colt's body, hopefully we'll have enough to piece this whole thing together and get out of here bright and early."

With two thumbs up from Rhett and Embry, the two men nodded and headed out.

Once they were out of earshot, Parker scoffed. "You don't have to be such an asshole, y'know."

Ash scowled. "The hell are you talking about?"

"With Rhett," he clarified. "She shares something about her family trauma and your first instinct is to shit all over it? Come on, Ash, that was a dick move and we both know it."

"I wasn't trying to *shit all over it*," Ash replied, using a mocking tone as he repeated Parker's words back to him.

"Uh huh."

Groaning, Ash threw his free hand in the air. "I don't know what you want from me."

Parker paused mid-step and sighed. "You want to be the leader so bad, but we lost Colt and now you're out here picking fights with the rest of the team? Not cool, man. You gotta step up and protect these people. *That's* being a leader —knowing when to support your team. And in that capacity, you're a sorry excuse for one." Shaking his head in disappointment, he walked off without waiting for Ash to keep up.

They took the stairs in silence, not a word uttered between them until they approached the bathroom, its wide door now only holding on by one of its hinges. In the center of it was a large, gaping hole, the edges of the timber shredded as though something had come bursting through it at high speed. The temperature on the second floor had a sudden chill, too. The hair standing on the skin of their arms indicated that it had dropped several degrees since they'd last been up there. The bathroom floor was still soaked in black water, pools forming where the tiles dipped from age.

Parker's fingers grasped at the blanket slung over his arm.

"Come on, let's get going. The sooner we're done here,

the sooner we can just go sit in the van until morning," Parker said. "I'm done with this place."

As he followed after his brother, Ash's eyes fell to where they'd left Colt's body.

Except it was no longer there.

"What the hell?" Parker's face was bent into a quizzical look of terror. "That's not possible."

"Are you sure this is where we left him?" Ash asked, his breath quaking as his mind questioned what his eyes were seeing. "It's not like he could just get up and walk away."

Parker's head swiveled, his flashlight double-checking the rest of the hallway.

"Positive," Parker determined. "This is definitely where we laid his body down."

For a moment, fear and panic crept into Ash's mind.

What if someone else really is *in here with us, and they took Colt's body?* Ash thought.

But they'd already done a search and came up empty.

Ash let out a constrained, disbelieving chuckle. "No way, this has to be a joke."

"Say that again?" Parker raised a brow, his mouth still open in alarm.

"Earlier, Colt said something about wanting to crank shit up a notch for season five. He wanted to introduce new tricks, new effects, something that would be scarier than anything else we've ever done," Ash explained. "What better way to do that than to fake your own mysterious death and make it look terrifyingly real?"

Parker's blank stare bore into Ash like a laser.

"What?"

"Ash, we *saw* his bloody, broken body. We carried it out of that disgusting tub and he wasn't breathing. I don't know what makes you think there's any way he could've faked all that," Parker insisted.

"You didn't hear him, Parker."

"Okay? I didn't need to. He's gone—now in more ways than one," Parker swallowed. Ire scratched at the back of his throat at Ash's insistence that this could possibly be a joke. "Colt loved a good prank, but he wouldn't take things this far. Whatever did that to him must've come back for his body to drag him into the darkness with them."

The last sentence echoed in Ash's mind.

They hadn't found anyone during their last search, but that didn't mean someone couldn't have been extraordinarily good at concealing themselves. This place was massive, so writing off the possibility wasn't exactly a good move.

But Parker's emphasis on *whatever* rather than *whoever* irritated Ash.

Ash groaned. "When are you going to give up this bullshit *I believe in ghosts now* schtick? For chrissakes, all these years you've been on my side about all this shit, but the moment Rhett tells some story about her house burning down you flip the script?" He scoffed, shooting daggers Parker's way. "What's that other thing leaders are supposed to have... oh yeah, *integrity*."

"I didn't flip anything," Parker defended, voice calm. "What I *did* do was consider that—given the circumstances

—there might be something going on that we can't explain away." His eyes surveyed the room. "Just like this," he gestured at the spot where they'd left Colt's corpse. "There's no way to explain his disappearing body unless you are willing to entertain the idea that some things in life are unexplained."

"So, you're saying that some creature from the black lagoon came and dragged him away? That's insane."

"And ruling out a very possible option is sane?" Parker countered.

"You're the one ruling out the possibility that he could be alive."

"The likelihood of that is even lower. We both saw the state of his body, there's no way someone could fake. Don't be ridiculous."

"Whatever," Ash grumbled. He could've used a stronger comeback, but for now that would have to do.

The room seemed to shrink as the stress within it escalated. Ash knew that Parker had a point, but he refused to acknowledge that fact and allow his brother any additional traction in their disagreement. If there was one thing they both could agree on, it was the need to locate Colt—whether he was alive or not.

"Either way, we've gotta find him," Ash decided, after he'd swallowed a chunk of his pride. "If we keep going with the investigation, we'll come across him eventually, right? There's cameras all over this place."

"I guess it can't hurt to try."

"That's the spirit."

"But if he really is alive, I'm going to kill him for real," Parker threatened. "I smell like death."

"Yeah, you reek," Ash agreed teasingly, wrinkling his nose.

"Hate to break it to you, but you don't smell any better than I do." Parker hooked his arm firmly around Ash's neck, playfully tightening around it as he led them back out into the hallway.

Things felt normal, just for a moment.

CHAPTER TWENTY-TWO

As Ash and Parker continued their investigation upstairs, they radioed for Embry to join them. Rhett opted to stay behind and monitor both the cameras and the mics, not only because she wanted to ensure that someone stayed behind to keep an eye on them from afar, but because she was afraid of what might be lurking after her in the dark. The others understood, of course, and focused on their game plan.

Each outfitted with a handheld camera, flashlight, and tactical vest (containing extra batteries, glow sticks, and digital recorders), the three of them agreed to split up and conquer each of the upper floors to cover more ground as quickly as possible. Ash took the fourth floor, Embry took the third, and Parker agreed to take the second.

As they crept up the stairs, their numbers slowly dwindled down to one.

Adrenaline pumping through his veins, Ash kept

climbing until he reached the top of the landing. The fourth floor had high, vaulted ceilings with dusty, cobweb-riddled beams that crisscrossed along the length of the ceiling. Of all of the floors, this one looked as though it had been practically forgotten. Antique pieces of furniture were covered in sheets. A grandfather clock sat opposite the staircase, staring down menacingly at whomever ascended into its territory.

"Spooky," Ash whispered to himself, turning the camera on and his flashlight off.

It beeped alive and the screen glowed in shades of green. His eyes traced everything that appeared as he wagered cautious steps forward in the dark. The floor seemed to stretch on forever in front of him, swallowed by the shadows that clung to every doorway. It was obvious that this floor had been barricaded for ages, locked away to rot with nineteenth century China cabinets and bug-infested, hand-woven carpets.

"Colt?" Ash called out, hoping to find his best friend alive and well.

Unlike Parker, he wouldn't be mad if it had all been a joke, he'd be relieved. Ash wanted nothing more than to know that the friend who is like a brother to him wasn't gone forever.

Something scuttled along the floor in the blackness, rattling the decaying floorboards under Ash's feet.

"Christonabike," Ash swore, uttering the words so quickly that they all melted together.

He *hated* the creepy-crawly bugs that they so often

found on location. The way they slithered around made Ash's skin itch with the thought of them touching him. Colt was the one that liked to pick them up and chase Ash around with them in hand. The memory tugged at Ash's heart, his eyes twinging as they welled up with tears.

No, he asserted. *Colt isn't dead. He can't be.*

Breath quickening, he stopped in his tracks. The blood rushing in his head pounded against both eardrums, as though a marching band were performing in the room with him. The banging of the snares, the blasting of the trumpets, the striking of the bass drums—a symphony of sounds played the soundtrack to his terror.

Ash cleared his throat and called out again, feigning confidence to hide the fact that his voice was shaking. "Colt? You there, bud?"

He took one step forward, pausing to listen for more signs of movement, trying to track whoever—or, *whatever*, if he were to begrudgingly open his mind—was shielding themselves in the shadows. Eyes squinting at the small LCD screen folding out from the side of the camera, Ash willed the shadows to clear enough to see what they were hiding.

"Come on," Ash muttered, zooming in and scanning. "Colt, if that's you, quit messing around!" He yelled, voice echoing as it spiraled down the hallway. "It's not funny anymore!"

Whatever it was scurried again, and Ash caught a wisp of what looked like fabric. It trailed after something into an open doorway. He didn't know exactly what he'd seen, but the noise was reminiscent of animalistic footfalls. The warning sounds of the camera battery dying whistled through the air like missiles in the night, ending with a deadening result. The screen shut off and darkness swathed over Ash, bringing with it a several degree drop in temperature.

"Shit," Ash whispered, patting down his torso to identify which pockets held the spare batteries.

Ripping the velcro on his left breast pocket, he reached in and pulled out one of two identical spare batteries. He struggled to swap them out, his hands fumbling over the camera body to find the battery door. This would be a time-consuming task regardless, but doing it in the dark added a layer of complexity to the job. Despite the fact that cameras were a big part of his career, Ash very rarely had to operate one—that was typically Colt and Parker's jobs. Now, he realized what a disservice he'd done to himself by not learning alongside them in preparation for moments like this.

After wasting too much time, with armpits drenched in sweat, the camera turned back on.

Breathing a sigh of relief, Ash once again looked at the screen to see if any movement was visible.

Again, the camera's shrill beep rang out.

"No, there's no way." Ash shook his head, eyes wide and brows furrowed.

The battery icon flashed and the camera powered down.

Ash let out a grating snarl as he fished out the final spare and swapped the batteries out once more.

"You better work," he scolded the camera.

It did.

He let out a sigh of relief, releasing the fist he'd balled up in rage while the other squeezed at the plastic body of the camera. Ash said a silent prayer, to whatever cosmic entity saw fit to reward them with this small victory, and reluctantly resumed his investigation of the fourth floor.

Frozen in place, hoping that whatever creatures were scuttling across the floor would leave him alone, he grimaced as his left knee ached something fierce. A cold spot had crept in, enveloping Ash's body like the closing of a casket. Guiding himself with nothing but his flashlight and the infrared light of his camera, he inched his way down the hallway toward the Headmaster's Quarters.

Moving closer, Ash kept his eyes peeled for any other signs of movement that might dart out from the doorways. Without warning, quick pattering darted across his feet and Ash yelped. He got a solid foot in the air as his flashlight clicked on and the light chased after a hairy, distended rat as it dived into a wide hole.

"Fucking hell!" Ash yelled, exasperatedly.

Fighting to catch his breath, adrenaline raced through his veins as if his body were a giant NASCAR track.

He composed himself, repeated a little self-soothing mantra, and inhaled deeply.

"You're fine. You're good. You're cool," he told himself. "So, chill the fuck out."

Out of the corner of the camera's frame, a dark mass

moved between doorways. He spun around quickly, pointing the camera at anything and everything. The first doorway: clear. The second doorway: clear. There was a chance his brain had manufactured it, prompted by the fear and adrenal hormones, but Ash wasn't going to make any assumptions given what he'd already heard on this floor.

Another step forward.

The screen on the camera flickered, losing pieces of the frame and glitching in a variety of shades and colors.

"Oh, come on, not again," Ash whined.

He smacked the side of the camera, which only seemed to make it worse. Rhett was going to kill him. The glitches spanned the screen with erratic movement, then inexplicably stopped and remained fixed on the screen. For good measure—and because he was already screwed—Ash smacked the camera again. This time, it managed to fix itself. No strange colors. No banding on the screen. Just the hallway in front of him.

A pattering of quick footsteps raced across the hall towards him.

The hair raised on his arms, his body recognizing the sound before his brain had time to process it. Every inch of his skin was burning, but the temperature of the room hadn't changed. His neck was white hot, as though lava might creep out if he were to slice the skin open. Reaching up to touch it gingerly, pain sliced through him and he let out a shrill cry.

If it was half as bad as it felt, he needed medical attention and fast.

Setting his jaw against the pain, Ash radioed the rest of their crew.

"Parker, Embry, are you there? I—"

With great force, the radio was knocked out of his hand and slid across the floor down into the annex.

Ash couldn't believe his eyes. How had it slid so far, when the annex was at the opposite end of the hallway? It was like a magic trick: there one minute and gone the next. He'd heard the radio slam into a far wall, its plastic body making a soft *thud* as it came to a stop against the lath and plaster.

Swift pattering charged toward him again, avoiding the flashlight's beam.

Spinning on his heel, Ash's heartbeat sped up again.

It was getting closer.

"Who's there?" His voice boomed as if he could out-intimidate whatever lay in wait.

It was moving faster, practically running straight toward him.

Ash's camera fell to the floor and smashed to pieces.

CHAPTER TWENTY-THREE

"**A**sh?" Parker's voice bellowed from the staircase, sending his brother into an instant panic.

Swiveling around, Ash gasped as his beam of light illuminated the other man.

"Fuck! You scared the shit out of me," he said, breathlessly.

Parker smirked. "Well, that's not so hard to do." He ascended the rest of the stairs until he was on the fourth floor. "You okay up here? I heard something crash, but you weren't answering your radio."

"Yeah, my radio fell." Ash pointed down at the floor. "And my camera. Hopefully they still work."

Parker stepped toward him and bent down to survey the damage. As he picked up the camera, additional pieces separated from the body of it and scattered across the floor.

The radio's batteries had flung out, but once Parker put them back in place, the device roared to life.

"The camera's done for," he replied, before speaking into Ash's radio. "Hey Em, can you meet us on the third floor? We're headed that way and we need ya." Handing the radio back to Ash, Parker added, "Rhett's gonna kill you."

"Don't remind me," Ash groaned. "By the way, do you see anything on my neck? Like right around here," he motioned, his fingers tracing the spot where he'd felt his flesh burning.

A brief glance was all it took to confirm.

"It looks normal to me," Parker noted. " Why?"

Confounded, Ash simply shook his head. " No reason."

The three of them fanned out as they crawled the third floor. Embry flanked left, Parker covered the right-hand side, and Ash focused his flashlight's beam on the center of their path. They moved in sync, slowly and deliberately. Parker hadn't mentioned seeing or hearing anything when he was on this floor earlier, but that didn't mean something wasn't lurking like it had been upstairs. Whatever it was, they were determined to find it.

Scanning each corner of the rooms they passed, nothing seemed out of the ordinary.

Or, at least, whatever *ordinary* was in the context of a creepy old reformatory.

Only a handful of steps away from the top of the stairs, Rhett's voice echoed in tandem through Embry and Parker's radios.

"Wait, stop!"

The three of them didn't move a muscle, awaiting further details.

When none came, Parker asked, "is everything okay?"

"I heard something," she said.

"Heard what?"

"It sounded like scraping, or maybe dragging. I'm trying to figure out which camera picked up the sound."

"Try to be quick, if you can."

"Working on it. Hold tight." There was a long pause, and then her Creole accent returned. "This is weird, but somehow it showed up on all of the camera mics at the same time."

"How is that even possible?" Ash asked aloud.

Parker waved him off as Rhett continued speaking.

"I'm not sure how that's possible unless it was *really* loud, but I'd be careful up there."

"Did the cameras catch anything on video?" Embry asked.

Another pause, and then a clear "nope" came through.

Radio back at his hip, Parker aimed his flashlight onto Embry and Ash.

"What do you want to do?" He asked.

Ash gnawed on the inside of his cheek, knowing what they had to do and simultaneously hating that there wasn't a better alternative.

"We need to split up," he stated.

Eyes locked onto his shadowy features, Parker and Embry stared at Ash and silently processed what he'd proposed.

"Need I remind you what happened last time we split up?" Parker asked, eyebrows raised.

Ash's brow creased as he gently shook his head. "Not on separate floors—on this one. We need to spread out and cover each wing." He pointed down the hallways on either side of their wonky triangle. "This used to be the dormitory floor, so there's more than a dozen rooms down each hall. If we don't split up, it'll take us twice as long to find Colt."

Assuming there was still a Colt left to find.

"No way," Parker rejected. "I'm not letting you traipse off alone again and get hurt even worse than you already have."

"Parker, I'm *fine*—" Ash defended, launching them into a yelling match.

"You can't even say that with a straight face, Ashton."

"Are you serious right now? I'm literally walking and talking and being *fine*!" Ash threw his arms open in exasperation.

"You've already hit your head tonight!"

"It's not like I got knocked out, it was nothing!"

"Nothing?" Parker laughed. "Nothing got your ass knocked to the floor, and you would've probably been eaten by that fat ass rat you saw if we didn't come rescue you."

"Oh, shove off!" Ash fired back, eyes dark and glowering.

"You're acting like a child."

"Would you two just stop it?" Embry yelled, stepping between them with her hands outstretched to part Parker and Ash away from one another. "You two make me miss *my* dysfunctional family, and I'm related to two serial killers!"

As if rehearsed, Parker and Ash stopped bickering and shifted their jaws in suppressed frustration. No one else was able to get on the other one's nerves the way that they could. Give them a pressure point to press and they'd be all over it.

"I'll go alone," Embry interjected. "You two are on my last nerve."

"Are you sure?" Worry pulled at the corner of Parker's mouth. "I'm not loving that idea, either."

"I'm fine, I swear," she insisted. "Now go, we've got a lot of ground to cover and I don't need either of you slowing me down." With that, she headed off down the dark hallway to the left of the stairs, down toward the Lower Boys' wing where the wards under thirteen were housed.

Exhaling a sigh, Parker's attention shifted back to Ash. He gave a wide shrug and shined his flashlight down the opposite hallway, the Upper Boys' wing.

"Guess it's you and me, little brother."

CHAPTER TWENTY-FOUR

"See? This isn't so bad," Embry said aloud, trying to convince herself that there wasn't anything creepy about the rusty metal frames of children's beds in echoey rooms that smelled like stagnant water, mothballs, and urine.

"It's just a kid's room," she muttered.

But it looked nothing like a typical child's bedroom.

The large room, triple that of even the grandest primary bedroom, was lined with rows of single beds, half of which were missing mattresses. Set up end-to-end, there were at least fifteen of them smashed into the space like giant corroded dominoes all staring ominously at the same wall. It was equal parts hauntingly beautiful and nightmarish.

Walking along two rows of beds, Embry's light touched each one she passed.

Sitting down on the edge of one of the beds, the springs

beneath its soiled mattress creaked as they took her body weight. Dust particles flew through the beam of light as she surveyed the room. Embry had always entertained a fascination with abandoned places, and had even done her senior capstone project in film school on an abandoned hospital. It was all about the shock factor—something that she was now getting a little too much of as she sat in this room. Her eyes weren't adjusting to the darkness, no matter how long she sat there. Miles of blackness stretched out around her.

The flashlight flickered as a darkness skirted around one of the bed frames.

Out of the corner of her eye, Embry was sure that she'd seen movement.

Her breath quickened and the room temperature began to drop.

The warmth of her breath turned to fog.

Unmoving, Embry's unseeing eyes shifted around the room.

A metallic clinking echoed around the room.

"Hello?" She called out, hoping one of the boys had turned back and entered the room to find her. "Parker? Ash?"

It was preternaturally silent.

A hot, sour breath slunk down the back of her neck, a stench like rotting eggs and burning garbage overwhelming her senses as a chill ran down her spine. Something was behind her, its unholy aura blanketing the room with a substantial heaviness.

Embry stood abruptly, backing toward the rear of the room as quickly as she could. She bumped into the beds as she moved, nearly hyperventilating. Her back smacked into the far wall and she sunk to the floor. Realizing the flashlight was still in her grip, Embry bashed the length of it against her palm until it turned back on. Swinging it to illuminate the path in front of her, Embry's eyes widened and a blood-curdling shriek left her mouth.

Something was crawling toward her, on all fours, limbs whipping through the air. Its keen claws scraped the floor as it writhed rapidly in her direction. Its face was covered in wet, dangling cords of hair, like ropes made of burnt gold that collected dirt and grime from everything it touched. A gaping mouth—or what looked like one—was nothing more than a rotting hole buzzing with hunger. Dark, luminescent eyes stared back at her, glinting in the dark. It was familiar in the oddest way, drawing her in like a fish with a lure.

And that's when she saw it.

That face.

She'd know that face anywhere.

Colt.

Embry's scream vibrated through the walls of Crenshaw Castle with such ferocity that it might've been louder by the time it reached Parker and Ash than it was when it left her mouth.

The echo reached their ears and that was it —they were running.

Ash's nostrils flared as pain spread through his knee. He pushed past it, arms pumping as he propelled forward, fear stretching from the crown of his head down to the soles of his feet.

Mouth tightened and teeth gritted, Parker had a six-foot lead on Ash. He scrambled down the hallway, past the staircase, and into the Lower Boys' dormitory. The first and second rooms he checked were empty. The third is where he found Embry.

Colt's rotting body had its hand around her throat, holding her against a wall as high as if she were levitating. Embry's face was turning blue, her body expending every last bit of energy as the life began to drain from her eyes. Pieces of her bubblegum pink hair were everywhere, like a dusting of glitter.

"Em!" Parker screamed, eyes so wide his forehead creases doubled in size and number.

The body that once belonged to Colt was falling apart. Bursting at the seams. His skin was falling off the bone, rotting away in shades of red and black. A horrific screech was leaking out from within somewhere unidentifiable, deep within the guttural folds of his skewered throat. His eyes were deep crevices, not bloodshot or recognizable but chillingly cold and devoid of life. A deep gash down the back of his neck oozed a rancid tar.

Nothing about his body looked like it should be functioning, let alone standing.

Yet, there he was choking the life out of Embry.

Making a split-second decision, Ash yanked his brother away, pulling him away from the doorway and across the hall into another room. As he slammed the door shut behind them, Ash stood against it, hoping to god the creature hadn't seen them. Hoping *Colt* hadn't seen them.

"What the *hell* is wrong with you!" Parker spat. "I could've saved her!" His hands were coiled around the front of Ash's shirt, twisting the fabric in the same way that he wanted to wring Ash's neck for pulling him away.

Ash's palms found Parker's shoulders, but he didn't fight back.

"No," he said, swallowing hard. "You couldn't have."

Their gaze connected, Parker's eyes searching and Ash's glassy and somber.

"The only way you could've saved her was if you sacrificed yourself—which you would've done because you're a selfless motherfucker." Ash let out a small chuckle, his head dipping as it hung in grief. "It was you or her, and I made a choice."

"The wrong choice!" Parker yelled, letting go of Ash's shirt to smack a hand against the door in outrage.

It made contact just a couple of inches from his head, and Ash couldn't help but flinch.

An unholy shriek screamed across the hall and Ash squeezed his eyes closed, as tightly as he possibly could. He couldn't think about what he'd allowed to happen to Embry, the suffering she must've been enduring as Colt's hand closed around her throat. He'd made a call in the moment and he had to live with the consequences. It had been her or Parker, and Ash chose his brother.

He would always choose his brother.

A piercing cry of pain swept through the air; Embry's final moment.

Parker's eyes welled up with tears, but he was enraged. He pointed at the door, gesturing through it toward their fallen friend.

"That's your fault," he muttered darkly.

The guilt hung around Ash's neck like a noose, tightening with every word Parker uttered.

It had been selfish, Ash knew that. But he wouldn't take responsibility for Embry's death. He didn't kill her. Seeing Colt like that, unrecognizable and possessed by something evil, Ash realized that there was something unexplainable in this place. Nothing they'd seen could be rationalized anymore, it was all too strange to be some convoluted prank or sneaky outsider. His desire for a realistic explanation of things had gone out the window, and he was ready to consider that this place was far scarier than he'd initially given it credit for being.

This was *real*.

Ash could no longer refuse to believe that there was no such thing as ghosts. At this point, there was no refuting the presence looming over Crenshaw Castle. To acknowledge that was to admit that there were things in the world that couldn't be explained by logic.

Rhett was right, he thought. *There's something here.*

Everything he knew was crumbling in real time and his head was spinning.

"I did it for you." Ash whispered the words more for his own benefit than Parker's.

Parker scoffed. "You did it for yourself."

It was more complicated than that, Ash wanted to defend.

There was only one person he'd been able to trust growing up: Parker. The idea of losing the only family he had left—after having written off their parents—was more than he could handle. It had triggered some part of his brain that told him to *act now and think later*, leaving Embry to fend for herself against whatever the hell was happening to Colt. He'd thought it had been compassion motivating his choice to save Parker, but maybe—

Colt's rotting corpse trudged down the hallway, obviously being puppeted by something evil. The heavy steps faded as he followed the corridor further, until it faded entirely.

They held their collective breath, terrified of giving away their position.

The movement was retreating, getting further away until they were no longer audible.

"I'm sorry," he uttered, both to Parker and for Embry.

"Sorry won't bring back Embry."

"Neither will punishing me for making sure you didn't die, too."

"That wasn't your call—"

"So?" Ash interrupted. "I made a choice and now we both have to live with that. So you can either hate me forever for it, or you can help me figure out how to get you, me, and Rhett out of here alive."

CHAPTER TWENTY-FIVE

Five had become three in a matter of hours, and it was only a matter of time before their lives were in jeopardy, too.

With Colt's re-animated corpse scurrying around Crenshaw's grounds, and Embry's body slumped in the corner of the Lower Boys' dormitory room, they had to be proactive now to avoid becoming the next victims.

"Par–er!" Rhett's voice shouted through the radio, broken up and glitching. "–sh!"

Clamoring for the radio, Parker raised his. "Go for Parker."

"P–ker, yo–ot cay–full owt–er!"

"Rhett, I can barely hear you," he sighed. "Come up to the third floor!"

"Whatever's going on here, we have to document it," Ash insisted. "It's the only way to get justice for what happened to Colt and Embry."

Rhett sniffled as she nodded hesitantly. On her wrist was a bright pink hair tie that she'd pilfered from Embry's side of the desk. As she began to speak, she rolled it between her fingers. "While I don't think messing with this thing is a smart move, I think you're right. If we have an opportunity to catch this thing on camera, to get closure for what happened to Embry and Colt, we have to take it."

The two of them looked to Parker, waiting for his buy-in.

"We might as well," he agreed, head turning to glance out the propped-open window, surveying the downturn the weather had taken.

Lightning had begun to plague the sky since they'd last trekked outside, the wind howling and whistling through the casement despite the stuffed fabric drowning it out. It was a wonder the roof hadn't caved in, though that was more than likely a testament to the quality of its original installment. Drops of water snuck in, sure, but it protected the place from flooding.

"I know I didn't believe it before, but I do now," Ash chimed in, his voice trembling as he collected his thoughts.

"Whatever this is… It killed Colt and Embry, and I couldn't stop it. We have to end this before anyone else gets hurt."

"We need to figure out what it is that's haunting this place," Ash said, looking at the list of names that Parker had written on the glass of the door. "That thing that killed Colt, or became Colt, or whatever the fuck happened," he went on, shaking his head as if he couldn't believe the thoughts flurrying in his own head. "It will come after us, too. I know it."

"I think we need to have a look around the Castle and see if we can find the old records room, because that's where we'll dig up the real dirt," Parker added.

Rhett walked over to the list and stared at it with rapt attention.

"Okay," she said, turning back to Parker and Ash. "Let's go find those records."

"Please tell me that you know where you're going," Rhett ventured, following between Ash and Parker as they wandered around the first floor looking for the records room.

Thankfully, Parker had had the foresight to locate and print a copy of the blueprints to Crenshaw Castle. Its enormous size meant that they could be searching all night, and recent events highlighted why that wasn't the most advantageous plan. The blueprints gave them a map to follow in terms of where rooms were placed, and helped them to identify what each room's purpose was. As they studied each floor's diagram, Ash discovered a room logged as the 'documents depository' on the basement level.

Not only were they surprised to discover that there *was* a basement level, they also realized it was an entire floor that they hadn't accounted for with their camera equipment. Given that they had the opportunity, it was worthwhile to explore that floor and see what else they found aside from the laundry facilities and storage closets.

"Yes, I know where I'm going," Ash said through clenched teeth.

"You have no idea where you're going, do you?" Parker whispered into his ear.

"I'm figuring it out!" Ash hissed in a harsh whisper.

Parker sighed, rubbing his temples with two pairs of index and middle fingers.

The deeper they went into the belly of the beast, the stronger the pungent smell of sitting water and sulfur became. Rats ran when they heard their footsteps echoing along the stone floors, the edges of their lights just barely catching them scurrying off in search of safety. Cobwebs clung to doorways and corners of rooms. Their shoes clomped slowly and cautiously as they wandered further into the dark.

Once they'd passed the industrial kitchen, they'd located the door that led down to the basement. It was sealed with an assortment of padlocks in different sizes and colors, a clear sign that they should not open it under any circumstances.

Thankfully, they'd brought bolt cutters.

Rhett did the honors, chopping through each lock like it owed her money. A cloud of dust swirled in the air as she swung open the door, choking the three of them in a series of coughs and croaking, throaty groans.

"Jesus," Ash rasped, waving away the dust with his hand. "Guessing this door hasn't been opened in a *really* long time."

"What was your first clue?" Parker teased, eyeing the pile of ruined padlocks.

Rhett shined her flashlight into the dark rectangular hole.

The light revealed a narrow, wooden staircase that dropped down to the basement level at a steep decline. From their viewpoint, it was impossible to see what was down there, but the smell grew stronger still.

"Ugh, what died down there? It smells like burning garbage and dead rats," Ash whined, pulling the neck of his t-shirt up over his nose in an attempt to block the smell from adhering to the inside of his nose.

"Probably the same thing that died in the rest of this place," Parker muttered, moving in front of Rhett and Ash. "I'll go down first, you two follow behind me. Okay?"

Who made him the leader all of a sudden?

"Sure, whatever," he shrugged.

Better him than me if there's a face-eating werewolf demon down there, Ash thought.

Descending the staircase, Parker was barely two steps ahead of the others when his weight proved too much for the tread of the stair he was stepping onto. It collapsed and he began to fall, leg plunging into the darkness below—only stopping when the bulk of his knee became stuck. He let out a clamorous yelp, arms flailing toward Ash for help. His flashlight dropped from his hand and clamored down the stairs with half a dozen loud smacks.

"Fuck!" Parker wailed, his arm slung over Ash's shoulders as his brother tried to lift him up. "Ow, ow, ow, OW!" He scowled, then snarled, "ow means stop pulling, Ash!"

"Okay! Maybe don't yell at the guy who's trying to rescue your damsel-in-distress ass, yeah?" Ash retorted. Balancing his brother's weight, his eyes focused on the stair that had given way. "Looks like there's probably shredded wood lodged in your leg. You're going to have to use your other leg to create leverage."

"Fuck," Parker reiterated, face flushing from the agony pulsing in his right leg.

"Yep," Ash nodded. "But we've gotta do it fast before you lose feeling in your toes or get blood poisoning."

Groaning as he shifted his weight onto Ash, Parker muttered the word, "fantastic," and slid his other foot underneath himself for maximum resistance.

"Ready?" Ash asked, not waiting for Parker's green light before counting them down. "One... Two... Three!"

Parker pushed while Ash pulled, a discord of grunts, straining, and panting as Parker's leg came free, torn fabric and spots of blood visible along his pant leg. Arm still slung across Ash's shoulders, he put weight on the injured leg to test how much pain he could tolerate.

"Okay, it's not so bad," he grimaced, pulling his arm back.

Ash's eyebrow quirked in response. "You sure?"

"Yeah, all good," Parker said with a wave, dismissing Ash's concerns. "Give me your flashlight," he called back, holding out a hand toward his brother.

Begrudgingly, Ash handed the Maglite over. "Don't drop that one, butterfingers."

Rhett let out a small laugh and the corner of Ash's mouth curled in amusement.

The light from Parker's flashlight illuminated the bottom of the stairs, awaiting their descent. There were many reasons for Ash's hatred of basements, the least of which being his childhood memory of getting locked in the one lurking under his childhood home when the door shut behind him and accidentally locked. With each step, the darkness enveloped them and Ash's stomach became like the waters of the North Sea, a violent body climbing and crawling with an unfounded anger.

CHAPTER TWENTY-SIX

Ash's weight shifted to the next stair and it creaked a little too loudly.

"Shhhh!" Rhett hushed from behind him, at nearly the same volume.

Scowling, Ash kept moving, following behind Parker's silhouette as the flashlight in his hand guided their way. Once at the bottom of the stairs, they turned the corner and the space opened up into a large room filled with antique filing cabinets and lined with dusty cupboards sporting brass hardware. There was a table at the center of the room with a handful of tufted leather chairs tucked against it, and several bookcases with first editions of medical texts and framed photos of grey-haired men in white coats. If it hadn't been for the papers scattered everywhere, cabinets doors left open, and cupboards left ajar, it might've actually looked like a functional office space.

"Not what I was expecting," Ash muttered, scanning the room in search of something that would stand out.

"What were you expecting?" Parker asked, shining the light around.

Ash shrugged. "A dungeon."

Each of them let out a small snort, in sync, as though the snark had been planned.

"It ain't that far off," Rhett added, stepping towards the nearest filing cabinet, a miniature flashlight the size of a butter stick clutched within her palm. She pulled open the top drawer and it stuck until she yanked, dust particles exploding into the air as the cabinet shook open. Rhett coughed, raising her shirt over her mouth and nose to keep from breathing it in. "God, what's with this place and all the dust?" She coughed again, wiping her watering eye with the back of her hand.

"Fingers crossed it's not asbestos," Ash joked.

He and Parker crossed the room, the former heading toward a large bookshelf and the latter to a second filing cabinet.

Ash surveyed the top shelf, eyes glossing over book titles he'd never heard of and trinkets he couldn't care less about. There was a strangeness to the assortment of items lining each shelf, like they'd been handpicked by a dozen different people with different tastes. A ceramic pig, shiny and plump and pink, stared back at Ash with its painted smile and broken coiled tail. It sported the same beady eyes as the piggy bank he'd had as a child, a lingering memory of his childhood that he couldn't shake.

"How exactly will we know when we've found what we're looking for?" He asked, pulling down a copy of *Gray's Anatomy* from 1858. "There were, like, a dozen names on that list of yours, Parker."

"Then we pull every file for every Oliver in Crenshaw's files," Parker replied, fingers walking along the edge of the file folders that lined the drawer. "Got one," he added, raising it above his head. Flopping it open, Parker read aloud, "Oliver Langley, born in 1894," and then promptly shut the folder and dropped it onto the large Mahogany table. "One down, ten to go."

It took almost an hour to dig up the rest of the files. Some had been alphabetized in the file cabinets, but much of the contents had been moved and folded over—presumably in the haste of someone who'd been looking for something specific as the building was closing. Some of the file folders had even been stuffed between books on the shelves, while others had fallen behind furniture pieces or were scattered around the room like sad confetti.

Parker, Rhett, and Ash sat around the table, the ten Olivers' laid out methodically in alphabetical order: Andrews, Bardot, Beckett, Cassady, Grint, Langley, McCowen, Preston, York, and Zabarowski.

"Any ideas for how to sort through these?" Rhett asked, picking at the corner of the folder nearest her, marked with

'Preston' written in a neat scrawl. "Three of them are faculty, but I don't know if that means we should scrutinize them more or rule them out completely."

Folding his arms atop the table, Ash leaned forward and rested his chin in the palm of his hand. "I hesitate to rule anyone out unless we have a good reason," he said, eyes tracing the G in Grint.

Parker nodded. "Alright, we'll keep them all in for now then."

"Wait a minute," Rhett piped up, eyes scanning the folders full of yellowing paper. "There's only ten here." She glanced between Parker and Ash. "Didn't you say there were eleven?"

"Yeah," Parker mused, forehead wrinkling as he ran through the mental list of names.

Ash spoke up before Parker could finish tallying. "Klein," he said, unmoving. "We're missing the folder for Oliver Klein."

They each muttered a variation of *what the fuck* under their breaths, and with a collective sigh they realized they had to keep looking if they wanted answers. Retreating to different corners of the room than they'd originally searched, the three of them pulled out anything and everything they could find from within the depths of every cabinet and drawer. Spiders frantically disappeared into dark crevices, their webs spanning the corners of every shelf. Dead centipedes lurked behind folders and cockroaches skittered the moment any bit of light filtered in from their flashlights.

Twenty minutes went by without any luck.

Then thirty.

By the time forty minutes had passed, Ash was grinning ear-to-ear.

"I got it!" he called back to the others.

CHAPTER TWENTY-SEVEN

Oliver Klein's folder was the thickest of them all, its tea-stained paper rippling and fuzzing at the edges as it broke down. Ash's thumbs brushed against it curiously before he set it atop the table between them. Electricity buzzed from the tips of his fingers down through his arms and sunk its teeth into his torso, boiling the anxiety that sat in his gut.

"All eleven accounted for," he said.

The stagnant air in the basement coated his lungs with dust as he took a deep breath.

"Alright then." Parker slapped both hands onto his knees before reaching for the seat of the chair to scoot himself closer to the table. "Let's start digging and see who has the potential to be our killer ghost, yeah?"

Ash wanted to object, but he couldn't come up with the right words.

Instead, his hand reached for the nearest file, the one marked 'O. Langley', and slid it toward his edge of the table. It wasn't noticeably thick, likely the history of a boy who hadn't spent much time incarcerated at Crenshaw Castle. As Ash opened it to reveal its contents, his gaze was met with that of a young child. No older than ten or eleven years old, there was a brokenness hiding behind his dark eyes. Ash's eyes shifted from the paper-clipped photo over to the rows of information scrawled along the top sheet.

> Oliver Langley, aged eleven years, was originally from Sandpoint, Idaho, but had relocated to Joseph, Oregon, when he was six years old. Born in 1923, his stockbroker father killed himself during the crash of '29. This tragedy had left the boy and his two siblings in the care of their mother, who developed schizophrenia and drowned his baby brother in the family's bathtub. Luckily Oliver and his sister survived, but they were remanded into their aunt and uncle's custody after their mother was arraigned and locked away within the walls of the East Idaho Sanitarium.

Skimming a few pages, his eyes landed on the boy's cause of death: forcible drowning.

Ash's eyes widened, a sigh escaping him as he mulled over the trauma this boy had endured in such a short life.

He'd narrowly avoided being drowned by his mother, only to drown within Crenshaw's walls a few short years later.

Two knocks against the table's top interrupted his train of thought.

"You good?" Parker asked, having noticed the pensive look on his brother's face.

"Fine," Ash mumbled. Another moment passed and he inhaled sharply, breaking his gaze that had once again drifted back to the boy's photo. "This shit is just… depressing as hell."

Closing the folder, he leaned back in his chair against the cracking leather cushion that ran parallel to his back.

If all of the stories splayed out on the table were this dark and dismal, getting through them all was going to be a test of how strong their stomachs were. After all, Crenshaw's history went back decades—spanned centuries since its inception—and the wards in the institution's care only arrived on its grounds when there were no other options available to them. That didn't bode well for what they might find in the rest of these files, save perhaps for those belonging to the staff members who'd also ended up on their list of Olivers.

After an hour of combing through the lives of each one, there were only three folders left at the center of the table. Rhett grabbed first, then Parker, then finally Ash reached for the final file.

'O. *Klein*' it read, in a similar flavor of cursive as they'd seen on all of the others.

Upon opening the thick file, there was no paper-clipped

photo as there'd been in all of the others. In fact, the entire assortment of papers seemed to be disheveled, as if whoever had been last to open it had sent all of the papers flying and hurried to put them back. The first sheet, instead of being the intake form as it was with all of the others, was a drawing—like the kind a child draws when asked to depict their family unit. Crude and dotted with flakes of dried-out crayon, it showed a small child between two adult figures, one in a dress with long hair and another in what looked like a suit and tie. It didn't look particularly menacing, but there was something unsettling about it that plunged into the depths of Ash's stomach to make a spectacularly elaborate and Olympic-quality splash into gastric acid.

Ash continued to finger through the yellowed pages, through detailed psychiatrist notes and behavioral reports, past family histories—

"Wait," he said aloud.

There was something in the family history that had jumped out at him.

Rhett and Parker looked up curiously, eager to hear what Ash had found.

At the top of the page, the patient's parents' names were listed: Archibald and Claudia Elwood.

Elwood.

"Oh my—*damn.*"

"What?" Parker asked, deep creases forming between his brows.

"Headmaster Elwood," Ash muttered, glancing up at

the two of them. "Oliver Klein was his kid. And it seems like…"

Before Rhett or Parker could inquire further, his eyes were glued to the pages again.

The family history ran through a gamut of medical and psychological questions.

Has anyone in the family had a history of schizophrenia? Manic-depression? Influenza? Yellow Fever? Scarlet Fever? Melancholy? Wilfulness?

They went on for several pages, asking everything from mental health to behavioral history to issues that may have permeated through the generations. Toward the bottom of the third page, Ash's eyes widened at the final question.

Have there been any instances of possession by evil spirits?

"Seems like what?" Rhett asked, after a too-long pause.

"Headmaster Elwood incarcerated his own son," Ash finally said. Confusion painted his face, twisting his features in horror as he read the scribbled handwriting. The more he read, the worse it became. "This is fucking disgusting."

Dropping the papers, Ash's hands went to his face and rubbed at his eyes in an attempt to make the words dissipate from his short-term memory. The way that any man could treat his own child like they were disposable—it made him sick.

"What?" Parker asked forcefully, grabbing at the papers to read for himself.

There, in black-and-white, it detailed how Oliver's worth was negated by his queerness.

A feeling that Ash knew all too well.

"Klein presents with a flawed sense of self," Parker slowly read. "Erratic behavior, including physical violence, harm toward himself, and claims of homosexual tendencies, lead authorities to the belief that Klein is a danger to himself and others."

"The hell did you just read?" Rhett asked, blinking.

Lifting another sheet of paper from the thick stack, it was Ash's turn to read aloud. "Ward 237 has been allocated— *allocated?* This place is fucking weird—to the Psychological Correction Initiative under the supervision of Dr. Walter Mellory." He cleared his throat before continuing. "All directives, notes, and procedure schedules can be found in the corresponding medical file for this ward."

Except, the medical file wasn't in the folder.

"Procedure schedules?" Rhett repeated incredulously. "That gives me probed-by-aliens vibes."

"For all we know, it's a log of talk therapy sessions," Parker added, as if there was a way to make any of what he'd just heard sound logical.

"Since when does anyone refer to talk therapy as a

procedure?" Ash snarked. "There's no way it's something that benign. This shit sounds medieval, like some kind of torture porn."

"If we want to find out, we need to find that medical file," Rhett concluded.

Ash nodded. "Agreed." Inhaling a deep breath, he let it out slowly. "Ghosts are bred from pain and traumatic deaths, right?" He still wasn't sure how much he believed in it all, but for right now he'd play into it. Everything that had happened to them so far was far from logical, so who knew what would prove to be true at the end of it all. "I don't know about you two, but this shit sounds pretty traumatic to me."

"We can probably nix half of these in comparison, but I don't think we should put all of our eggs in one basket," Parker argued.

Ash's stomach gurgled, acidic black coffee and nicotine stirring in its contents. He knew it unwise to go into an investigation without having eaten some kind of meal, regardless of quality or nutritional value. Instead, he'd slammed the largest Americano he could get his hands on and told himself he'd eat later.

Unfortunately, later had shown up with a vengeance.

"We need more information about this Psychological Correction Initiative and the guy running it—" Rhett searched the page, pointing at the name with her index finger. "—Dr. Mellory. If he was the one in charge of this thing, then he'd have squirreled away some notes or something. Some kind of proof that he was heading up a glorified torture program slash conversion camp."

"We should start by finding Oliver's missing medical file," Ash stated. "Otherwise we'll never know exactly what they put him through."

Even as the words came out of his mouth, he wasn't sure he *wanted* to know. The more they discovered, the closer it would all hit home for Ash. Echoing the same homophobic flavoring as his own father, Headmaster Elwood's treatment of his own son burned at the back of Ash's throat. How could anyone treat their own child like they were less-than? Stow them away in a child-sized prison and experiment on them or do whatever heinous acts had been documented in Oliver's medical file—ones that Ash was certain would've violated the Geneva Convention.

"Okay, then let's find it," Parker said with a nod, pushing his chair back as he rose to his feet. "If it exists, it's here somewhere."

"We've already looked through everything in here, it's all patient records but nothing medical," Ash said. "It's like all of the medical files were either taken or—"

"—or hidden," Parker finished, eyes flitting from one corner of the room to another.

He stepped away from the table they'd been sitting at, stepping toward the one piece of furniture that didn't quite seem to belong as well as the others: the bookcase. It wasn't flush to the wall, but rather sunk into it like something was pulling it from the other side. Reaching out for its edge,

Parker's fingers traced along it where the wooden trim met the plaster wall.

As he watched his brother try to pry it open, Ash got an idea.

"Wait," he murmured, following after the other man.

Once at his side, Ash began to pull off everything that sat along each shelf. He pulled down dusty leather bound books, brass statuettes, framed photos and tintypes of people that had been long dead. Everything came clattering to the floor in his haste, and even Parker took a step back as glass shattered at their feet and book spines split in two.

"Jesus, Ash, what the hell?" Parker exclaimed.

"It's gotta be some—" The statue of a figure's head tilted as he pulled it forward, but didn't fall off the shelf. Instead, a metal piece was revealed that connected it to a mechanism on the other side of the bookcase. A soft click was all the sound it made as the entire piece of furniture swung slowly inward. "Bingo," Ash whispered.

"How the hell did you guess that?" Parker asked, staring into the blackness in front of them.

Ash chuckled. "Believe it or not... *Scooby-Doo*."

It had been a fan favorite in their house growing up, especially among Ash and Colt.

Despite being a fond memory, the thought brought up feelings of Colt. Colt's death had left a scorched hollowness behind inside of him that he couldn't ignore. It snaked around his insides and burrowed into his gut like a labor of moles hunting for sustenance. It climbed into his throat but he hastily swallowed it down, the heaviness sinking back down as he pulled his flashlight out of his back pocket. The beam illuminated in the darkness, but its light was swallowed whole. The edges of what lay within it were only slightly visible, with nothing but outlines and silhouettes of things that could easily be mistaken for other things.

"Of course," Parker laughed with a shake of his head. "Fucking *Scooby-Doo.*"

CHAPTER TWENTY-EIGHT

Small footsteps clattered from behind as Rhett stepped into view beside them.

Shining her own flashlight into the dark, she asked, "so, are we going in or what?" Then, without waiting for a reply, she took the lead and stepped into the hidden room first.

"Careful," Parker muttered after her.

"I got it," Rhett called back, waving him off with her free hand before the blackness enveloped her, leaving behind a rocky silhouette for their flashlights to chase after.

Ash gave her a three second head start before he entered in after her, eyes fixed on the dimly lit patch of light guiding his feet from tripping over anything that might reach out to grab for his ankles in the dark.

"You think there's a light in this place?" Rhett asked, shining her flashlight upwards as she scanned the walls for a switch.

Just as she let out a disappointing *hrmph* at the lack of switches, a loud crack echoed through the cavern-like space.

"Sorry!" Parker called out. The tinkling of broken glass clattered as Parker's foot swept the pieces aside with the side of his shoe. "Ash, toss me your lighter."

"That only works if I can see you to know where to throw it," he chirped back.

Sighing, Parker shined his flashlight up at his own face. "See me now?"

"Yup," Ash said as he hurled the small piece of plastic at his brother's shadowy face. It spiraled toward the other man as it whizzed through the dark, making abrupt contact with the other's forehead.

"Ow!" Parker scrunched his eyes shut as it bounced off, lucky reflexes trapping the lighter against his side before it could fall to the floor. "If you could pitch a ball like that, you wouldn't have gotten kicked out of Little League," he said, rubbing his forehead.

"My lack of pitching ability wasn't why I was kicked out of Little League," Ash laughed.

Parker clicked the lighter and held it up to an old gas lamp hanging from his other hand. The small flame took hold of the gas mantle and he turned the release knob to slowly grow the flickering open flame. Its soft glow lit up a portion of the colossal room as the three of them found an antique exam table situation at the center of one section.

"What the hell is this?" Rhett's eyes grew large and glassy.

"Best guess? We just found Dr. Mellory's laboratory," Parker said.

"This place closed in the sixties, right?" Ash asked.

"Seventy-two."

"Then this place was probably retrofitted for electricity at some point. We just have to figure out how to turn it on..." Ash's voice trailed off as he looked around. Assuming their generator could handle a little bit more of an electrical load, turning on a few lights to aid their sleuthing wouldn't be a problem.

"If any room was going to have it, it would be this place," Rhett agreed. "After all, Mellory couldn't torture little kids if he couldn't find them in the dark."

"Yeah, it's tough to use an electric bone saw without, y'know, *electricity*," Ash quipped. Picking up the rusted tool, he shined his flashlight onto it like a spotlight and tilted his head. "What are the chances they used this on Oliver?" He wondered aloud, mouth moving faster than his brain ever could.

"You'd think a little tact would slip out now and again," Parker chided Rhett. His eyes dropped down to the saw in Ash's hand and his brow creased as they pulled together. "And put that shit down, it's probably contaminated with hundred-year-old bacteria."

"You could suck the fun out of a funeral, Parks." With a roll of his eyes, Ash put the saw back where he'd found it and returned to the hunt for Oliver's medical file.

As they made their way deeper into the center of the vast room, new pieces of furniture entered into their field of vision. Another exam table. Wooden cabinetry and rows of shelving. Lamps—some of which had burnt-out bulbs, while others had been shattered or were missing entirely. On the one hand, everything had aged at exactly the same rate, looking like a time capsule that had been abandoned to rot and fester like an infected wound. On the other hand, it was exponentially creepy knowing that this place had been used as a torture chamber for unsuspecting wards.

"Uh, guys?" Rhett said, a good twenty feet away from them and facing a back wall. "I think I found the medical records."

As they approached, their flashlights illuminated a large set of cabinets that overtook the entire wall from floor to ceiling. Antique brass hardware adorned each drawer pull, with an old sliding ladder fixed to the wall. Reminiscent of an old library, each drawer had a placard with a handwritten label that denoted both a chronological and alphabetical organization system.

"Whoa," Parker said as he stood beside Rhett. "That's... a lot."

"Guess we'd better dive in," Ash concluded, scanning the drawers for the right combination of dates and letters.

Dr. Mellory's accounts of the trauma Oliver endured were rigid and clinical. A sanitized version of the agonizing pain detailed in the handwritten list of *evaluations* that seemed to go on for page after page after page after—

"This shit is *sickening*," Rhett spat, leaning back in her chair as every emotion left her body except for one: profound sympathy.

They'd split Oliver's massive file amongst the three of them, in order to get through it as quickly as possible, but even a third of it was heavier than they were expecting.

Parker sighed. "You can say that again. This doctor clearly had a few screws loose if he thought experimenting on children was okay." He shuffled the papers in his hands, eyes widening in disbelief the further down the pages he read.

"I knew it would be bad, but…" Ash let himself trail off, swallowing the words that were too hard for him to utter out loud.

Resentment, like an engorged pill bug, rolled itself up into a tight ball and clung to the space in his throat just beneath his larynx. This file, and the torturous acts described within it, read like pages ripped from the journal of Ash's past. There was an unmistakable kinship fluttering between himself and this boy he'd never met. Ash could never comprehend the suffering Oliver had endured in this place, but he recognized the pain of a father's betrayal. It sliced like a knife to the gut; six inches of polished steel making a home in the bowels of its latest victim.

As Ash sat there attempting to digest what he'd read without spewing chunky vomit all over the mahogany table, the pill bug in his throat began to multiply. Two, then four, then sixteen, then forty-eight, then hundreds. They crawled under his skin and he could feel the tightness in his neck as he strained to breathe. His anxiety was climbing and sweat started to bead at his brow.

Parker wagered a glance in Ash's direction. "You good?"

The words didn't even enter an ear, but swerved past Ash's head completely.

"Hellooo?" Parker waved across the table. "Earth to Ash."

"Huh?" Ash responded, dazed. His mind was still cloudy, but it was beginning to clear. "Yeah, I'm good. Fine. Never better."

Everything about Ash's body language said *don't ask,* but that had never stopped Parker before.

"Oh yeah, sure you are," He scoffed, looking briefly at Rhett and then back at his brother. "Nothing says *I'm okay* like saying it three different ways, in a weird tone, and looking paler than Casper."

Fingers rubbed at his eyes as Ash tried to focus on Oliver's demons rather than his own.

"I know this stuff is mega-dark," Parker continued, "but you can't let it get to you. At least not right now, not when we've got to—"

"Can you just shut up, please?" Ash shouted, thumbs pressing firmly at his temples while his elbows dub into the table. "I–ugh, I need some quiet. There's too much goddamn *noise.*"

Rising to his feet, Ash hurriedly heads back out of the

large room and toward the staircase to get some air that didn't smell like mildew and rat droppings.

"Whoa, hey!" Following after his brother at a jaunty pace, Parker reached for his brother's arm as Ash stepped onto the second stair. "Where are you going?"

"I can't breathe down here," Ash rasped, pulling against the other man's grip but getting nowhere.

Instead, Parker's grasp tightened and his face softened with concern. "What's wrong with you?"

"Nothing, I—" Ash yanked his arm away, finally breaking free. "I need you to back off, Parker. You're..." He sighed, raking his wavy hair with his hands and staring at his feet as he collected his thoughts. "You're overstepping."

"*Overstepping?*" Parker questioned, hawking the word out like rattlesnake poison.

"Yeah," he barked back, jaw set and neck vein popping. "Don't forget that this is *my* fucking team, Parker."

You're the cameraman! Ash wanted to scream.

"I'm supposed to be the leader here, not you."

"Then be one!" Parker hissed, throwing his hands up. "No one is stopping you. But when I see you getting stuck in your head with that lost-as-shit look on your face, it doesn't exactly instill a whole lot of confidence, man." He sighed. "You can't get pissed at me for trying to help you, there's no sense in that. Either be a leader or don't, but make a choice and stick with it."

Ash leaned against the grimy wall and let the crown of his head fall back until it was resting on the cool stone. He expected Parker to walk off and get back to work, but instead the both remained still.

A few moments passed and then the silence was once again filled by Parker minding his brother's business.

"What the hell is going on with you?" He asked.

Ash scoffed exasperatedly. "You mean aside from two of our friends getting brutally murdered and having to read about this fucking kid being tortured for being gay?"

"Yeah," Parker answered, sarcastically. "Aside from that." His tone wasn't helping anything, and he knew that, but talking to Ash could sometimes be like trying to convince drywall to animate itself and do a funky chicken dance.

"How about the fact that you're railroading me with Rhett?" He suggested.

"Excuse me?" Parker retorted. "You know what, I'm *so sorry* for stepping up and trying to get to the bottom of this shit," he condescended. "You need to grow up, Ash. Your version of being a leader is doing whatever the hell you want because you think it's some kind of power move. Real leaders prioritize the group and do what they gotta do to get shit done. If that's what you wanna be, then more power to you—and I'll back you one hundred percent—but don't walk around feeling sorry for yourself because you're insecure about being a shitty leader and wanna act out when somebody else steps up and does it better."

Ash's eyes stung as he took a deep breath, his ego reeling and bruised as he attempted to stiff-upper-lip his way out of talking about this. After all, that wasn't actually what he was upset about. Sure, it hurt being replaced, especially by your own flesh and blood, but there was so much about Ash's relationship with their father that Parker didn't know. Bits and pieces that Ash didn't want him to know, for fear that he'd have to relive it all through the eyes of his brother, complete with the pity he knew was waiting on the other side.

Jaw kicked out to the side as he mulled over the pros and cons of spilling his guts, Ash took a deep, centering breath and shook a few fallen hairs out of his eyes.

"I don't know how to make this any clearer, P." His teeth clenched and he forced a frustrated burst of air out through his nostrils. "I *really* don't want to talk about this with you right now, so back off."

CHAPTER TWENTY-NINE

Continuing up the short staircase, Ash reached the door and grabbed the handle to pry it back open and away from the thickly-painted frame. Only, this time, it didn't budge. Brows digging into the bridge of his nose, Ash twisted it harder and shoved his shoulder into the door as hard as he could. Again. Again. Pain radiated down his arm as he stared, dumbfounded, at the door.

"What the hell?" Ash whispered to himself, rubbing at his now sore shoulder as he looked for what might be causing the door to be stuck shut.

The longer he stood there, trying to wrap his head around the stuck door, he was bombarded by thoughts of Oliver's needless suffering at the hands of his barbaric father and Crenshaw's homophobic staff.

Seething, Ash flung his leg back and kicked the door as hard as he could.

"Whoa, everything okay?" Parker called up the stairs, bending into view with his arms still crossed over his chest.

"Uh..." Ash breathed, assessing the situation as the red in his vision faded. "No, definitely not."

"Well what's the problem? Too many spiders?"

Ash rolled his eyes. "The door's locked, wiseass."

"It's probably just stuck," Parker offered. "Put your shoulder into it."

"You wanna come try?" Ash motioned to the door that wouldn't budge, looking forward to watching his brother fail to do what he'd already tried to do without success.

With a sigh, Parker placed a hand on the rotting handrail and trudged up the stairs. He shouldered past Ash and surveyed the door before wrestling with the doorknob like he wanted to steal its lunch money and shove it into a locker.

"It's probably... just... stuck..." Parker grunted, throwing his body against the heavy door repeatedly. Each time his arm made contact with it, groans slipped out through mouths twisted into pained expressions.

"Oh yeah," Ash said, sarcastically, allowing himself the pleasure of a few muffled chuckles. "You're definitely making progress, don't let the unmoving hunk of wood fool you."

"Can it," Parker barked, over his shoulder.

Ash watched as his brother's hands stretched across the entire surface of the door, searching for somewhere he could slot it to wedge the door open or pry it off of its rusted hinges. He wanted to believe that there was something logical to their being trapped down there. Perhaps the door had swung shut from the storm winds, or maybe the rain dripped perfectly onto the hinges to make them slick enough to slide. There was no limit to the ridiculous scenarios his brain could cook up to avoid allowing himself to consider the possibility that this, too, was paranormal in nature.

"What are you two doing over here?" Rhett asked, her brow creasing as she stepped toward the staircase, leaning over it with her sleeved forearms. "I was wondering what was taking so long. Fighting with a door? That's... different."

Glancing toward her, Ash smirked and used his head to motion toward Parker. "It's stuck shut and *The Incredible Hulk* over here is trying to break it down."

"Hmm," Rhett hummed. "Doesn't look like it's going too well."

"Would you two quit it?" Parker asked. "I can't focus with all the yapping."

Ash scoffed. "Not sure a lack of focus is the problem," he mumbled, shoving both hands into the front pockets of his pants.

"Uh huh..." Rhett said, unamused. "Anyway, since you both left me alone in the other room to come screw around with an old door, it seems like I was the only one of us who *actually* spent their time wisely." A wicked grin began to form at the corner of her mouth, the kind that showed she knew something that they didn't.

Yet.

Parker grunted as he pushed on the door from every angle imaginable.

"So you found something, huh?" Ash smiled. "Care to share with the class?"

Clearing her throat, she nodded.

"Turns out that Oliver Klein's medical records were the missing piece," Rhett said. "And the shit he was put through... it's a direct match to what we saw with the bodies. Not to mention that it ties to some of what Maura had seen here, even some stuff she didn't say on camera."

Furrowing his brow, Ash tilted his head. "What do you mean? You talked to her off camera?"

"Well, yeah," Rhett shrugged. "Just briefly, but she mentioned some pretty disturbing stuff. Said she'd even seen some past tour visitors get attacked." After a moment, she waved a hand as if to dismiss that tangent entirely. "Anyway, that's not the point. The shit that happened to Colt and Embry? I think Oliver was trying to send us a message."

Parker's final exhausted grunt came as he slammed his shoulder into the door again before slinking down to sit atop the top step, heavy breaths inhaling and exhaling.

"You done now?" Ash asked pointedly, eyebrows raised. "Pretty sure that we're not getting out that way."

Staring daggers at the other man, Parker huffed. "At least I tried."

"Can we table the passive-aggressive banter for a minute?" Rhett interjected, eyes darting from one Novak to the other and back again. Opening one of the file folders, she began to recite something that was written in it.

> *Despite efforts to reduce the patient's clinical aggression, all measures thus far have proven ineffective. Patient will be moving on to electroconvulsive therapy for further experimentation and analysis.*

Ash's face fell as the realization of what those words meant wafted over him.

"Shock therapy?" Parker asked, before Ash's brain could catch up.

"Exactly," Rhett nodded. "They were going full-out with the conversion torture in this place. Mellory's notes read like a how-to manual for ridding kids of their homosexual tendencies and reported *behavioral problems.*" Her eyes rolled as she finished the sentence, in complete disbelief that anyone could use hearsay as a prescription for child abuse.

Raking back a few stray hairs with his fingers, Ash nodded slowly as he processed.

"Okay, so if this really is Oliver's spirit, then everything in those files would be plenty of motive for sticking around to wreak havoc," he agreed. "But what I can't figure out is... why us? Why does this thing want to take us out when we hardly even got any footage before everything went haywire?"

"Could be that we disturbed some shit by being here,"

Parker added, forearms resting atop his knees. "They stopped doing tours for a long time, right? Maybe that calmed it down. Obviously Oliver's still pretty pissed off and he's taking it out on us."

"That doesn't make sense, though," Ash said, shaking his head. "Why would he want to go after us when we didn't do anything to him? Everyone who was involved in those experiments is long dead by now."

Rhett gnawed on the inside of her cheek, her mind going back in time to her family's own ghostly tragedy. Pain was a powerful motivator, both for the living and the deceased. The pain that Oliver went through was intense, and the resonance of that pain still echoed through the halls of Crenshaw Castle. It was tangible, uncomfortable, like an ache that never went away.

Oliver was surely reaching out to them, but what was he trying to say?

"We need to take another look at the bodies," Ash blurted out.

Both Parker and Rhett did a double take as their focus honed in on their third musketeer.

"Huh?" they grunted in unison, mutually curious as to where he was headed with that train of thought.

The bodies were the key—of this, Ash was certain.

The closer they inspected the bodies of Colt and Embry, the more information they could gather to piece together Oliver's message. They knew now what he'd been through at the hands of Crenshaw's medical staff, and the sadistic Dr. Mellory, but what they didn't yet know was how it all tied back to them. There was a reason he was choosing to reach out to them, and Ash's mind raced with possibilities all while still fighting against the idea that this was actually happening to them.

He'd expected a lot of things to happen tonight, but finding a real, bonafide ghost wasn't on that list.

"Colt and Embry are the only ones who came face to face with Oliver's spirit, right?" Ash asked, before clearing his throat. "That means their bodies might be clues. Or, at least, there might be clues left behind *on* their bodies."

Parker didn't move, instead choosing to lower his gaze toward his feet where he dropped a hand to pick at the laces.

It was hard enough the first time they'd seen the husks of their former friends. Pulling Colt's body out of that tub had been hard enough to do once, his waterlogged skin and swollen appendages flopping and sloshing. Watching the light drain out of Embry's eyes as Colt's reanimated corpse snuffed it out.

Turning it over in his mind's eye was enough to turn Ash's intestines into a Bavarian-style pretzel. All it was missing was a beer cheese dip accompaniment.

"We don't know that there will be any clues," Parker piped up.

Ash recognized the queasy tone of voice slipping out from between his brother's lips. Parker was afraid of what they might see if they looked closer than they had the first time, allowing themselves to pick apart every cut and bruise and fold of papery skin. Those images might never leave their memories, tainting every good one that was filed away.

He was right to be afraid.

"We don't know there won't be," Ash countered. "What would you rather us do, sit on our thumbs and wait to die next? We're sitting ducks in here as it is."

Parker looked to Rhett for reinforcement, but was instead met with a shrug.

"He's got a point," she admitted. "If we stay down here, we're never getting out of here alive."

The three of them sat in the subsequent silence, bathing in it while Rhett and Ash waited for Parker to deliberate the merits of staying versus revisiting Colt and Embry's bodies for a pair of amateur autopsies.

"Fine," Parker inevitably sighed, momentarily rueing his brother's existence. "But any sign of trouble and we're hanging up the coroner's coat. Got it?"

Raising his hands in mock surrender, Ash bowed his head. "Trust me, we aren't gonna be slicing and dicing. Just some good, old-fashioned, amateur detective work."

"Whatever you say, Nancy Drew," Parker retorted, raising to his full height to descend the stairs. "Which way is out, then?"

A smirk curled at the corner of Rhett's mouth.

"I think I know a way," she said.

CHAPTER THIRTY

An intrusion of cockroaches skittered between a frenzy of arms and legs in the pitch black as the trio crawled through a ventilation duct that was barely large enough for them to squeeze through. It was a newer addition to the old building, wedged between brick and stone as the modern convenience became one with its decrepit surroundings.

Ash crept forward at the head of the group, calling back to the others without being able to turn back to see them by the light of his flashlight. "Doing okay back there?"

"Oh yeah," Parker grunted. "Loving it."

"Ten out of ten, would recommend," Rhett squeaked.

"I'll be sure to add that to our Yelp review," Ash chuckled. "I think it's just a little bit furth—*EEUUUGHHHH!*"

As Ash pressed on, a cockroach caught itself between his palm and the metallic surface beneath it. Its exoskeleton crunched beneath his hand and thick, viscous membranes squished against Ash's skin like mucus. It slid between his fingers and sucked the bug's antennae and legs into its juicy tissue.

Panicking, he halted abruptly and Parker's head ran into his rear, prompting him to push Ash forward in disgust.

"What are you stopping for?" His voice boomed in the small quarters of the duct, despite it being no louder than his usual speaking voice.

Furiously wiping his hand along the thigh of his pants, Ash groaned and moaned as a cacophony of sounds and expletives trickled out of his mouth.

"It's just a little bug, relax," Parker. "There's probably a lot more where that one came from."

"Disgusting," Ash muttered under his breath.

After sufficiently cleaning his palm of the cockroach guts to the best of his ability, Ash forged on while the two behind him cackled like a pair of hyenas. Finally, they reached the end of the ventilation duct and cold air wafted toward them. It licked at Ash's face and he closed his eyes as it swept through his hair.

For one brief moment it felt like fingers curling against his scalp, the way that Teddy's used to when they'd lay beside one another. It had been so long since Ash had thought about the way it felt to be with Teddy, but being at this location was bringing everything back all at once, like it had shattered the dam within him that held back everything from that time in his life.

It's not fair to Erick, he told himself. *You can't keep dwelling on this, you gotta move on.*

Parker nudged him from behind. "Ash!"

"S-sorry," he stuttered, remembering what he was doing when his mind ran away with him. "Careful, there's a lip on the edge here," he instructed, slowly lifting himself out with help from the ledge beside the duct's opening.

Ash dusted himself off as Parker and Rhett slowly climbed out, shaking off all remnants of spiderwebs and filth that clung to his clothing and the memories of Teddy that held his heart in a tight grasp.

"Looks like we're in…" Parker started, looking around for a hint at their location within the large fortress that was Crenshaw Castle.

Something glinted in the dark and caught Rhett's eye from across the room.

"The Headmaster's office," she said, pointing at a moldy portrait hanging on a far wall.

"No, that's impossible," Parker argued definitively. "The headmaster's office is on the fourth floor, we were in the basement."

Ash shrugged. "Guess we climbed up a few stories."

"We never went up," Parker asserted, jaw tensing as the vein in his neck pulsed with unease. "We were level the entire time, we should've ended up in the laundry or one of the storage rooms."

Shining his flashlight around the room, Ash made his way toward a nearby window. Despite it being boarded up from the outside, a small gap between two boards allowed him to peer out into the night. The beam of light broke through the rain to find a patch of sparse grass four stories down.

"I don't know what to tell you, man." Ash turned toward the others. "Unless the ground around us eroded, we're definitely on the fourth floor now."

"At least we know where we are," Rhett mused, making her way over to the large desk that sat in front of warped built-in bookshelves highlighted in different shades of mold and water damage. "We can work our way back down from here and find Colt and Embry along the way." Her voice trailed off quietly, head tilting as she surveyed the books and paraphernalia left to rot on the shelves by the room's final occupant.

Parker frowned, eyebrows colliding into folds of skin. "It doesn't make any sense," he muttered. "Any chance that window opens?" He asked, jutting his chin outward.

Inspecting the edges with his fingers, Ash shook his head. "Nope. By the looks of it, this shit has been painted over a thousand times." He gripped the edge of the lower pane and pulled hard, yanking against it with all his might. "And it ain't budging," he huffed.

"Screw it, let's just go find Embry and Colt and get this over with," Parker insisted.

Rhett rifled through the desk drawers, ignoring the both of them. The lower drawer stuck as she pulled on it, the rusted shut lock attempting to keep her out. Crouching, she pulled a bobby pin out of her dark mess of hair and bent it to fit it into the hole as best she could. A few quick movements and some muscle were all it took until a faint *click* unlatched the inner mechanism.

"Gotcha," Rhett whispered through a proud smirk, pocketing the pin and opening the drawer.

Its emptiness was more than disappointing.

She sighed, but the longer she looked at the barren, flowery drawer the more something felt off about it. The dimensions didn't make sense given the size of the drawer and the way that it fit into the body of the desk. It was too shallow, so there had to be a false bottom hidden inside it.

Nails digging against the sides, she found a loose corner of the silverfish-eaten contact paper and pulled on it. It ripped with each tug, but Rhett was in for the pound already. The paper scrunched beneath her fingernails, disintegrating each time she scratched some of it away. The rips revealed a thin, black ribbon, riddled with the same tiny, bite-mark-shaped pits. Wrapping the fabric around her index finger, Rhett gently lifted the false bottom to reveal a jumbled mass of old photographs.

She chose one at random from the top of the pile, gingerly lifting it from the drawer to examine it more closely. A group of boys stood together, their dejected expressions full of sorrow and gloom as they stared back at Rhett. Their eyes were as dark as the ink the photo was printed in.

"What'd you find?" Ash asked from his spot at the window, noticing that she'd paused.

As he stepped toward her, the wood floors creaked beneath the soles of his shoes.

Rhett aimed her flashlight into the drawer below as he approached.

"A stash of old photos," she said. "They've been in here a while, judging by the outfits."

Kneeling beside her, his light illuminated the bottom side of the drawer that had been removed. "A false bottom," he chuckled as he picked it up, the ribbon dangling as his eyes gave it a once over. "Someone thought these photos were worth hiding..." he mused. "I wonder why..."

Without another word, Ash abruptly stuck his hand into the pile at the bottom of the open box. His fingers wiggled as he fished around, popping up between the gaps like worms in the sand of an extraterrestrial desert. Retrieving a fistful of silver halide prints, the creases and signs of wear were extremely visible as he turned the papers over in his hands. A few had been marked with Spencerian script, the neat and precisely executed lettering a perfect example of the kind of penmanship taught in institutions like Crenshaw at the turn of the twentieth century.

"Nineteen..." Ash read, squinting as he struggled to make out the last two numbers. "Sixteen? Nineteen eighteen?" Passing the photo off to Rhett, his eyes narrowed at the others in his hand.

"Nineteen-sixteen," Rhett confirmed.

Flipping it back over, the photo shared eerily similarities to the previous, notably in the attire worn by the children. However, in this one, a man was standing at the back of the group with his hands menacingly resting atop the shoulder of a morose-looking child at his side. Sweat dripped down the back of her neck as a cool breeze swept through the room, sending a chill that ignited a barrage of goosebumps on her arms.

The beam of Rhett's flashlight shifted to their resident historian.

"Why does this guy look so familiar?" She asked, holding out the photo toward Parker.

One quick look was all it took.

Parker's eyes widened. "That would be because his portrait is downstairs."

She did a double take. "Elwood?" Holding it as close to her face as she could without it touching her nose, she scoffed. "No way."

"He was much younger there," Parker admitted. "But that's definitely him. Probably a couple of decades before he became Headmaster, if I had to guess."

As Parker continued, Ash collected the rest of the photos and laid them all out on the floor in a chaotic array.

"Elwood was a teacher here before he ever became Headmaster."

"Not sure why the guy who seemingly hated children wanted to work with kids as his life's calling," Ash snorted, still crouched over his arrangement of the photographs.

Rolling his eyes, Parker let out a huff. "Says the skeptic host of a ghost hunting show."

"Host of nothing if we die in here," the younger Novak retorted, shuffling the order of the photos until he was satisfied. "There," he concluded, surveying the puzzling masterpiece.

"'There *what?*" Rhett asked, leaning over the edge of the desk to peer over Ash's shoulder with her flashlight illuminating his work.

The trio peered down in the dim light at the collection of old snapshots, eyes straining through the dark as they looked for similarities and inconsistencies—anything that might make sense of how the images were all connected.

Ash's gut had been right.

There was a bigger picture hiding in plain sight.

"All of these photos..." Rhett hummed. "The same kid is in all of them."

"What do you mean? There's tons of different kids in all of them," Ash said, pointing at various photos to make his point.

"No," Rhett dismissed. "The same *kid* is in all of them—a singular kid."

She reached for the closest of them, fingers grasping the aged paper as her thumb slid across the child at the bottom left of the group pictured. "Him."

The child's shock of blonde hair stuck out a square peg trying to fit into a round hole amongst the sea of brindle-haired children in shades of sepia. While not quite a uniform, their outfits were similar enough to inform a pattern. Collared, sailor-style tops adorned each child's torso, some featuring stripes while others were one solid color. The trousers were a mix of short and long, shades spanning a range of dark tones that could've been any color under the sun.

Ash scrutinized the image, zeroing in on the boy whom Rhett had pointed out.

There was an eerie familiarity that sank into his chest, but the boy's face wasn't one he recognized.

No, Ash thought. *It's not his face—it's his expression.*

The deeply uncomfortable way his lips pressed together was all too familiar.

He looked exactly as Ash had in every posed family photo that had been taken during his childhood.

"There's something going on here," he finally said, motioning with a wagging finger between the boy and Elwood's looming figure.

"What about it?" Parker asked, quizzically.

It was no surprise to Ash that his brother hadn't picked up on it.

The two of them had lived far different lives, despite growing up in the same household. Parker, the golden boy, could do no wrong. Ash, on the other hand, couldn't seem to get anything right. Even if he did, their father would never have admitted it, anyway. Not when there were a plethora of choices to pick apart; his choice of extra-curricular clubs (none), the effort he put forth in his classes (he was lazy and average at best), athletic prowess (or lack thereof, in his case), and even the friends he spent time with (Luther Novak had never been a fan of Colt Pereira).

By the time he turned thirteen, Ash had become an expert in parental disappointment.

Now, he could recognize it anywhere.

"I think that's Elwood's son," he said. "That's Oliver."

CHAPTER THIRTY-ONE

There was little record of Oliver's time at Crenshaw Industrial Reformatory. Save for the medical files and intake questionnaire, it was as if he'd never been there at all. The boy seemed to have traveled through the institution like a ghost.

"Someone had to have gotten rid of his file," Rhett concluded.

The three of them had torn the Headmaster's office apart looking for hidden filing cabinets, more secret hiding spots, and Prohibition-era stashes built into the walls and furniture. Sadly, nothing turned up. When they were done, the room looked like a hurricane had hit it at one-hundred-and-twenty miles per hour. Papers were strewn across the floor, drawers left hanging open, peeling wallpaper ripped halfway down the wall. Even broken glass shined as it reflected the beams of their flashlights, the result of Ash's reckless and destructive search methods.

"I doubt there'd be anything in there that would tell us anything more than we already know," Parker offered. "His medical file was damning enough."

"Sure," Ash shrugged. "But the student file is the one that would have his photo in it. Without that, we're only speculating that the kid is Oliver Klein."

Rhett cleared her throat to gather her teammates' attention. "Who cares?"

The Novak brothers each slowly raised a hand without looking at the other.

"No," she dismissed with a shake of her head. "What I mean is... why does it matter whether we know what Oliver looks like? If Elwood put his son here, we know they had a fucked up relationship, right? I don't know about you two, but that's good enough for me. Ash was right earlier."

Stunned silent, Ash's eyes widened.

Had she actually said what he thought she just said, or did he hallucinate the words that had just come out of her mouth?

"We need to find Colt and Embry's bodies," Rhett continued. "If we do that, we might find a clue or something that tells us what Oliver wants from us. Then, maybe—and that's a *big* fucking maybe—we can survive this godforsaken place and get the hell out of here, alive."

Heading down from the fourth floor to the second, they crept slowly with their bodies clumped together in a wonky pinwheel. They descended the stairs at half-speed, wielding their flashlights like luminous sabers despite the fact that they'd be useless if anything actually did go bump in the night again.

A sinister soundtrack straight out of *The Texas Chain Saw Massacre* played on a loop in Ash's ears. It thundered alongside the increasing rate of his heartbeat throbbing into his throat, warning him that all it took was one false move and every ounce of blood could spill right out of him and onto the floor.

"Left up here," Parker instructed, nodding his flashlight in that direction for Rhett.

She'd been the only one of them who hadn't witnessed Embry's murder, or seen Colt's body firsthand, and for that Ash was admittedly jealous. It was proving impossible for him to scrub the images of their final terrorizing moments from his brain, a task he assumed was some kind of karmic retribution for a terrible decision he'd made in his past. The time he ended things with a girl by cheating on her with her brother, perhaps.

"Maybe I'll just wait in the hall," Ash said as they approached the doorway to the dormitory room where Embry had taken her final breaths. "I really don't want to see that again."

"If we're going, you're going," Rhett teased, grabbing a fistful of his shirt and pulling him into the room alongside her.

Without warning, Parker stopped short, lifting his light until it was illuminating the same spot they'd watched Embry's body sink down to in a pile of broken flesh and bones. There was nothing but a dried pool of blood, evidence of the altercation except for the one thing they came for: Embry.

"What the fuck?" Ash blurted out. "No. No way. Not fucking possible."

"Her body," Parker muttered. "What happened to her body?"

"We *saw* what happened to her body," Ash corrected. "The problem is that it's not where we left it."

How has this happened twice in one day? Ash questioned, realizing that it had to be an unseen pattern.

Rhett stepped toward the bloody puddle to examine it, and noticed that there was a significant channel moving away from the site of the slasher set and toward the door they'd just entered.

"I'm guessing she wasn't in any condition to drag herself across the floor?" She asked.

"Breathing was out of the question," Ash croaked.

"Colt," Parker said, eyes glued to the trail of Embry's blood. "He must've dragged her body out after we barricaded ourselves in the other room."

"Not Colt," Ash spat. "Whatever that *thing* was in his body, it wasn't him. He would never do something like that."

Colt might've been dead, but Ash owed it to his friend to protect his memory. Cold-blooded killer, he was not.

Those were his hands inflicting the damage, but the light behind his eyes was long gone. There was something evil inside of him pulling the strings, even if Ash wasn't ready to accept that possession was possible beyond the flavor executed in movies like *The Evil Dead*.

Nodding slowly, Parker's thoughts swirled around in his head like a tornado.

"You're right," he agreed. "But if her body is gone, there's a good chance his body isn't back in that bathtub waiting for us to find it."

"Meaning...?" Rhett inquired.

"Oliver's killing us and then using us to do his bidding," he answered.

A clamorous crash echoed from out of sight, reverberating through the air.

"You two heard that, right?" Rhett stiffened, her eyes shifting in the darkness as she attempted to find the direction in which the sound had originated. "Please tell me you both heard that and that it wasn't an auditory hallucination."

"Uh huh," Ash grunted, at the same time that Parker said, "I heard it."

"What the hell was that?" Rhett asked, slowly and cautiously rising to her feet.

Ash clicked his flashlight onto the higher setting and shined it down one hallway and then another, eyes constantly moving as shadows slipped away and new ones appeared. There were three directions from which the sound could be emanating, but from where they stood it was impossible to tell which way was the right choice.

"Rethinking my idea to split up?" Ash asked, eyeing Rhett.

"No," she snapped.

Parker cleared his throat. "I think we should."

"What?" Rhett asked incredulously, blinking as though she couldn't believe what she was hearing. The man whose middle name might as well have been Logic was suggesting that they *split up*? Unbelievable.

"Ash is right, we should split up and look for the source of that sound," he reiterated.

"*Ash is right*?" Rhett repeated. "You can't *actually* think it's wise to split up when there's something actively hunting us. Hell, potentially *two* something's hunting us at this point."

"We're trapped in here," Parker rebutted. "What else can we do aside from looking for another way out? Maybe that sound was coming from somewhere with another doorway or a window that hasn't been boarded up. We have to try, right? We'll take our radios and it'll be fine."

No matter how much sense he made, Rhett didn't want to agree with the sentiment.

"I don't see why we can't try *together*," she argued.

"It'll take three times longer," Ash added, picking at the skin around his thumb's cuticle. "If we split up, we can cover more ground quicker. I don't know about you, but I want to spend as little time as possible in this shitty portal to the fifth fucking dimension."

"I really hate the idea of going alone," Rhett whined. "I'd rather it take longer than us get murdered separately, chasing a sound that was probably a lure to get us to do this exact thing." Without waiting for either of the brothers to say anything more, she held up her flashlight and stalked off toward the hallway on the right.

"Rhett," Parker said, softly. "I know you can handle this. We'll be quick about it—in and out. Then we can be done with this place and leave it in our rearview."

Rhett groaned and let out a deep sigh. "Fine. But if I die, it's on you," she said, pointing at Parker.

"That's it? Wow, she never listens to me like that," Ash commented.

Parker looked at him and a small smirk crawled onto his face. "That's because nothing sounds reasonable coming out of your mouth."

With that, he strode off toward the hallway on the left, leaving Ash to follow the final pathway that snaked through the lower level of the building toward the kitchen.

Ash let out a snarky slew of canned laughs, his flashlight shining ahead of him.

"Whatever," he muttered under his breath. "Nothing reasonable, my ass."

CHAPTER THIRTY-TWO

"This is just great," Rhett grumbled, walking further and further into the dark.

Rarely did Rhett bother trying to argue against anything the boys decided, mostly because they never listened to her anyway. She could rattle on until she was blue in the face, and every word she said would go in one ear and out the other. Even now, the one time she was begging them not to do something with every fiber of her being, they opted to go ahead and do it anyway.

"We're so done for," she whined.

Cockroaches and beetles scattered as the beam of light swept the hallway with her every step. Spiders clung to their massive webs, holding hostage the corners of every room and the arch of every doorway. The building was still —too quiet—as though it was holding its breath as she roamed its insides.

Rhett knew this place was alive, and now thankfully Parker and Ash did, too.

There were echoes of life in Crenshaw Castle, and they were bloodthirsty.

Of that, Rhett was sure.

As for everything else, the jury was still out.

"Just keep going," she told herself, aloud. "The sooner you check it out and confirm there's nothing, the sooner you can meet back up with the guys."

As soon as she stopped speaking, a loud clang clattered down the hallway. It sounded like a frying pan being thrown across a room, slamming against everything it could on the way to the floor.

Rhett whipped around, her arm swinging the flashlight toward where she assumed the sound had come from, but she couldn't be certain. Everything around her was vibrating like neverending ripples along the surface of a crystal clear pond.

"Who's there?" she called out.

Silence rang out like bees buzzing in her middle ear.

Louder, Louder, LOUDer, LOUDER.

And then it stopped.

All sound stopped, instantaneously—unnaturally.

"Hello?" Rhett asked.

This time, she couldn't hear herself utter the words.

Her fingers plunged into her ears, trying to dislodge whatever might've gotten itself stuck in there and stole her hearing.

Without warning, she could once again hear the skittering of insect legs and the fluttering of bat wings. Scuffing a boot along the floor to confirm, Rhett sighed with relief that her missing sense had returned.

"Rhett," a distant voice called out.

Her head spun toward it and a chill shivered up her spine and across her body, the skin turning to gooseflesh. The already cold air dropped a few degrees, enough that Rhett could see her breath dance out in front of her with every exhale. Shaky breaths hiccupped in her chest as she wagered another step forward.

"Rhett?" the voice echoed again.

It sounded like...

"Ash?" Rhett called back in response. "Is that you?"

Distant footsteps tapped across the floor and then disappeared.

Her heartbeat pounded in her chest, quicker with the passing of each minute.

"Rhett!" the voice sounded.

"Ash!" She mimicked.

"Come this way, we found something!" Ash called.

"Oh, thank god," Rhett sighed, panic dissipating from her veins.

Hearing Ash's voice was far better than some disembodied one lingering in the shadows. She had to have been down there at least half an hour, maybe longer. Her watch battery had died a few minutes into her separation from the others, so she couldn't be sure. Knowing that the others were onto something gave Rhett the first bit of positive energy she'd had all day.

A few minutes passed, but she couldn't see either of the others' flashlights.

"Ash?" Rhett loudly asked. "Parker?"

"Rhett!" Ash yelled, his voice further away than it had been earlier.

"Slow down, I can't find you!"

"Come this way, Rhett! We need you!" His voice rose and fell in a melodic sing-song of tones, like this was a game of hide-and-seek and she was losing.

Parker made his way through the front room and into the dining room, careful to check every door and window that he passed. Not a single one budged an inch, despite his best efforts. Even the ones with the oldest boards nailed across them, looking like they could be picked apart by the tines of a fork, remained in place.

His search continued, taking him to the next spot on his list: the laundry room.

As expected, it was every bit the disappointment he assumed it would be.

A row of laundry sinks outfitted with attached washboards lined one wall, while another was filled with hung ironing boards and shelves that stretched up toward the ceiling. There were old irons, spools of thread tossed haphazardly in disintegrating baskets, folded linens and towels with centimeters of dust buildup. Clotheslines stretched across the room, populated by dozens of wooden pins, which provided a place to dry laundry when the weather outside was less than accommodating. A godsend in the Oregon wilderness, without a doubt.

Other than bugs and grime, there was little else worth investigating in the laundry room.

The room was windowless and doorless, with only one way in and one way out. Nothing in there was going to tell Parker anything he didn't already know. It was a mix of the old and the new, with washboards and washing machines, dryers and clotheslines—but there was nothing that stuck out as anything more than ordinary.

"This was a bust," Parker sighed.

As he turned to leave the room, the beam from his flashlight illuminated human features distorted in the bright light. They twisted as the figure reached out for him, its long, slender fingers wrapping around his arm.

Yelping, Parker's back slammed into the door frame as he backed away from the creature.

"Dude, chill!" Ash yelled, pointing his own flashlight at his face. "It's me!"

On the verge of hyperventilating, Parker's wide eyes and rapidly thudding heartbeat quickly turned into a tight-lipped scowl.

Parker smacked his brother's arm so hard that the other yowled in pain. "Didn't anyone ever tell you not to sneak up on a guy when he's walking around alone in a haunted mansion?" Parker huffed, blowing out a deep breath of air through puffed-out cheeks.

"Not sure I'd call this a mansion," Ash mused, glancing around.

"The hell are you doing over here, anyway?" Parker asked. "You should've ended up in the kitchen by now."

"I dunno," Ash shrugged. "I followed the hallway around and it led me here."

"Weird," Parker hummed.

"My thoughts exactly."

"Have you seen Rhett?"

"Nope, I figure she's still exploring her end of the place. Have you?"

"No, but if you ended up here, she should've too."

"She could've gotten lost," Ash offered. "This place is a maze, especially in the dark."

A shrill, guttural scream exploded in the air, turning the heads of both men. Their flashlights shined down the hallway, the light dying out as it was swallowed by the dark. The two of them looked at one another, silently asking whether they'd both heard the same thing. Both of them gave a small nod in acknowledgement of the unspoken question, afraid to be the first to utter a word after the shriek that had just rang out.

"Did that sound like–" Ash started.

"Rhett's voice," Parker finished. "We gotta go find her." Pulling out his radio, he lifted it to his mouth and pressed the Talk button. "Rhett, do you copy?" After waiting a moment, he spoke again. "Broussard, you there? We heard a scream, was that you?"

The other end remained silent, without even a hint of static.

Eyes meeting Parker's, Ash swallowed hard. "I don't think she's okay."

CHAPTER THIRTY-THREE

Rhett's arms pumped at either side of her body, with clenched fists and throbbing fingers. Ash's voice was getting further and further away, despite how fast she was running toward it. There was an endless amount of space between her and him, like her vision was stuck in a dolly zoom, except that he was never in her field of vision.

"Slow down!" She screamed, through ragged breaths.

Ash's laughter bounced towards her in echoes, but it wasn't his normal laughter. This was like a crowd full of Ashs, all laughing in unison from somewhere up ahead of her.

A lifting wood plank caught the toe of Rhett's shoe, sending her in a forward somersault that was interrupted midway by her face slamming into the floor. She let out a piercing wail as a warmth slithered down her face. Closing one eye, her fingers wicked away the slick blood that was pouring out from a cut along the edge of her scalp. Lacerations along her arms and legs were beginning to bleed through the torn fabric of her clothes.

Lifting herself up, glass shards cut sharply into her hands, slicing them like a hot knife through butter.

"Aaagh!" She screamed, fighting every urge to collapse onto the floor again.

Picking up a piece, it glittered like translucent, deadly confetti between Rhett's fingers. Had it been there before she'd tripped, just lingering in the dark, another lingering leftover from the past? Or did someone put it there and lie in wait, waiting for the perfect moment to watch her fall into their booby trap? Either way, she hadn't seen it coming. As observant as she liked to think she was about her surroundings, how had she missed that?

"Ash!" Rhett called out.

No one answered her.

Instead, the silence played games with her head, sounds appearing then disappearing without warning. The waves of sound crashed into her like those massive breakers found at Mavericks, knocking into her with blow after forceful blow.

A shadowy figure, blacker than black, creeped toward her, its body contorted and bent into a four-legged creature whose humanistic features were lost in the dark. Each emaciated limb cracked and jerked as it moved toward Rhett, who scrambled to back up until there was nowhere for her to back into.

It had cornered her, like a fly in its spidery web.

"Oh god," Rhett heaved, rising to her feet as her hands grasped at the injured parts of her. "You're not Ash."

Ash and Parker followed the hallways back around until they were back where they started, and then trekked after Rhett. The deeper they went into the building, the stranger it felt that they hadn't come across any sign of her.

"We should've found her by now," Parker grumbled. "Radio her again."

Before speaking into the radio, Ash cleared his throat. "Rhett, you there?"

A low light at the end of the hall glowed like a beacon.

"Hey, wait, I think that's her," Ash chirped.

The two of them bounded down the hallway, passed battered furniture and moth-eaten rugs, until they arrived at the source of the light: Rhett's abandoned flashlight. It lay strewn on the floor, as if dropped in the haste of her departure.

Parker leaned down to pick it up, turning it over in his hands like it contained hidden clues to her whereabouts.

"Try again," he said, jutting his chin out toward the radio at Ash's hip.

"Rhett, come in—" As Ash spoke, his voice echoed in multiples of two alongside a screeching distortion of feedback.

In tandem, both Novak brothers covered their ears and grimaced.

The moment it stopped, a lightbulb went off in Parker's head and his eyes widened.

"Do that again," he instructed. "But this time, press the call button."

Ash obliged, and a ringing tone sounded off from somewhere around them. Each time the chiming ended, he restarted it, ensuring that they wouldn't lose track of it as they slowly stepped around the space.

The melody rang and rang until Parker found it, tossed a dozen feet away from the flashlight.

"This explains why she wasn't answering," he sighed.

"Might also be related to why she screamed," Ash added.

"*If* it was her that screamed. We still don't know if that was her."

"Who else would it be, one of the *other* paranormal investigators locked inside this building with us?"

Parker frowned at his brother, his features bathed in disapproval. "Either way, we need to find her before something else does."

"Okay, so... I guess we head down this way?" Ash pointed the beam of his flashlight down the hall in the direction he suspected Rhett would've continued down. "If I was her, I'd go that way."

Parker motioned forward with his hands. "Lead the way, Magellan."

Small chuckles escaped Ash as he started down the

corridor, watching his step and looking in every doorway that they came upon.

After twenty minutes of walking and conducting room searches, the pair stopped in their tracks. Droplets of half-dried blood and shards of glass stippled the floor like polka dots. Yet, there was no other sign of Rhett aside from blood that may—or may not—have been hers.

"What do you think?" Ash.

Parker's face was white as he crouched down and looked at the crime scene. "I think this means we need to hurry."

With haste, the two of them ran down the passageway, following every curve and yelling out Rhett's name in hopes that there would be some sign of life.

"Rhett!"

"Yo, Broussard! Where are you?"

"Tell us you're alive, Rhett!"

"Rhett, say something! Anything!"

The soles of their boots stomped heavily as they galloped deeper toward the building's center. Shadows played tricks on their eyes, jumping out at them from the edges of their vision only to disappear as soon as they focused on them. Sounds echoed around them as they descended into the depths of Crenshaw, voices swirling in a caterwauling discord. The voices wormed their way into their heads so deeply that even palms pressed over their ears couldn't block them out.

Muffled conversation drifted from out of sight, and Ash

spun around in all directions, wielding his flashlight as though it were Michael Myers' knife.

"What?" Parker asked, an eyebrow raised skeptically.

"The voices..." Ash frantically turned each time he heard a whisper.

Mouth ajar and forehead creased, Parker didn't hear anything. "What voices?"

That was the wrong question.

"Not what... who," Ash distractedly replied.

It was on the tip of his tongue.

He knew those voices, and could identify them anywhere.

"Colt," he whispered, eyes darting around like he'd gained the ability to see clearly in the dark. "I heard Colt."

Parker's tongue swiped across his bottom lip as he braced himself. It was no surprise that his brother was struggling with Colt's death. Not only had it happened right under their noses, but he'd been forced to see his body —to pull the soggy limbs and bloated face out of an icy bath. It was a lot for anyone, but he knew Ash like the back of his hand. He shoved everything deep down, all the hurt and pain and suffering, and hoped it would eventually go away. Ash was afraid to face the truth, to truly acknowledge that Colt was gone; to rectify the guilt that was eating at him.

And now that guilt was manifesting as auditory hallucinations.

"Ash, I don't know what you think you're hearing but it's not Colt," he said, using the gentlest tone he could manage.

"It is," Ash snapped, eyes wide as they frantically continued their search. "And Embry! I hear Embry, too!" With jarring movements, he craned his neck and erratically shifted his body weight from one foot to the other with robotic sways.

Parker placed a reassuring hand on his brother's shoulder.

"Rhett, is that you?" Ash whispered to the dark, seeming not to feel his brother's touch at all.

Grip tightening, Parker tugged his little brother toward him. "There aren't any voices, Ash. It's silent in here, like it's been for..." Looking down to check his watch, he realized that morning he'd swapped out his chronograph for his Apple watch and it had died just like his phone. "Probably hours, by now."

"No!" Ash insisted. "I hear them!" He brought a finger up to his mouth and pursed his lips, exhaling in a bout of shushes. "Be quiet," he warned in a hoarse whisper. "They can hear us, too."

"Fine, I'll humor you," Parker sighed. "What are the voices saying?"

Ash's face twisted up, like a six-year-old being asked a far too complex question. "I can't tell. Some of it sounds angry, but then there's this laughter. I think Rhett wants us to go that way." Outstretching an arm forward, he pointed down a winding corridor ahead of them that split off from the pain hallway.

"What's down there?" Parker asked, allowing himself to indulge in Ash's delusion.

"I don't know," Ash replied softly.

"If you're hearing Rhett, that can't be good."

"Why do you say that?" The innocence of his question caught Parker by surprise.

"Because Colt and Embry are dead. If you're hearing them *and* Rhett, I don't think we're going to find her alive."

Ash started to laugh, a few seconds of giggling halted by an abrupt pause.

The two looked at one another and Ash's face fell.

"Parker?"

"Yeah?" He answered.

"Rhett said we need to run."

CHAPTER THIRTY-FOUR

Breaking out into a sprint, the two of them rallied their remaining energy and took off toward the voices that Ash claimed to hear.

"After we survive this," Parker huffed, trying to keep up his speed. "We're gonna talk about the fact that you don't believe in ghosts, but you *do* believe in hearing voices that aren't there."

Ash's strange daze seemed to be lifting, at least as far as Parker could tell.

"If we survive this, I'm done with this ghost hunting bullshit," Ash laughed, breathlessly. "We don't get paid enough to die." But it would certainly give him the break from the show that he'd been looking for.

Parker let out a chuckle that even he didn't expect.

"Deal," he said, just as Ash slowed to a stop and held an arm out in front of him. "What's wrong?"

Peering into a doorway, past an ajar door halfway off its hinges, Ash took a deep breath.

"Hang on," he whispered.

Extending a hand, his fingers brushed against the wood and gently pressed the door until it squealed open. The ominous energy spilled out at their feet, flooding the hallway with enough malevolent energy to raise the hairs on both of their necks. Ash crossed the threshold and eased himself into the room, with Parker cautiously waiting in the hallway for his return.

"See anything?" Parker asked.

"Not yet," Ash replied, sweeping the room with his flashlight.

A soft sound began to grow as he stepped around what appeared to be another old bathroom. This one, however, was in far worse disarray than the others they'd seen. Broken sinks littered porcelain along the tile flooring, a pale mauve desert that came to life when the light shone across each slab's mottled surface.

Clearing the room from left to right, Ash froze as a pair of shoes appeared in his light's beam. Lifting the light slowly and carefully, a pair of legs sprouted from the shoes. The fabric engulfing them was saturated, and water dripped from the creases and folds. Rising further, the light rolled over the back of the torso and up to the head, which was matted with dark hair.

It was Rhett.

Hunched over as she faced away from him, her body shook back and forth with tiny, jerking movements. Soaking wet hair knotted into itself and draped over her neck, clinging to every bit of pale skin it could find. Her hands covered her face, though Ash had a dreadful sense in the pit of his stomach that she was smiling underneath them. There was an inhuman quality that emanated outward from her in oscillating flutters.

"Uhh, P-Parker?" Ash stuttered, his blood turning to ice in his veins.

"Yeah?"

He didn't want to look away, for fear of what might happen if he took his eyes off of her, but Parker needed to see this.

"Get in here," Ash instructed, using his flashlight to light the way for the other man.

Parker stood beside him looking lost. "What did you need me for?"

"Look at this."

Moving his light back to the corner of the room, it shined a bleached purple hue across shattered ceramic.

"At what?" Parker asked. "Are you shopping for new bathroom tiles? Because I wouldn't go with those ones."

Glowering, the cogs in Ash's mind started to stick.

"No, that's—I saw something. *Someone.* Rhett was standing right fucking there two seconds ago," he insisted.

Looking at him like he'd grown a second head, Parker nodded slowly. "Sure you did, bud."

"No, shut up. I'm serious. She was *right there!*" Ash outstretched a pointed finger.

"Hearing shit, check. Visions, check. What's next, are

you going to smell her perfume? Come on, we're wasting time that we could actually be using to find Rhett."

"She was right fucking here!" Ash urged. "Why don't you believe me?"

Parker rubbed at the pain between his temples, fighting every fiber of his being to remain composed as he participated in this ridiculous argument. "Because flesh and blood people can't walk through walls, Ashton." Incredulity took over his face. "Since there's only one way in and one way out of this room, either she wasn't real or there's a trap door in the floor that we don't know about."

Ash heard something skitter across the floor outside of the bathroom.

"Wait, shhh," he instructed. "I hear something."

"Again?" Parker sighed.

Until he heard it, too.

The clattering of quick footsteps, not quite a run but an arrhythmic jog, echoed down the winding hallway.

"What is that?" Parker whispered, straining to listen closer.

"Rhett," Ash breathed, the soft whisper of her name stinging the tip of his tongue.

Without another word, Ash dashed out of the washroom and toward the source of the sound, with Parker trailing after him uttering words he couldn't be bothered to process. This was his opportunity to catch up to her, to save her from the fate he couldn't rescue Colt or Embry from. Pushing his body faster and faster and even faster still, Ash couldn't give up. They rounded each twisting corner as they followed the hallway around. A glowing warmth was getting brighter, until finally they were face to face with two large, wooden doors that loomed over them.

Parker spun around, attempting to orient himself with their familiar surroundings.

"We're back in the foyer," he concluded, throwing his hands in the air and letting gravity pull them back down to his sides. "We lost her. Great, how did that happen?"

Slowly turning around, Ash's gaze followed the staircase up to the second floor, whose banister curved around a lofted portion of the level that hung over the main entrance.

"Parker," Ash whispered, voice trembling as he frantically tapped against his brother's arm. "Turn around."

An extension cord—one of *their* extension cords—tied around a bannister of the open second floor dangled Rhett's body down halfway to the first floor, swinging in slow, repetitive movements like a pendulum. Upside-down, legs in the air, the cord wrapped tightly around one leg while the other hung limply. Blood stained the front of her shirt, dripping down her face and pooling beneath her swaying head as her hair painted a gory mural on the floor. Dull, lifeless eyes stared back at them, her broken jaw crooked and inhuman.

Instantly drawn to the handful of gashes sliced across her torso, Parker's mouth remained agape in horror. It took a moment for his brain to process what his eyes were seeing.

"Oh my god," he gulped, practically tripping over himself to rush to Rhett's side. "Okay, okay, it's okay, we're gonna get you down," he whispered. Turning back to look at his brother, Parker pointed up to the second floor. "Ash, go up and cut her down!"

Ash stood frozen in place, fixed on the decaying expression of their fallen friend.

"She's gone," he said, head shaking. "Look at her face, man... She's long gone."

Finger's sliding against the slick, matted hair stuck to Rhett's neck, Parker felt for a pulse against her carotid artery. One second passed, then two, and then his face went as white as a sheet. His chest rose and fell at a quickened pace. Hands trembled. The vein in his neck hardened, threatening to pop at any moment and splatter everything in a bright green ectoplasmic goo.

"It could've been an accident," he said, looking upward at the bannister.

"An accident?" Ash criticized. "What, she tripped and fell on a bunch of knives before tying a rope to herself and jumping over the bannister? No way."

"Not helping!" Parker yelled, still cradling Rhett's head in his hands. "Just get her down, Ash!"

Jaw clenching indignantly, Ash headed for the stairs and ascended them two-at-a-time until he reached the landing of the second floor. Scanning the rotting floorboards, nothing appeared to be out of the ordinary. It looked as it had when they'd first roamed the halls, aside from some splintered wood bits that had broken off of the bannister from the friction of the rope rubbing against it. Fingers touched the cool metal of the blade in his pocket, and he pulled out the compact pocket knife and flipped it open.

As he sawed back and forth against the rope, the woven material began to break apart and shred into a sprinkling of dust that drifted through the air down toward Parker and Rhett.

The dead weight on the rope worked in their favor. By the time the blade was three quarters of the way through it, the remaining section snapped and Rhett's body fell through Parker's arms and thudded to the floor.

Parker's boots stepped across pieces of hair, a sand-like crunching sound accompanying every movement. Neither of them had noticed at the time, but Rhett's hair had been chopped off mid-shaft.

Images of Embry flashed through Ash's mind as he descended the stairs to find his brother crouched, inspecting Rhett's body as her broken limbs splayed out in awkward angles. The unusually angelic expression on her face was jarring, highlighting just how gone she truly was.

"This is strangely familiar," Parker remarked, moving bloody hair away from her neck to reveal three gashes striped down it. Grimacing at Ash, he sighed. "Colt and Embry had similar markings on their necks. I don't know what it means, but it's gotta be significant somehow."

"Or it's a result of bad aim by whoever attacked her," Ash countered.

"Your skepticism is showing, brother," Parker said as he looked down at Rhett's face one more time. "After everything we've seen tonight, I would've thought you'd have come around."

The truth was that Ash *was* coming around, and he was terrified by that fact.

Everything about their chosen career—traipsing around the country visiting long-forgotten places that had become fodder for gory local legends—had been designed to point out the flaws in the paranormal. Their job was to make others believe that what they were seeing was real, but if *they* succumbed to their own lies then what was the point of it all?

"Yeah, well, I guess some things never change."

Parker took a deep breath. "And some things do," he said, knees cracking as he rose to his feet. "We've gotta keep moving."

They roamed Crenshaw for over an hour, but each time they turned down what they thought was a familiar hallway, it would lead them somewhere they weren't expecting. A second floor staircase landed them back in the Headmaster's office, just as disheveled as it had been when they'd been in there earlier. Another hallway led to the bathroom where Colt's bloated corpse had been found. The doorway into a dormitory somehow now opened into the laundry facilities in the basement.

Eventually, sick of their continuous walking with nothing to show for it, Ash sighed and leaned against a wall. Parker kept walking, but turned around the moment he no longer heard the echoes of his brother's footsteps behind him.

"Come on," he insisted.

"No, man." Ash shook his head and slid down to the

floor with his knees bent. "I'm done walking around like a chicken with its head cut off." He gestured around them. "This isn't working."

"And your suggestion is to give up? How is that any better of a solution?"

In refusal to share a counterpoint, Ash's eyes closed indignantly.

A thumb and index finger dug into the corners of Parker's eyes as fire rose in the back of his throat and lashed out at his tongue.

"Ash, get up," Parker demanded.

"No," Ash replied without opening his eyes. "Not until we have an *actual* plan that might *actually* fucking work. Until then, you know where to find me." He held up two fingers in a peace-out move, his desire to move as high as his desire for a root canal.

Parker groaned, fists clenched to avoid ripping out his hair.

It was then that it hit him.

There was one thing that might get Ash up off of his ass.

Taking a deep breath, he interlaced his fingers and faced his younger brother. "Remember that show we used to watch with Colt?"

"Which one? We watched a lot of shit, Parks."

"*Supernatural,* that ghost hunter show that ran for ages. You remember the main characters, Sam and Dean?" Parker asked.

"Yeah, sure." Ash shrugged. "Why?"

"Do you remember how they'd get rid of a ghost if it was haunting somebody?"

"Digging up the bones and burning them."

"Yeah, and they'd salt the bones before they lit them on fire," Parker corrected. "I think that's what we need to do with Oliver's remains. That might be the only way to keep him from continuing to haunt this place."

A blank, expressionless stare spread across Ash's face. "So, your idea is to try something we saw on a television show ten years ago? Yeah, sure, that sounds brilliant," he muttered, the words muffling as his head dropped onto the crossed arms resting atop his knees.

"Come on," Parker nudged. "It's better than sitting here doing nothing with our thumbs up our asses. If it doesn't work, then we try something else."

Lifting his head, Ash blinked the sleep away from his eyes and sighed. "What's the point? We can't get out of the building anyway. Whatever this is has us trapped here. We're never getting out, it'll just keep making us get lost."

Groaning, Parker bent down to meet his brother's gaze. "Quit being a Debbie Downer," he said, extending a hand to help the other man up.

Despite the heaviness in his gut, and the petrifying fear that they wouldn't make it to sunrise alive, Ash apprehensively agreed and took Parker's hand.

They'd seemingly misplaced the third floor staircase, so circling the floor was their best chance at finding a way back down to the infirmary where they hoped to find Oliver's burial records. Assuming those hadn't been pilfered like so much of the institution's other belongings had at the time of its closure, it was their best bet for identifying his remains and using the Winchesters' famous method of ghost removal.

A distant door slam reverberated down the hallway and both Novaks froze instantly.

"You heard that?" Parker gulped.

Ash nodded, wordlessly, just as Parker's flashlight began to flicker.

"No, no, no," Parker groaned, slamming the flashlight against his palm in an effort to knock the batteries back into place. "Do. Not. Turn. Off!" As if on cue, the beam died just as he commanded it to remain on.

"Shit," Ash hissed.

Without the light, it was like being trapped in a cavern. Traces of moonlight slipped in through the cracks between the boards on the windows, but the two of them strained to see where they were going. A dark mass scuttered behind them, out of sight but still too close for comfort. Heavy footsteps followed shortly after, speeding up as they grew closer and closer.

"We've gotta move!" Parker uttered, wrapping a hand around his brother's arm and dragging him along at full speed.

Gravelly voices whispered after them, accompanying

the trampling footsteps that chased after them. Not a word of it was coherent, spoken in a hurried, twisted language all its own. The murmurs pursued them relentlessly, angry tonality asserting a rising anger through the nonsense verbiage.

As they sprinted down the winding hallway, Ash's legs began to weaken. Like running through water, each movement was slow and pulled him in every direction except forward. A warmth pooled in his feet, numbing them and filling his shoes with a sloshing pudding.

"This way," Parker pointed, yanking them both to the left.

Ash's head spun, his vision fogging as a daze flooded in like headlights.

"Thomething's mot wight," he slurred, mouth not cooperating as he struggled to keep up with Parker. His tongue was swelling fast, taking up more space in his mouth than there was to fill. "Thuh'th hathetheng thoo neee?" Heart racing faster and faster, Ash began to hyperventilate.

Parker shoved them both through a doorway, slamming it behind them and silencing the voices that were hounding them.

Breathing ragged, Ash felt his face with both clammy hands. His tongue no longer felt too large for his mouth, nor did he hear anyone on the other side of the door.

"What the fuck?" he whispered to himself.

"What were you saying back there?" Parker asked. His lungs were working overtime, too, and he leaned against a wall to collect himself.

"I..." Ash began, before stopping himself. Eyes flitting across the room, he realized where they were.

They were back on the fourth floor again.

Back in the Headmaster's office.

"We never found the stairs," Ash uttered, brain working overtime to make sense of the path they'd taken to arrive here. "We shouldn't be in here right now."

"We need to find a way out of here," Parker replied. "Look around for blueprints to the building, they've got to be kept in here somewhere."

"Blueprints to find what?" Ash asked.

"If we're going to get out of here, we have to find a way to the outside that isn't through a locked door," he explained. "Blueprints can show us how to get to the roof." A quick glance revealed the other man's hesitancy. "Roof access equals us going home. Sounds good? Okay, start looking for a lamp or something we can use to see."

Slowly, their squinted eyes traveled the room in tandem in search of a light source.

Then they both saw it.

CHAPTER THIRTY-SIX

The bookshelf didn't look as it had the last time they'd been in this room. While it still was filled with molding books and knick knacks, it didn't fit against the wall with the rest of the built-ins anymore. In fact, it concaved on one side, angled in the dark and creating a deep shadow that called to them.

"What is that?" Parker whispered, moving towards it while hugging the wall.

Ash followed, choosing to walk through the room, instead. He'd almost reached it when his foot kicked something, sending it skittering across the floor and into the side of the desk. Bending down, he crawled across the floor on all fours and felt around for what had been sent flying by the toe of his boot. Each time he laid down a hand, dirt and grime stuck to his palm like they'd been coated in maple syrup. Grimacing and letting out a disgusted groan, he kept going until finally he'd reached the prize.

Picking up the cool plastic, his fingers rubbed against elastic fabric. Holding it up, Ash held it up under a beam of moonlight where he could identify it.

A headlamp!

Hastily, he pulled it atop his head as a nimble finger turned it on.

"Whoa!" Parker yelled, shielding his face with his forearm as the turn of Ash's head sent the light's wattage directly into his retinas.

"Sorry. At least now we can properly see what's behind door number two."

"Hang on." Parker held out a hand, the other wrist-deep in a filing cabinet against the wall. "I think I found our map."

He pulled out a rolled-up set of tattered papers, tied around the center with a piece of twine. As Parker unfurled it, faded handwriting and straight lines of varying sizes littered the page. Ash peered over his brother's shoulder and, for the first time, the two of them realized just how large the building was.

"This place looked way smaller when I was viewing this on the computer," Parker mumbled, unsure what to look at first as he shuffled the pages until the fourth floor's blueprint was on top of the pile.

Rooms upon rooms were packed into each floor, and this one was no different. What *was* different, however, was the layout.

Parker pointed to their current location. "If this is where we are... and this is the weird hidden bookcase room," he glanced over his shoulder to ensure that the bookcase remained open, "then what's *this?*" Moving his finger, he indicated a space directly behind and above the Headmaster's office.

"Only one way to find out," Ash said, taking a deep breath.

The two of them strode toward the newly found door, with Parker a few steps behind and blinking rapidly to rid the spots from his field of vision. A faint breath of air escaped the crack between the hidden door and the rest of the shelving, its temperature quite a bit colder than the room they were standing in.

As Ash pressed the door inward, the hinges creaked loudly with every centimeter of movement.

"Be careful," Parker warned, watching his brother stick his head inside the opening to look around inside the space. "If you fall through the floor, we have no idea where you'll end up."

"Relax," Ash whispered back, venturing completely through the doorway. "It looks like some sort of... staging space? Reminds me of our old attic, but way smaller and totally empty."

The space was small, similarly sized to a walk-in closet one would find in modern homes. At the far back was a landing and a steep, narrow staircase that led up to somewhere that couldn't be seen from where Ash stood. As Parker crept in behind him and the two of them slowly made their way toward the stairs, the door slammed shut behind them and both men nearly jumped out of their skin.

Instinct took over as they reached for one another, knuckles pale white as both of their hands clenched the other's clothing as tightly as they could.

"I really hate this place," Ash muttered, letting go of Parker and refocusing his attention on the task at hand. "Let's go up there, it might lead to another way out."

Before even a syllable of argument could be uttered, he took off toward the stairs and climbed toward what he hoped was a fireman's pole or spiral slide that could carry them safely back down to the ground floor. Anything was better than wandering around until their legs finally gave out. The headlamp lit up a few feet in front of him, but as it dimmed the shadows near the walls crept around in silence. At the top of the stairs was a crawlspace, just wide enough for a human body to slide through (assuming they hadn't had a big lunch).

"Are you still claustrophobic?" Ash wagered, preparing to slide headfirst through the small opening.

"Uh huh," Parker mumbled, sweat already gathered along his hairline. "Just as claustrophobic as I was when we climbed through the ducting."

Ash chuckled. "Just try and... think about something else. Baby pigs in rain boots or something," he offered, pressing himself into a position where he could maneuver his way through.

Clenching his teeth, Parker swallowed hard as his nostrils flared. The taste of bile was slowly worming its way up his throat as he debated the pros and cons of following after Ash through what might as well have been Crenshaw

Castle's birth canal. Each movement forward resulted in pained groans and heaving breaths. The best he could do was cross his fingers that the tunnel was a short one.

"Have I mentioned," Parker huffed, "how much I hate small spaces?"

Ash laughed and his head hit the ceiling of the crawlspace, leading to a groan and momentary pause to rub the part of his head that he was sure would be bruised the next day. Without warning, a rotten odor spilled out from the crevices around them and Ash scrunched his nose in disgust.

"Ugh!" he spat. "What died in here?"

"If that was you ripping ass, I'm going to make you regret it the moment we're out of here," Parker groaned, glowering at the back of Ash's legs as he followed behind the other man.

The spoiled smell grew stronger the farther into the tunnel they went.

"Quit grabbing my foot, Parker," Ash called back. "I know it's dark in here, but back off a smidge."

"The hell are you talking about?"

"You're right on top of me, dude. Give me a little space so you aren't crowding me."

"Ash, I'm a good two feet behind you, I don't know what you're talking about."

Deciding it wasn't worth the argument, Ash dropped it and sighed forcefully. The two of them would continue arguing in furious circles if he chose this hill to die on, and it simply wasn't worth it.

Not when they were so close to getting out of this godforsaken place.

This time, Parker's elbow crunched down on his calf and Ash let out a painful yelp.

"Goddamn it, what did I just say?" he exploded.

"Ash... that wasn't me. I—*AAAGHHH!*" Parker's scream rang out through the small space as something dug its claws into his ankles.

Twisting as best he could to look back, all Ash could do from his position was to forge forward in order to turn around and help.

"Hold on, Parker!" he bellowed, forcing himself through as quickly as he could.

The sharp talons of whatever had a hold of Parker were sinking deeper into his flesh, curling around his bone and shredding the muscle. Heat rose in his chest and the sound of his own pain rang in his ears like a gong being struck over and over. Reaching ahead, Parker scraped for every inch of movement that he could manage. His nails dug into the wood, cutting his nail beds and splintering into his fingertips. Hot, sticky blood pooled into his cuticles as he scraped his way toward where his brother had disappeared.

A handful of feet ahead, Ash's head had poked out and into the opening of yet another room. This one was roughly the size of the Headmaster's office, but it was stacked with boxes and old furniture and items that likely hadn't seen the light of day in years. Falling to the floor inelegantly on his way out of the tunnel, Ash clambered to his feet and dove back in the other way to reach for Parker.

"Grab my hand!" Ash instructed, eyeing his brother near the end of the tunnel.

Pulling while Parker's bloody hands grabbed hold of Ash, they grunted and groaned until both were free and lying haphazardly on the dirty, creaking floor. Each of their chests rose and fell with haste, heartbeats thrumming in their ears and throbbing at their necks.

"What the hell was that?" Ash breathed.

Parker shook his head, though Ash couldn't see him do it. "No idea, but I really don't want to stay and find out."

CHAPTER THIRTY-SEVEN

After a moment, once they were certain that whatever had been in the crawl space wasn't going to jump out after them, the brothers sat up and looked to see where they'd found themselves now.

"Well this is a let down," Ash admitted, a bit disappointed. "After all that, I was expecting some kind of secret lair or something at least moderately interesting. This is just a bunch of old crap."

"I'm gonna try the windows on this side," Parker said as he figured out how to balance on his bleeding legs and pointed to the right.

Ash nodded, shaking the headlamp and wobbling the beam of light in wonky up-and-down motions. "I'll check these ones."

Of the four windows, not a single one budged behind the two-by-fours that had been nailed over them a dozen times each.

"If we can pull the boards off, we can break the glass and climb up to the roof," Parker suggested, before quickly rummaging around the boxes and sheet-covered furniture cluttering the room. "Do you see anything that might help?" he asked.

"Uhhhh," Ash drew out, surveying the room.

The room was packed full of stuff, some of which looked out of place in juxtaposition. There were tools and bed frames with a litany of straps attached, and items that looked like torture devices. If the medical staff at Crenshaw had been abusing its wards through medical experimentation, the evidence of their crimes might very well have been hiding in that room.

Goosebumps ran the length of Ash's arms as he shook the thoughts away to focus on the task at hand. Now wasn't the time to investigate the horrors done to the children in Crenshaw's care—at least not until they could save themselves and survive to tell the tale. Only then could they come back with police to cart away the horrors.

Ash stepped toward a pile of boxes and opened one. A cloud of dust exploded as it opened, flurrying in front of the headlamp's light and covering his face and the front of his shirt in microscopic muck. Heavy coughs and several deep clears of his throat later, his lungs were finally able to fill with air that didn't threaten to choke him out.

"Nothing in here," he coughed, shaking his head and awkwardly stepping toward another box.

This time, prepared for what might happen, Ash pulled the neckline of his shirt over his mouth and nose before popping it open and checking inside. A long section of braided rope was coiled in a figure-eight and knotted around itself.

"Found some rope," he called over to Parker, lifting it up and shining the headlamp on it. "It's not long enough to reach the ground from here, but it's something." Popping open another box, Ash found a box filled with folded white sheets. "There's a bunch of sheets, too. We could try tying them together and see if they'll be long enough."

"Perfect, I found a crowbar," Parker said, a proud grin across his face.

He strode over and grabbed the rope from Ash's hand, unwinding it before dropping it to the floor to work on the boarded-up window. Wedging the crowbar between two boards, Parker yanked down on it heavily until the force pulled the nails out of the frame. Repeating the action until he could see out into the pitch black Oregon wilderness, Parker used the edge of the tool to cut around the painted-over edge and carefully pried the single-pane window open. Despite its squealing and stuttering, the opening yawned widely as a breeze swept in that smelled of pine and freedom.

Swiveling back to his brother, Parker waved him over with an outstretched arm and four twitching fingers.

"Come here," he beckoned. "I need your light."

Ash had been so busy digging around in the boxes that he'd completely forgotten his brother was prying off the boards in the pitch dark. Careful to watch his step, he made his way to the window with the heap of sheets and shined the headlamp's beam down into Parker's hands as he tied the rope into knots and fixed one end to a hefty pipe that ran beneath the windowsill.

Tugging on it to ensure that it would bear weight, Parker slipped the rope through his hands until he reached the other end.

"Hold still," he warned, reaching to wrap it around Ash's waist.

"Whoa!" Ash backed up. "What are you doing?"

"You're going to rappel down," Parker answered, as if the question had been the stupidest one he'd heard all day.

"The hell I am," Ash huffed. "You can rappel down and I'll lower you."

Tilting his head, Parker stared blankly at his brother.

"First of all, you're not strong enough to lower me down. Second, I'm injured." He pointed to his leg, crimson stains bleeding through the denim. "If anybody's gonna be able to climb down and run for help, it's you. Not to mention, you've got the headlamp." Parker teasingly tapped the light atop Ash's head as a worried smile crept across his face.

Ash desperately wanted to argue, to refute his brother's logic, but his stomach rose into his throat as he realized Parker was right.

"I'm not leaving you here," he said with a defiant shake of his head.

"Good thing I'm not giving you a choice then," Parker rebutted, dipping his chin toward the pile of bedding at the other man's feet. "Start tying those sheets together."

Grabbing the makeshift rope with both hands, Ash

shook his head again. "No, you're going first. You said it yourself, you're injured. We're triaging this shit." Eyes locked onto Parker's, he refused to look away. "Either you go first or we'd both better get comfortable up here, because we'll be staying a while."

The staring contest between them didn't last long, interrupted by a sigh.

"Fine," Parker conceded. "But you'd better be right behind me."

A light chuckle slipped between Ash's lips. "Trust me, I'm not staying up here any longer than I have to."

Parker secured the length of rope tightly around his own waist while Ash got to work knotting the ends of each sheet together as quickly as he could. It was eerily silent in the attic—too silent. The lingering sense that they weren't alone up there hung in the air, electrically charged and full of violent possibilities.

Once he was finished, Ash removed the lamp from his own head and smoothed out his hair.

"Here," he said, attaching it to Parker and tightening the elastic straps to ensure it didn't fall off while he was hanging off the side of the building. "You're gonna need it."

Every bone in Ash's body knew that sending Parker out there first was the right call. All their lives, Parker had been the responsible one while Ash had been the screw-up. At the end of the day, Parker was the one that could save them. But even if he couldn't, he was the one who deserved to survive this nightmare. Ash hadn't been able to save Colt, or Embry, or even Rhett, but he was going to try his damnedest to save his brother from a similar fate—even if it was the last thing he ever did.

"You sure you'll be okay up here?" Parker asked, eyeing the other man carefully as he checked over the length of tied sheets.

Ash nodded. "I'll be fine. Don't worry, I'll follow right behind you once you're on the ground. Scout's honor," he swore, jokingly holding up Spock's famous tri-pronged handshape rather than the one commonly associated with the Boy Scouts of America.

"Uh huh," Parker begrudgingly mumbled, shifting toward the opening and carefully maneuvering himself out the window feet-first. The knotted bed sheets twisted in his grasp as he held onto them for balance, slowly putting more of his weight onto them as he climbed out onto the side of the building. Clinging to the edge with white knuckles, Parker glanced down and the ground telescoped in real time, like an optical illusion designed to simulate the effects of car sickness. "Oh fuck," he whispered, turning back to face the side of the building and inhale several large breaths.

"You good?" Ash asked, peering down at his brother from the safety of the attic.

"Peachy," Parker coughed, chest tight while fear clawed at his back teeth. "Let out some slack," he instructed.

Nodding, Ash loosened his grip on the length of the fabric, just enough to lower Parker down a foot or so.

Then, he heard the other man yell, "shit!"

Quickly wrapping the makeshift rope around a metal

pipe to retain the tension, Ash looked over the edge again. Parker was hanging there, the fingers of both hands holding on to the splintering floorboards for dear life. His face was pinched into a look of pain and panic.

"Parker!" Ash yelled, thrusting an arm into the chill night air for his brother to grab onto. "Are you alright?"

Looking up to respond, Parker's expression shifted. Terror glazed over in place of the fear, as though his fingers had ceased feeling anything at all.

"Ash!" Parker screamed. "Look out!"

But it was too late.

CHAPTER THIRTY-EIGHT

A contorted creature scurried on all its limbs toward Ash, mouth agape as it unleashed a screech that rivaled nails on a chalkboard in both pitch and volume. Like a spider, it crawled with speed and an intimidating size, a black mass moving through the dark so quickly that Ash's eyes struggled to keep up.

Then the light of the moon illuminated its body.

Rhett.

A sharp breath filled Ash's lungs and he wanted to hyperventilate. This was Colt all over again—his body tortured into a new, demonic form. Nothing about this thing was Rhett anymore, and yet it wore her face. As if pieced together by Leatherface himself, her flesh tore in places where it had stretched beyond its limit. Thick, blackened blood oozed all over like oil turned to sludge.

"Ash, run!" Parker yelled, slapping his brother's hand away.

Turning back, with terror in his eyes, Ash scrambled. "Not without you! Grab my hand!" He thrusted his hand toward the other man, but Rhett's corpse reached him before he could grab hold of Parker.

Carrot-sized fingers stretched out of a monstrous palm, razor-sharp nails tearing through the air like knives as they outstretched toward him. Ash shifted away from her a moment too late as Rhett lunged. He cried out in anguish, arms flailing in an attempt to keep her nails from slicing through his carotid artery. He ducks to miss one swipe of her arm, but the other follows right after and slams into the side of his head and sends his body careening into the wall with another blaring shriek.

Ash was thrown so hard that his limp body fell to the floor, extremities splayed like a discarded rag doll.

Eyes locked onto his unmoving brother's unconscious frame, Parker swallowed hard as his heartbeat pounded in his ears. It was now or never. Fight or flight. Yet, there he was, hanging over the edge of a broken windowsill with nothing to break his fall.

The evil overtaking Rhett's body led it forward with heavy, intentioned steps.

"Ash!" Parker shouted, hoping—to whatever cosmic force was listening—that the other man would jump up from his momentary slumber and save himself. "Get up!" He strained, the corners of his eyes blurring as they leaked. "Get the fuck up, Ash!"

Rhett's head swiveled toward Parker, her cold, dead, jet-black eyes boring holes straight through him as if he wasn't even there. She exhaled a putrid musk that wafted toward him, so disgustingly nauseating that Parker had to do a double-take to make sure it wasn't *actually* green in color.

"Ash!" He called out again, voice straining and shaking as his decomposing crewmate stalked toward him.

A guttural groan snaked out of her throat as her focus zeroed-in on Parker. Her hulking form seemed to shift in the darkness, changing shape with each passing minute like a kaleidoscope. The angles of her shoulders overextended, bones broken and shattered beneath the cracked patchwork of her skin. Everything about her appearance was wrong in the most tangible way.

Back down on all fours, Rhett's body twisted toward him, joints cracking and snapping as her hurried movements swiftly writhed towards him. In just a few steps, she was right in front of him. Snarling just a few inches from his face, the knife-like talons that had once been her fingernails were grazing against his cheek. Then one sliced through his flesh and a river of crimson liquid poured out and muddied his already filthy shirt.

Parker cried out in pain, using all of his strength to hold himself up as his weight pulling on the tied sheets slowly bent the pipe they were wrapped around.

He didn't have much time to make a move.

A haunting smile emerged across half of her face, revealing a mouthful of yellowed, fissured teeth. At least, Parker assumed they were teeth. Everything about her features was marred in some way, fractured by the unholy malevolence that had taken hold of her empty shell.

Trying one more time, Parker screamed for his brother. "Ash! Wake up!"

The words echoed in Ash's head as though he were in a tunnel, complete with fog and all. Groaning, he pushed himself up slowly until his knees were bent beneath himself for support.

Snarling, Rhett snapped an arm out at Parker and grabbed a fistful of fabric and flesh in one fell swoop. Amidst his screaming, he managed one final act of protection. If he could do only one thing for his brother now, it was to remove one less obstacle on his path to survival.

Ash blinked as he reoriented himself amongst the scattered light and violence. Only once his eyes were fully open did he realize what was happening.

"Parker, no!" He screamed, scrambling toward the open window.

"*Run!*" the other man instructed.

Then, without warning, Parker grimaced fiercely and set his jaw. Letting go of the sheets, his hands were now tightly gripping the tattered clothing that draped over Rhett's body. He kicked himself off of the side of the building and used his own weight as leverage to pull Rhett's body over the side with him. The sheets tied around the pipe were yanked loose, and they slipped through the air before following Parker and Rhett's bodies as they fell through the dark down to the rocky ground below.

"No!" Ash hoarsely wails, watching his brother's body disappear into the night below.

CHAPTER THIRTY-NINE

Fingers wrapping over the edge, Ash peered out in search of another way down. His vision was full of tears that had only halfway been wiped away with the back of his sleeve. In a matter of a few hours, he'd managed to lose the two closest people to him—Colt and Parker. Not only that, but he'd lost his entire friend group, their whole film crew, in the course of a single night.

And the night wasn't even over yet.

At this point, all he wanted was to curl up into a ball and pretend none of this was real.

But he couldn't.

From his position, there only seemed to be one potential way down: a broken window that hadn't been boarded up. Luckily for him, it was one floor below and roughly one expansive room over. Climbable, or at least worth attempting. That, or he'd have to get comfortable in the attic because he would be stuck there indefinitely. There was no way he was crawling back through the crawlspace that had led them there.

"You've got this," Ash whispered to himself, a shoddy attempt at a pep talk. Usually he was pretty good at instilling himself with confidence at the drop of a hat, but he was finding it tougher to manage while mourning his entire support system. "Do it for Parker," he said, taking a few deep breaths to regain control of his shaking hands.

Exhaling loudly, he rubbed his hands together and clapped before limbering up his shoulders with a swift shimmy.

Lifting himself out of the window, careful to avoid looking down for any sign of his brother's body, Ash pressed himself against the side of the building and found a handhold to grip as the toes of his shoes stepped along the edge of the building's brick ledge.

He could do this, Ash was sure of that.

It couldn't be much harder than when he'd climb trees as a kid, right?

Inch by inch, Ash slunk along the side of the building, taking the smallest breaths he could manage to keep his chest from rising too high. Just as he'd reached the halfway mark, a colony of bats surged toward him and swarmed the side of the building. Ash furiously tried to slap them away, but a few of them sunk their teeth into his neck and nicked his ears. He yelped in pain but kept moving forward, determined to escape the throng of creatures and deliver himself safely through the window below.

"Just a few more steps," Ash grunted, fingers in so much pain that his grip was weakening by the second.

Feeling the side of the window with his shoe, he felt around for the edge of the glass. The sharp edges were dull against the numbness growing at the ends of his fingers like gangrene. A slippery stickiness dripped down them, but a quick wipe against his pants was enough to retain his grip for the moment. Slithering down, he kicked his feet in and launched himself through the opening until he landed shoulder-first onto the dense wooden floor.

The wind was knocked out of him and he coughed up a mixture of inhaled dust and speckles of blood. Swallowing down whatever disgusting mixture remained in his mouth, Ash lifted himself to his feet. A sharp, familiar pain at Ash's side radiated across his torso. Pressing a few fingers into the soft bruises forming beneath the surface, the aching of a broken rib or two was confirmed.

Groaning, but unwilling to give it any further thought until he was safely outside the city limits of Hokisam, Ash inhaled a shallow breath and checked his surroundings.

Beds, at least half a dozen, lined the far wall, separated by thin moth-eaten curtains. A locked cabinet with a shattered glass panel at the front held a few sparse, labeled vials. In the corner, a desk had a dozen clipboards scattered across its surface.

This was the infirmary.

Clutching his side, Ash stepped toward the door slowly. Creaking echoed above him and he paused with bated breath. Footsteps shifted, clamoring together as at least half a dozen pairs of feet moved about. They stampeded across the upper floor and then ceased altogether. Standing there, in the silence, the hairs on the back of his neck rose.

Turning on his heel, Ash surveyed the room once more now that his eyes had adjusted to the darkness. The desk seemed the obvious place to start, the clipboards calling to him as possible clues. His mind wandered with possibilities of how Oliver was connected to it all, and the pieces started to fall into place.

"Oliver," Ash mused. "I know you're here somewhere," he murmured, his first conscious admission that the supernatural was, in fact, *real*. "But where?"

There was an answer to that question hidden somewhere within the walls of Crenshaw Castle, Ash could sense it deep within himself. Something wasn't right with this place, and there was a gnawing in the back of his mind that told him Oliver was at the center of it. There was just the matter of the *how* and the *why*.

Sifting through the paperwork rotting on the table, disembodied voices whispered through the chill air like a memory frozen in time. The words were hard to make out, but the voice was so young. So full of pain. It called out, agonizingly, the last few words clear as day.

"He can't do this to me!"

It was so loud that Ash spun around, heart racing, looking for who could've been in the room with him. The empty room stared back at him. A few still moments passed, and then the same voice spoke again, this time uttering the words so close to him that he could've sworn he felt someone's hot breath against his ear.

"*It isn't real.*"

CHAPTER FORTY

A sh stumbled backward into the desk and its metal legs squealed against the floor as it jerked forward. The weight shift aggravated his broken rib, sending another shockwave of agony pulsating through his body. He slammed his fist against the table and it rattled, masking the profanity that slipped between his lips as he bit down hard on the inside of his cheek.

"Oliver?" Ash sputtered, as if the voice had insinuated its identity. "What the fuck isn't real?"

This entire investigation had been a frustrating case study in what was real versus what was an illusion. There was no telling what was real anymore. The fact that a creepy voice from nowhere was inciting the question in the first place was reason enough for him to believe that it was all in his head. That, somehow, all of the time he'd spent inside this institution was driving him to the brink of his own sanity.

"WHAT ISN'T REAL?!" He demanded again to the empty room, his booming bellow echoing around the room like a bouncing rubber ball.

Bottled rage exploded as tears streamed down his face, erupting in a bout of destructive anger. Sliding his arms across the table, pain be damned, Ash shoved everything atop the desk to the floor. The desk itself was next, his adrenaline pumping as he flipped it over and yelled as loudly as he could. The curtains separating each infirmary bed were next. He yanked them down and threw them aside, then locked his eyes onto his next target: the drug cabinet.

Ash prepared to push it over, but to his surprise it didn't budge.

Surprise gave him pause, enough to pull him from his *Hulk*-like state of destruction.

Trying again, its unmovable status reasserted itself.

Sighing, Ash raked his fingers through his hair to get it out of his eyes. Crouching down, he examined the bottom of the cabinet. Screws twisted through the wood of the cabinet and secured it to the floor.

If there was ever something to hide, ensuring its security was of the ultimate importance.

The more he pulled on it, the less it seemed to move, and the more Ash's frustration grew. As he sat on the floor, staring at the cabinet, he turned Oliver's words over in his mind. At least, the words he assumed had been spoken by Oliver's disembodied voice. What had the voice meant by '*it's not real*'? And how did that apply to one specific thing rather than Ash's entire experience in this godforsaken place? Staring at the cabinet, he considered the fact that there was no reasonable motive to bolt the cabinet to the floor. It was already outfitted with a lock, and the room had likely been monitored at all times. What reason was left?

"It's not real," Ash whispered.

The back of the cabinet, he realized, was wallpapered with a strange pattern. Beyond that, though, the corners and one edge were starting to lift from age and the deterioration of the glue. Something shined at the corner of the lower shelf, but it was too small to see clearly. Climbing to his feet, Ash didn't take his eyes off of it as he stepped closer. Reaching for it, his fingers peeled at the corner of the paper.

"It's... not..." Ash reiterated, pulling at it until he revealed a hinge. "Real."

His eyes widened as he stretched back the paper until he reached the bottom of the upper shelf, which was attached to the back of the cabinet rather than secured to the sides like he was expecting. Upon further inspection, each shelf was reinforced against the back and hid inconspicuous gaps at the sides. It was an unusual construction for a cabinet, all things considered, but then again Ash wasn't a carpenter.

Using his knuckles, he rapped them against the back of the cabinet in several places until the final knock echoed to indicate a hollow space tucked behind it—a hollow space that shouldn't have existed behind a cabinet that was secured to a wall. Ash felt along the opposite edge until his fingers traced bubbles in the paper. Or rather, a latch masquerading as a blemish in the application.

The back side of the cabinet swung open the second it was unlatched, as though it had been waiting ages for the opportunity to welcome someone else into its secret hiding space. It stretched back further than Ash expected, likely expanding into a room next to the infirmary that had been walled off from the hallway to maintain its secrecy. A room hidden away from prying eyes, only visible to those who knew where to look.

Reaching into his pocket, Ash remembered he still had his lighter with him. It wasn't as useful as a flashlight, but it was better than nothing. Fingers fished around for the plastic lighter until he managed to pull it out, and his thumb swiped against the spark wheel. A tiny flame appeared, the light from which highlighted how little fluid was in the reservoir.

Grimacing, Ash knew he had to hurry and make it count.

Careful not to trip over the raised lip that jutted up from the bottom of the cabinet, he ducked down and climbed inside. The warmth of the light from the BIC in his hand reflected off of a myriad of shining surfaces, all glinting in the dark like the dusty stars of a long forgotten galaxy. The air was thick and rank, like stagnant water and rotting eggs. Fighting the urge to vomit, Ash pulled the neck of his shirt up over his mouth and nose and groaned with disgust.

An antique surgical table at the center of the small room shone in the orange light. Leather straps attached along either side draped down to the floor. This room was different from the infirmary. Menacing, even. The air vibrated against Ash's skin with a low hum that teased something sinister. Aside from his general discomfort with all things medical, there was something about an old school makeshift surgery room that didn't sit well with him. That and the fact it was hidden, as though whatever the room had been used for was so evil it shouldn't be seen by anyone other than the perpetrators of the acts themselves.

And their victims, of course.

Ash took a few steps around the room, looking for anything that might help him piece things together, and that's when he heard it.

The voice.

Oliver.

"No! No! No!"

A shrill scream rang through Ash's head and he raced to clamp his hands over his ears as if that might stop it. The flame extinguished as the lighter fell to the floor. The piercing cry was a bullet train slamming into his frontal cortex. He dropped to his knees in stabbing pain, squeezing his palms against the sides of his head forcefully as he yowled.

"You'll all pay for this," the voice whispered.

Then, as quickly as it had appeared, the pain vanished.

Slowly releasing his hands from his ears, Ash waited

hesitantly in case it returned. But it didn't. Instead, the room seemed to turn itself upside down and throw him around inside of it. It was as if gravity had malfunctioned. Everything in the room was immediately tossed across the room with dangerous speed, disrupted in a surge of chaos that lobbed metal surgical tools and medical instruments all over the place. A pair of scalpels slashed into Ash's limbs as surgical steel clamps slammed into the side of his head.

Landing on his side, broken ribs smashing into the ground, he yelped as agony flooded his body all over again.

"Fuck!" Ash yelled, the bitter taste of fury coating the back of his throat. "I'm so sick of this shit!" He picked up a pair of metal clamps and chucked them as hard as he could, thinking it would make him feel better.

It did, a little.

"What do you want?" He screamed into the void.

And then he saw it.

Sitting up abruptly, like he was being yanked forward by invisible strings, Ash's vision went white. As color faded back into view, the room he was in did, too.

Only, it wasn't the same.

Everything sparkled under the overhead light like it had been freshly cleaned. White-clad doctors and nurses milled huddled around and spoke in hushed voices as they prepared their instruments for whatever—or whoever—was coming. Ash stared in an attempt to memorize their faces, wishing Parker's eidetic memory was beside him for this strange hallucination. Even more, he wished Erick was there to console him after the string of losses chasing after him.

As he mulled that thought over, the hidden entrance door swung open and a woman entered. She cradled the upper half of a sleeping young boy, followed by a man who had the boy's ankles in his hands. As the man's face was illuminated from the shadows, Ash's stomach dropped through to his knees. It was a good thing they weren't able to perceive him, or else he'd have shat himself, too.

"Ah, Headmaster," one of the doctors crooned behind a cloth mask. "We've been waiting for you."

Headmaster Elwood assisted the woman in hoisting the child onto the surgical table and as they began to strap him down, Ash realized who the boy was... Elwood's son, Oliver Klein. Jaw on the floor, he stood to get a closer look. Oliver's angelic face twitched as they secured the leather straps with brass buckles. His eyes blinked open and the terrifying image of masked physicians encircling him caused immediate panic. He attempted to thrash against the restraints, but the attempt was futile.

"What are you doing to me?" Oliver screeched, breathing ragged and unsteady.

"Saving you from yourself, my boy," Elwood retorted gruffly. "I can't have you traipsing around the grounds like some Uranian sodomite perpetuating heinous acts against the others. You'll corrupt the rest of the children, and we can't have that. These devilish, homophile thoughts that have consumed you must be eradicated!" His voice boomed. "This evil, effeminate proclivity within you, ..." Elwood eyed his son up and down, a disappointed shimmer catching in the light. "It makes me sick," he finished, spitting out the final word like poison.

Turning to the doctor, the Headmaster nodded and then exited the room the same way he'd entered.

The light faded from Ash's eyes and he collapsed back onto the floor in a pile of his own limbs. The only movement for a solid minute was the rising and falling of his chest. As he woke from his daze, the fleeting memory of what he'd seen felt like a nightmare too real to forget.

The corners of his eyes stung with tears that were quickly wiped away by his dirty sleeves. If he'd thought his own father was a homophobic asshole, Headmaster Elwood's treatment of his son had proven that Luther Novak could be far worse.

Ash's stomach contents churned as he looked on, the sickening scene unfolding accompanied with Oliver's screams and a doctor ordering sedation by way of a comically large syringe. As the boy's objections were silenced, and he quietly slipped into a medicated slumber, the scene and everyone in it glitched like a bad video game and then zipped itself up and disappeared into the ether.

Once again, he was all alone in the dark, fumbling for his lighter that had spun out somewhere on the floor. Feeling around with his hands, Ash crawled on all fours while the fugue-like state of dizziness swirled around in his head like a burgeoning storm. The sound of cracking stone and falling rock echoed around him. Only a few feet from where he'd started, Ash's hand slipped into a sunken portion of the floor. Managing to catch himself, his hands carefully felt around the edges of the disintegrating floor, feeling the gaping hole in the stone floor grow in size before him. Careful not to fall inside, Ash's fingers stumbled over the plastic lighter and he scrambled to pick it up and ignite the flame. Illuminated, the cavernous hole seemed to go on forever, swallowing the light within it the deeper it went.

"We're the same, you and I," Oliver's voice crackled again. *"We'll never leave this place."*

There wasn't time for Ash to question what he thought he'd heard.

From the depths of the tunnel's shaft, a tentacle-like hand coiled out and wrapped itself around his hand like a python strangling its prey. The tighter it constricted its fingers, the more he resisted. Blackened nails dug into the soft flesh of his forearm and a grisly, pained groan slipped through through his gritted teeth.

Never leaving wasn't an option in Ash's mind.

He was going to get out of there, one way or another.

Feet kicking out in search of a point of leverage, Ash's attempts were futile. Instead, another hand crawled out of the hole and reached for him.

Then another.

And another.

Dozens of hands lunged for him, their elongated fingers carving into him like a rotating saw blade spinning at full speed. Each slice elicited agonizing pain, drowning him in his own screams. The longer he fought, the more the hands multiplied. Soon they were grasping at his ankles, compressing his legs and waist, and stretching up to his throat.

He could no longer resist.

As the phantom hands receded into the gaping pit, they dragged Ash along with them.

CHAPTER FORTY-ONE

A pulsating hum vibrated against Ash's cheek. Gently, at first, and then it grew stronger.

"Ash," a familiar voice cooed.

Eyes blinking open slowly, Ash became aware of just how far down he'd fallen—all while being terrified to look down at his own appendages. Every part of his body ached with the force of being run over by a Mack truck, crushed bones and all. Each time the rhythmic shudder rolled across the floor, Ash grimaced in anticipation for the wave of pain that accompanied it.

"Aaghh," he groaned, joints cracking as he rolled over onto his back.

At the edge of Ash's peripheral vision, something darted past him. Feeling for the lighter again, he sighed. In the heat of his kidnapping, it had been lost, and once again he was without any glow to keep at bay whatever might be hiding in the shadows.

"Who's there?" He asked, breaking a notorious horror movie rule: *never* ask 'who's there' when you're alone in the dark.

If you have to ask, chances are you're not alone.

As if taking a breath, everything creaked around him. The walls, the floor, every inch of the space Ash now found himself in. It exhaled and the dirt beneath Ash's body shifted. Scrambling to his knees, and backing up furiously, the movement turned into tunneling and it headed straight for him like a heat-seeking missile. Falling backwards onto his hands, Ash crab-walked as fast as he could until his back smacked into the wall.

The tunneling grew faster and faster, and then—

It disappeared.

Panicked breathing became the soundtrack to Ash's terror as he sat there, chest rising and falling as a bass drum thumped between his ears. His eyes were starting to adjust to the darkness now. A whistle swept through the air like a brief wind, interrupted by a deep groaning. The ground moved beneath him again, only this time something had risen from within it. The silhouette of curves and smooth edges lifted, and Ash strained his eyes to see through the dimly lit air of the space between him and whatever it was. As if sensing his struggle, a soft glow began to emanate from within the mass of tangled shapes.

Wagering a crawled step toward it despite his immense fear, Ash held his breath. The faint light illuminated what was now perceptible as a human skeleton. The remains were intact, though it was clear they were not recent.

Scrapes and fractures in the bone revealed a traumatic history, and the size of the figure seemed far too small to be that of an adult person. Ash reached out a hand to touch the remains, and as quickly as the thought had flashed into his head, his entire body stiffened with instant regret.

"Oh, fuck," he blurted out, retracting his hand so fast that he lost balance again, careening back and landing on his ass as a puff of air was forced out of his lungs.

An ice cold chill shot through his veins.

It was small. Too small to be the remains of an adult person, that much was obvious. As the glow began to pulsate and flicker, Ash's eyes were glued to the skeletal remains as if he expected them to rise from the dirt and lunge toward him. The longer he stared, the further the fear broiling in his stomach burned up into his throat. Until finally, it was gone, and with it went the remaining light. With nothing but the sound of his own breath to interrupt the stagnant silence, Ash's nerves were fraying at the edges like a worn afghan.

Staring into the dark, the heaviness of something lingering beside him grew.

Hot, snarling breath beat onto the side of Ash's face and down his neck. His spine stiffened as he cemented himself where he sat, afraid to move even a millimeter to glance in the direction of the heat's origin. Ears pricking at the soft sound of a light clicking, Ash's chest tightened like it had been wrapped in tight layers of plastic.

Click. Click. Click.

A flame ignited beside Ash's head.

The glowing orange flame originated from the lighter he'd dropped stories above, grasped within a scarred and bloody hand.

Eyes wide, they met those of the creature beside him—a pint-sized demonic presence that was eerily familiar in the worst way. Rotting, mottled flesh hung like curtains along greying bone. The stench of death wafted off what was left of its body, moving in waves toward Ash and invading his nostrils as though they were a new land to colonize. A high-pitched ringing slashed through the air, sending Ash's stomach dropping.

As he searched the crevices of his memory, it hit him.

"Oliver," Ash whispered. The name wormed its way out, pulled from his diaphragm unwillingly like a fish skewered by a line. "You're the one doing all of this, aren't you..." He managed, more of a statement than a question. Gulping at the fear in this throat, his raspy breaths quickened as he pushed his back into the wall of the crawlspace.

The creature's face contorted, revealing a handful of cracked Chiclets in shades of green and yellow beside bare gums and squirming maggots whose ivory bodies twisted and wiggled in the flickering of the flame.

But then it was gone.

The lighter went out, the only light in the tight space extinguished just as Ash was putting the pieces together. A pang of relief flooded his chest as the dark enveloped him again. Relief that he didn't have to look at that *thing* anymore. Relief that he could focus on the pounding of his heartbeat rather than Oliver's dead eyes staring into his soul. Something dropped beside him, and he tapped his fingers along the ground until they curled over the lighter and he shoved the device back into his pocket.

Best to hold onto that for safe keeping, he thought.

"I know it's been you," Ash whispered hoarsely into the pitch black. "What they did to you... it was fucked up. Completely fucked. I know that's why you're still here." Eyes unable to focus in the dark, Ash kept his head on a swivel as he looked from corner to corner. "Just tell me—"

Slim, bony fingers coiled around his throat as a heavy force lifted Ash off of the floor and shoved him against the wall. Clawing at the tightening digits crushing his esophagus, Ash gasped for air as he dangled in the air, feet barely grazing the dirt on the floor as he frantically kicked his legs. Hot breath coated the side of his face and he tried desperately—and unsuccessfully— to recoil away from it. Without warning, just as his vision was starting to tunnel, a series of images flashed across Ash's eyes like he was watching a familiar movie that he couldn't name.

A body, coarsely wrapped in dirty sheets.

Blood, everywhere. On the walls, on the floor, splattered across an antique physician's light overhead.

The closing of a door, and a padlock securing it shut.

As the last of the images faded to black, and the last of his consciousness was slipping from his fingers, the remaining ounce of air was knocked from Ash's lungs and the tightness around his throat dissipated. He fell to the ground and inhaled a puff of dust in a frantic play for oxygen. Erupting into a coughing fit, Ash crawled a few steps and then collapsed into a pile of his own arms and legs.

The images he'd seen hadn't been a coincidence. He was willing to bet every dollar in his six-figure bank account that his vision had been Oliver's doing—a way to show Ash what he wanted, or perhaps what he needed from him. Heartbeat battering his eardrums like the drumbeat of an Ice Nine Kills song, an ache began to form right behind his eye sockets like a burning metal rod had been thrust into his skull. A pained groan exited Ash's mouth through his parted lips, teeth gritted and nostrils flared.

Slamming a fist onto the ground, he took a deep breath in.

"Gotta get out of here," Ash whispered to himself. "Get the fuck up and find a way out." His body didn't seem to agree with that game plan. "Come on, Ash." The pep-talk wasn't working and it was fueling the fire under his ass. "Get up!"

The connection between his body and brain somehow reconnected and he was able to tuck his legs under himself to sit up on his knees. The injury to his leg was only getting worse, and it pulsated angrily with the pressure he was putting on it, but even that was no match for the swollen golf ball on his head that was temporarily sealed by a layer of crusty blood. He was a human blood bag being slowly drained of all that was keeping him alive.

Ash knew what he needed to do to get out alive.

In fact, he'd made a mental list of his next three steps:

Step One: Find a way out of this room.

Step Two: Locate the body Oliver had shown him and lay it to rest.

Step Three: Live to salvage what was left of their footage and dedicate that final episode of *Phantom Files* to Parker, Rhett, Embry, and Colt.

Crenshaw Castle was no longer simply a building abandoned in the Oregon forest, left alone to rot. Instead, it had been a dormant beast that became inhabited by the vengeful spirit of Oliver Klein. Whatever had remained of the boy's soul was threadbare by now, clouded by the smoke and brimstone burning eternal in the portal to hell that had opened beneath the grounds of the possessed institution.

The longer Ash thought about it, the more his status as the last man standing seemed a laughable tribute to his time as the *Phantom Files* frontman. All of the years he'd spent trying to convince their millions of viewers to believe in the paranormal—while remaining a skeptic himself—had delivered him to this very night, face-to-face with the fucked up spirit of a twentieth century kiddo who was now leading him toward a rotting corpse. The remains most likely belonged to the headmaster's son, Oliver, or at least that's what Ash was being led to believe.

It took longer than he would ever willingly admit to escape the crawlspace he'd been pulled into. Dirt crusted along every inch of his clothing, piling in his pockets and coating his skin. Several coughs crept into his throat and croaked out, the abrupt jostles exploding dust and specks of mold out into a spray from where they'd collected on his clothes and in his hair. Right about now Ash was cursing his own ego for believing he didn't still need the inhaler he refused to carry around. It hadn't made the asthma go away, but it did increase his confidence by a point or two. That wasn't worth the struggle to breathe that he was currently facing, but there was nothing he could do about that right now.

Instead, Ash was climbing through a pair of broken wooden boards into a room that didn't look like it was supposed to exist. If he'd been blessed with his brother's eidetic memory he might've remembered the layout of the building's blueprints to corroborate that theory, but he didn't need to—everything about this room felt... wrong.

The far wall was lined with mortuary cabinetry, each one numbered and featuring large metallic hinges and a hefty handle. The only furniture not attached to the walls was a singular item at the center of the room, catching Ash's interest as though it were under a spotlight. The flat surface was covered with a large sheet that was once presumably white but now carried decades old strains of bacteria and disease that had woven themselves into the moth-eaten fabric. Spots of black mold were spattered across walls and buried into the cracks in the baseboards. The stagnant air was musty, dank with mildew and clinging to his damp skin. The scents of old paper and decaying history were crawling into his pores, gnawing at his insides like the rats that chewed through the walls.

"So they did have a morgue," Ash whispered, sweat dripping down the side of his face.

It made sense to him that Crenshaw Castle would have a morgue on the premises, despite the lack of one on the building's blueprints. After all, the closest nearby town wanted nothing to do with Crenshaw's troubled youth. It was enough of an imposition that the reformatory was within a sniper's distance of Hokisam, but to allocate the city's resources to what many locals considered a 'drain on the state' was more than a slap to the face—it was a personal attack. In response, locals chose to turn their backs on the institution and those within its walls, which had obviously led Crenshaw's leadership to determine they needed increased self-sufficiency. A morgue was on the more sinister end of that spectrum, but a necessity nonetheless.

As Ash stepped toward the center of the small room, his fingers looped between folds in the sheet and he yanked it off with one quick sweep of his arm. A substantial steel table was revealed as the fabric drifted to the ground, its surface dull from years of use. There were channels along the sides that followed its gentle sloping all the way down to a drain.

The voice he dreaded wormed into his head once more.

That's how they drained the blood, slow and painful...

A quick convulsion rattled Ash's upper body, cricking his neck as more images flashed into his vision. White coats smeared with claret stains, their hands grasping instruments and scalpels over pallid flesh. A heart monitor slowing to an unnatural pace. Blood splashing over the edge of the table, the quantity too much for the table's channels to withstand.

Scarlet waves careening over the edge, each drop landing on the floor and cracking through the air like thunder.

Too much for the human body to lose all at once, a different voice echoed.

Ash threw up his hands to cover his ears, as if that would be enough to stop it. As though there was anything that could stop it. His eyes squinted shut so hard that they were watering, anguished tears streaming down his face.

"Stop it!" He screamed, falling to his knees.

Stripes of vermillion flowed down pale limbs as they flopped over the sides of the table. Sharp blades sliced as electric saws whirred to life. The snapping of bones echoed over and over. Bright lights eclipsed by blurry faces, masks obscuring half of their faces.

Then the hands and masked faces were bleeding into one another, melting like a roll of film on fire, until they were gone.

No blood, no people, just... nothing.

The once white-hot room went cold again, blanketed in jet-black.

Ash's mind was once again his own, void of any extraneous thought or image or anything Oliver was trying to plant inside his head.

Ash was alone with his thoughts again, but this time he didn't feel physically alone.

As he sat on the floor, contemplating the likelihood that he'd ever find a way out of this nightmare, a light flickered on. A fixture was hanging above the mortuary table, a subtle swing to its movement. It was the same physician's light that he'd seen in the vision Oliver had first shown him. It flickered again as he studied it, like a neon light in the front window of the local watering hole, beckoning him closer. Rising to his feet, Ash reached up to touch it and—

Tap-tap.

Ash inhaled sharply as his attention turned to the tapping sound emanating from across the room.

"Hello?" He asked, hoping there wouldn't be a response.

Gripping the light, Ash tilted it toward the sound, illuminating several rows of freezer boxes that lined the wall.

Most were unlocked or left ajar—except for one.

CHAPTER FORTY-TWO

W hether or not Ash actually *wanted* to find a dead body hiding within the vintage human popsicle storage drawer was a toss up, but for the sake of escaping Crenshaw with all of his limbs intact he secretly hoped he'd find something that had once had a heartbeat. Given that the door had remained locked all of these years, the odds were in his favor on that one.

Pockets of dust and rotten sawdust flitted down through the air and sprinkled the top of Ash's head. It clung to his filthy hair and sweaty brow, eventually fluttering across his eyelashes as though he were wandering through a snowstorm.

"Huh?" Ash muttered as his gaze shifted upward.

Floorboards overhead creaked and whimpered as something moved across them at a wicked pace, like a cluster of arachnids sloshing over and under one another toward their prey. Except that these sounds were utterly unnatural in every way. The spidery gesticulation was a whirlwind of weighted shifting and deranged grunting, the slapping of hands against walls alongside an unholy screeching.

It was *them*, Ash knew.

The bodies of his coworkers, his friends, his brother.

They were coming for him.

"Fuck," he whispered hoarsely, scrambling toward the locked freezer door. The hefty iron padlock was rusty, but it was still strong enough to keep Ash out despite how hard he yanked on it with every ounce of his bodyweight. "Open, goddammit!" Exhaling a ragged breath, Ash's focus shifted to his surroundings in search of something he could wield to sever the shackle.

Ash...

Ash?

Aaaaaaash...

ASH!

The voices had infiltrated again, but this time Oliver's wasn't one of them. First it was Rhett's in a slow, hushed whisper. Next was Embry's, a question in a raspy, throaty tone that was unlike anything he'd ever heard come out of her mouth. Then it was Colt's, singing his name melodically like he used to when they were kids playing hide and seek. The third was Parker's, coming through as though he was yelling for his younger brother's attention. Each one was just slightly off, as if they'd been recreated from a distorted recording. It was like they were manufactured just for him, to lull Ash into a false sense of security—or into the impossible belief that he could possibly get them back at the end of it all.

It was too late for that.

Curling his fingers into a fist, Ash slammed the side of it against the freezer door and yelled, "Back *off!*" A growl rose from the bowels of his chest, riding out the anger that had been brewing in his gut. Being hunted was one thing, but the taunting was the final straw.

Surveying the room, Ash locked onto a set of drawers at the edge of the overhead light's reach and he flew toward them with superhuman speed, yanking each drawer open one by one until a set of implements caught his eye. One in particular, a shiny hand-pump embalming instrument, looked sturdy. As he picked it up and turned it over in his hand, the weight of the cold metal smattered a satisfying snarl upon his face.

The way out was starting to shine like a light at the end of a long tunnel.

It took three smashes of the tool against the aging padlock before it broke free from the handle of the freezer door. It hurled to the floor, narrowly avoiding nicking Ash's foot in the process, and spun off into the corner where it disappeared.

Shaking a thought of where it'd gone from his head, Ash took a deep breath and grasped the freezer door's handle. This was it—the moment from his vision. Heart racing, he flung open the door and peered into the empty metal hole.

"What the fuck?" Ash frustratedly blurted out, his

eyebrows digging into the bridge of his nose. In disbelief of what he was seeing, he reached a hand in and patted it around, tapping atop a slide-out metal surface and discovering that, once again, there was nothing to be found.

Something skittered across the floor near his feet and Ash panicked, jerking his arm back and smacking his elbow hard on the lip of the drawer. Mouth agape, arm coiled against himself, Ash's face crumpled into a silent scream as stars spun in his field of vision. The pain vibrated up his arm and across his torso, ripping through him like a chainsaw on the highest setting.

The walls of the small room were buzzing, but Ash attributed that to his throbbing elbow.

He shouldn't have.

While he was busy nursing his injury, the space around him was dwindling. Each wall was moving, little by little, inch by inch. It was as if the building was inhaling and exhaling around him, like he was standing within Crenshaw's lungs—the James to its Giant Peach. Ash began to feel smaller than he had in a long time. Even smaller than Luther was capable of making him feel.

The five of them had wrongly assumed that this place was just like every other they'd visited—full of dust and nothing more—but now four of them had paid the price for their wrongful assumptions. What else had they been wrong about? Ash knew that Elwood's son was part of this, but perhaps his mistake had been in assuming that Oliver *wanted* his body to be found. Or that Oliver had been nothing more than a victim.

From where Ash was standing, he was a calculated hunter.

If I were the arbiter of this destruction, Ash realized, *then I wouldn't want anyone to find my body and rid me of this place forever. I'd want everyone who entered to suffer the way I did.* It wasn't the best way to spend eternity, but it would satisfy the bloodthirst. *Spending my eternity causing the same horror that I went through... that's true revenge,* he realized. The words rolled through his mind and his eyes grew wide.

Oh my god... He gulped.

It was the oldest trick in the book and they'd all fallen for it.

Like a pack of fucking amateurs.

The visions were a *trap.*

Ash pulled open every door he could find, scrambling through the labyrinthine hallways that seemed to stretch on with no end in sight. Miles and miles of creaking floors and yellowed peeling wallpaper passed by in a blur, his vision tunneling toward the glow that always seemed to be *just* ahead of him.

"Help!" He tried to scream, though the voice that squeaked out was hoarse and strained.

The end of the hallway finally appeared just as Ash's legs were beginning to wobble. He hadn't run this much in his entire life, but there wasn't much he wouldn't do at this point. Anything to get out of this place and never look back. A tingling sensation was climbing up his legs, now. A warning that he'd soon lose all ability to outrun what lived inside this house of horrors.

His only chance was to try and break through the front door, to use whatever he could find to pry it open. To do that, Ash realized, he'd have to find his way back to the foyer. The only problem was that there were far too many dead ends and moving parts in this house of horrors.

With that, the sole remaining—well, *living*—member of *Phantom Files* took the stairs two at a time towards the floor above. Each movement slipped an inch or so beneath the soles of his shoes, but Ash steeled his resolve and climbed harder. The slipping grew subtly wider, a few inches stretching across the width of the step. The rubber soles of his boots stuck a bit more each time it made contact with the tread, as though the wood had been coated in a honey-like substance.

Nearing the midway point toward the upper level, Ash's legs began to tremble. Then it spread up to his torso and then along his arms. Was this what it felt like to lose control of your body after who knew how many hours without food or water? Did hallucinations by dehydration include a bout of the shakes? Before the questions could settle too deeply into his mind, Ash felt the staircase railing vibrate under his grip. The wood splintered and cracked and Ash shoved himself toward the other side of the stairs, leaning onto the other railing in hopes that it would stay put.

This was definitely *not* a hallucination.

Paralyzed with fear, Ash could barely move his feet. It

was as though they'd been cased in cement, and were suddenly too heavy to lift even with the aid of both hands and every ounce of his strength.

A moment later, the center of the staircase began to squeal like a boiling tea kettle. Twisting and creaking, the wood split open and the entire wooden pathway burst into a cavernous, black hole that reeked of death. The sweet, putrid smell carried with it notes of decaying fish, rotting eggs, decomposing pumpkins, and heady mold as it wafted up into Ash's nostrils and begged for his insides to slosh around and spew everywhere in a disgusting offering. Instead, his lips remained tightly pressed together in hopes that he could keep his gag reflex in check.

Just then, the center of the stairs ripped open in an unholy roar. A deep chasm screamed below, the torturous sounds slithering over one another in the dark. Ash grimaced as his grip tightened on the railing at his back, not daring to take a step for fear that the wood might further snap and drop him to his death. From the depths of the dark abyss, it almost looked like something was... *moving?*

"What is that?" Ash whispered to no one.

Despite his fixation, his eyes couldn't focus on the movement. Against Ash's better judgment, he leaned forward to peer over the edge. Something was down there, that much he was sure of. Arm stretched out behind him, fingers still coiled against the railing and holding on for dear life, Ash tilted his chin forward as far as he could.

"Hello?" He called out, knowing damn well that you

were never supposed to acknowledge the creatures that lurked in the darkness.

"Hello, brother," a grisly, familiar voice snarled from the chasm.

Ash threw himself back against the railing, his spine straightening and fist clenching.

Reaching up from the depths of the open pit, an unhuman hand with sharp claws and burnt flesh dug into what remained of the rotting wooden staircase. A second hand followed suit, so charred that it appeared blackened with soot. The two limbs hoisted a monstrous creature that was wearing his brother, Parker, as a meatsuit. At each joint, Parker's body had exploded open and the creature's jagged flesh poured out in a mess of sharp points and matted hair. It wore Parker's face like a decrepit Halloween mask, torn open at the mouth and cheeks hanging limply beneath deep eye sockets. The lopsided grin it bore resembled anything but Parker.

A lump hardened in Ash's throat.

"You're not my brother," he managed.

The creature surveyed itself and gave a weak shrug.

"Close enough," it responded, its voice like sandpaper against Ash's eardrums.

Ash clenched his teeth so hard he thought they might crack right then and there. It took everything in him not to look away, to focus on the anger and channel it. Parker deserved better than to be worn by this creature like a dime-store costume that was four sizes too small.

"What do you want?" he screamed, eyes welling up with tears.

The creature's head tilted to one side as it stared back at Ash.

"Isn't it obvious?" Its voice multiplied in a shrill, gritty cacophony.

Ash swallowed but the lump only grew.

"We want *you*."

CHAPTER FORTY-THREE

U nlike every movie he'd ever seen where the victim gives the bad guy an opportunity to explain their motive in some bullshit monologue, Ash had no interest in sticking around. Instead, he turned and stumbled as quickly as he could down the crumbling staircase.

"No, no, no, no," he muttered hastily with every step.

This was *not* happening.

He was not about to be the sacrificial lamb to the slaughter for whatever royal 'we' had taken over his brother's body.

Absolutely fucking not.

"You can't run from us," the demonic voice called after him, bearing a mockingly sing-songy intonation. "We wove quite the web to bring you here."

"The fuck I can't," Ash retorted under his breath.

The further he ran, the more lost he became. Ash spun

in place in the middle of an unlit corridor, uncertain of which direction was the one that would lead him back to those exceedingly tall wooden doors at the front of the foyer. Eyes squinted as if that would aid him, Ash gave up and took off in a random direction.

"Aaaaaash," the voice rang out. This time it sounded exactly like Parker. "You're only delaying the inevitable!"

Out of breath and running out of time, Ash felt along the walls for another way up to the floor above. His memories were fuzzy now, and recalling anything from the building's blueprints was impossible.

"Goddammit, Parker," Ash groaned, voice cracking with a grieving ache. "You're the one with the fucking photographic memory. *You* can do this shit, not me." Why had it been him left to deal with this mess? Ash was capable of plenty, sure, but a demonic asshole parading around in the skin of his friends... That would've been beyond anyone's capabilities, right?

A sticky growl echoed down the hallway.

"I can smell you, Ashton!"

Ash's stomach dropped straight through him, tensing every muscle on its way down. As he sat there, chest rapidly rising and falling as his nerves got the better of him, Ash came to a grim realization. The longer he stayed in one place, the greater the chance that he'd be discovered and probably devoured by what awaited him down the long hallway. Unfortunately, the room he'd found himself in was pretty bare—even by *abandoned-for-decades* standards. There were no beds, no desks, nothing to indicate what the room's purpose had been once upon a time. But something at the edge of the floor caught his eye: deep scratches in the wooden flooring seemed to disappear into the wall.

Heavy footsteps thudded from the hallway behind Ash, growing closer and closer.

"Fuck it," Ash muttered, quickly crawling toward the scratched up floor.

His fingers traced the carved indentations, but he knew that there wasn't time to ruminate on what had caused them. For all Ash knew, the creature wearing his brother like a catsuit had been behind that, too.

"There is nowhere you can run, you know..." the voice cooed, this time sounding nothing like Parker's. "Your fate has already been determined. You're *mine.*"

A creaking groan echoed as it moved closer, paralyzing Ash in fear.

This was it.

Ash's palms banged against the wall repeatedly as he looked for a seam where the wall might break away and reveal a way out of here that didn't include going out the way he'd come in. With panic and fury, he mustered every ounce of strength that he had left in his exhausted frame. Just as the wall was starting to give, the door to the hallway burst open and flooded the room with a rancid stench.

Only, this time, it wasn't a perverted version of Parker that stood in front of him.

It was Teddy.

Ash's eyes widened as they sized up the sight of his former love. It had been years since he'd seen Teddy, because the other man had disappeared without a trace during their senior year of high school. Every facet of the life they'd imagined —going to college together, sharing a sunlit apartment filled with all the things they loved, even adopting a dog that could snuggle up to them at the end of a long day—was gone in an instant.

He'd never gotten over losing Teddy, but even worse, he'd never been able to mourn or get closure. Teddy had never been found alive and his remains were never discovered. It didn't help that Teddy's parents had died in a car accident a few years before he and Ash had met. As far as their local police department was concerned, he was simply another orphaned, queer runaway who wasn't worth their time and resources. They stopped looking for him almost as quickly as they'd started.

Yet, there he stood, looking exactly as Ash remembered him.

"H-how is this possible?" He stuttered, blood rushing like a river in his ears.

"Oh, Ashton," Teddy sighed. "How I've missed you."

Teddy strode toward him and then paused, kneeling to be at eye-level.

Ash scooted backward.

"You're not real," he said with certainty. "What are you?"

This was not Teddy. It couldn't be his sweet, lovable Teddy.

Another sigh escaped Teddy. "Y'know, I've been planning this reunion for a long time. Ten years, if I'm not mistaken." Slowly, he reached out and brushed his icy cold hand against Ash's leg. "I thought you'd be excited to see me. You used to be so thrilled to see this form."

Coiling away, Ash cringed at the other's touch. "You're not him," he insisted, squeezing his eyelids tightly shut. "You're not Teddy and this isn't real." It was his mantra now, the repetition an instinct now rather than a choice. "This isn't real, this isn't real, this isn't r—"

"Enough!" Teddy roared, lifting a finger to Ash's lips. His face had contorted, with sharp brows dipping down through the center of his face as jet-black eyes drilled forward.

The nail at the end of Teddy's finger had been replaced by a length claw that poked into the soft flesh of Ash's philtrum and drew blood. Despite the pain, Ash didn't dare wince. He knew that whatever this thing was, it could split him open before a single word tumbled out of his mouth.

"I'm trying to make this easy for you," Teddy said, setting his jaw. Every soft feature began to darken, slowly and then all at once. "We had a deal, and it's time for you to uphold your end. But we both know you've never been one to take the easy path, have you?"

Why was this thing playing with him?

What was it trying to gain?

"You know nothing about me," Ash spat back.

A soft chuckle slipped out from between Teddy's split, bloody lips. It grew and grew until it was unhinged, unnerving laughter like that of a supervillain from a kids' cartoon.

"What's so fucking funny?"

"You were never the brightest crayon in the box, but still... I expected more from you, Ash." Teddy's finger dragged across Ash's skin and down his cheek, leaving a bloody line in its wake.

Ash winced, a weak groan slipping out as Teddy's hand grasped his jaw in a vice-like grip. As much as he wanted to look away, his gaze was locked onto the dizzying dark portals that Teddy's had become.

"The Teddy that you know, *this one*," Teddy hissed, using his free hand to gesture down the length of his deformed shape. "He was just another vessel for me. I've been sticking around, in one form or another, to keep tabs on my investment. After all, you don't get to sell your soul and not make good on your end of the agreement."

A sadistic grin spread over Teddy's face, displaying jagged yellow stones in place of the perfect white teeth Ash remembered him having. Nothing about him was as he remembered, which only threw his head further into a dizzying spin.

"Me?" Ash questioned, the word mashed through Teddy's deathgrip on the lower half of his face.

Teddy pushed Ash's face away as he let go. "It's a shame to think about the time I wasted gaining your trust in this form, just for that fucking oaf to ruin it." An irritated burst of air shot through Teddy's nostrils. As if getting into character, Teddy pulled himself together. "Look at me, dwelling on the past," he chuckled. "You're here, and the plan worked, so I'll count that as a win in my little black book."

"Huh?" The quizzical sound slithered out of Ash before he could think about it. Whatever Teddy was talking about, he didn't have time to ponder it right now.

Rubbing along his surely bruised jaw, Ash stared at Teddy as a mix of apprehension, confusion, and anger brewed in his gut. All he wanted was to run, but Teddy's enlarged torso was entirely blocking the doorway. Darting his gaze toward the wall he'd been pounding on when Teddy caught up to him, Ash noticed that the wallpaper had begun to curl away from an edge that had once been invisible. Part of the wall was depressed, revealing that a hinge at the other end of the panel allowed it to swing open with enough force.

Returning his focus back to Teddy, Ash carefully positioned his body toward the panel.

"All's well that ends well, I suppose," Teddy said. "In the end, you're still where you belong. Right here, with me. *Forever.*"

"Not a chance," Ash muttered.

A moment later, his feet were slamming through the opening in the wall and breaking open a new way out. What awaited him on the other side was a mystery, but it had to be better than the freak show that was right in front of him. Teddy's villain monologue be damned, Ash leaned over and threw himself feet-first through the cavity.

CHAPTER FORTY-FOUR

Wincing in pain, teeth gritted, Ash counted four deep slices across his bicep. Teddy had attempted to catch him as he vanished through the gap in the wall, his claws out and ready to skewer him, but he'd been too late. Unfortunately for Ash, he hadn't gotten away unscathed.

Now, he was crouched in a space that was only a few feet tall. It was dusty, coated the inside of his nose and throat with every breath until he lifted his shirt over his face as a mask. Breaking into a coughing fit, Ash knew he couldn't stay there. He needed to find another trap door. Patting down his pockets, he found the lighter he'd stashed earlier.

"Solid work, Past Me," he congratulated himself, still coughing, as he lit the flame.

The tight crawl space illuminated in an orange, flickering glow. Dust swirled around the stagnant air, heat trapped with nowhere to go. Ash's heartbeat thrummed in his ears as the blood rushed to his head. He had to get out, and he had to get out *now*. In a flurry, Ash pounded on every inch of the walls around him. Moving from one corner all the way around, he shuffled from side-to-side. Just as Ash was starting to give up, the creak of a loose floorboard vibrated beneath his feet. Dropping to a squat, Ash dug his nails at the edges of the plank and lifted it out of place.

As a blanket of warm light washed over the interior of the cranny, its contents were on full display: a wad of bills in a money clip, a rusty key, and a couple of folded papers. Ash reached for the papers, which were now brown with age, and carefully opened them with one hand while the other held the lighter steady. Scanning each word to ensure he read it accurately, Ash deciphered the mix of typewritten text and smudged cursive scrawl.

"Oregon State Board of Health Certificate of Death on the Premises of Crenshaw Industrial Reformatory," Ash said, reading the title along the top of the first page.

An old photo was paperclipped to the upper corner, only it wasn't the kind of photograph that Ash expected to find attached to a death certificate. Rather, it looked like one that belonged in a frame on the living room wall of a family's home. Oliver, clad in a pair of Mary Janes, dark-colored trousers, and ivory sweater, stood in front of the looming figure of his father. Archibald Elwood's cold body language insinuated that the relationship between himself and his son was deeply fractured.

A sharp pain prodded Ash inside his chest as he studied

the image. Sighing dismissively, he turned to the second page. The document detailed the manner of Oliver's death, stating that his official cause of death had been acute hypoxia and that it had been ruled an accident. If what Ash had seen in his vision was true—and that was a *big* if—this otherwise perfectly healthy boy's death had been induced by a long list of experimental procedures and abusive tactics.

What Ash couldn't figure out, though, was what this stuff was doing hidden in the floorboards. Had someone stashed it there and forgotten about it? Perhaps it was part of the efforts made by Crenshaw's staff to cover their tracks. No death certificate, no body—

"The body," Ash whispered, an epiphany striking mid-thought.

Reaching down to pick up the rusted key, he turned it over in his hand.

"If I was trying to hide a body..." he mused. "I'd stash it somewhere no one would think to look..."

The real question was where could the boy have been hidden where it wouldn't have been uncovered already either during renovations by the Schuyler Foundation or someone else who decided to snoop around on the grounds. That was unlikely, considering that if they'd stumbled across a decomposed corpse it would've been headline news. Unless, of course, it was on the portion of the property that was sectioned off for the cemetery. A body in a cemetery wouldn't be unexpected, let alone newsworthy. It would be business as usual.

It was perfect.

Oliver's body had been hidden in plain sight all along.

Folding the paper back as quickly as he could, Ash shoved it and the key into the front pocket of his crusty pants. His clothes were so mottled with dirt and blood that he was simply grateful he couldn't smell himself. Even his hair was matting together, with some bits stuck to his scalp while others poked out wildly in all directions.

Gone was Ash's camera-ready appearance, taking with it his skepticism.

Armed to the teeth with nothing but a lighter and a key, he got to work going over every inch of the suffocating space with a fine-toothed comb. One hand with a death grip on the lighter while the other carefully pressed into the walls every which way, Ash knew there had to be a way out. But with every passing moment, the flame of determination threatened to fizzle out. That is, until a fingernail caught the edge of a wood panel and a chunk of it gave way, lodging underneath the keratin like a massive splinter.

Yanking his hand away, face twisted and contorted, an unholy howl wailed out of him.

"*Gaaahhh*-dammit!"

His fist slammed into the wall and echoed with the cracking of knuckles. Tears filled Ash's eyes as the last of the oxygen was sucked out of his lungs. Unfortunately, there was no time to dwell on injuries—no matter how much it throbbed or bled. It took a few quick, shallow breaths in and out before he worked up the strength to shove two grimey fingers in after the shard of wood. The moment he successfully pinched the splinter between his nails and pulled it out, his skin stained scarlet with the dribbling of fresh blood.

"I'm so sick of this shit," Ash grumbled, resorting to kicking the toe of his boot against the bottom of every plywood panel. "Fuck this fucking pla—"

A thunk preceded a muffled scratching as Ash's foot caught in the wood. Expecting to find a hole that led to another floor, he wrenched his leg free and crouched down to inspect the damage. The lighter's radiance didn't reveal a space between floors, as Ash had expected, but rather another wall that had been sealed in—and it featured a sunken lock that was almost as rusted as the key stowed in his pocket.

A wave of relief washed over him at the thought of finally having caught a break.

Grabbing the rough edge of the panel to keep himself steady, Ash kicked away more and more until he was certain he could squeeze through. Digging into the pocket with his swollen, bloody hand, the pain didn't even register anymore. His mind and body had more or less disconnected, everything operating separately as they conducted their siloed processes. All of the time spent in this building was taking its toll on him, from the way everything seemed to be its own shade of grey to the amount of sweat lingering on his forehead and drenching the back of his neck.

Tingling fingers fiddled with the key.

It slid into the lock and Ash gave it a quarter turn.

With bated breath, he waited for the soft metallic latch to give way.

Click.

Ash almost didn't hear it over the sound of his own heartbeat in his ears, but he did. He heard it and committed it to memory so that he could forever remember the sound that meant freedom. Glancing upward, he half-expected to see the creature coming after him. He hadn't been in there long, but the fact that Teddy—whoever, or *whatever*, that was—hadn't followed him down couldn't have been a good sign.

Throwing the door open, a biting breeze swept past and sent a chill down Ash's spine.

For the first time in hours, the air was fresh.

It smelled like Oregon Ash and Ponderosa Pine.

The tunnel took Ash down a winding path that eventually led to an old tool shed on the back of the property. Everything inside of it appeared undisturbed, as if it had been entirely forgotten despite the fact that there were docents and staff inside the institution's gates regularly. Cobwebs clung to corners and draped over a thick layer of dust coating every surface. Like a time capsule, this shed was frozen in time. It revealed remnants of decades past, of technology long forsaken and items belonging to those who had long since passed.

A small, rectangular window framed Ash's view of the adjacent cemetery through the cracks of its broken pane. Each headstone was a reminder of someone whose final days had been spent within the institution's walls. Children who would never again return to their homes or live normal lives with their families. In the end, they were just kids who had made mistakes.

Shifting his attention to the array of tools hanging on wall-mounted hooks, Ash considered his options and the fact that there were laws against digging up graves. While he wasn't sure what the punishment for that crime would entail, he was fairly certain it was probably a felony.

After a moment, he shrugged.

"Screw it," he said as he grabbed the handle of an old shovel.

As he pushed open the door to the tool shed, the bottom scraped along the wet mud until it built up into a mound and stuck in place. Whether it was the task of exhuming a body or the fact that he hadn't eaten in what felt like days, Ash's stomach was doing backflips and bubbling like a boiling pot. He was supposed to be approaching the finish line of a sprint, but instead he was on the verge of shitting himself mid-marathon.

The crisp night air enveloped him the moment the door swung open. He'd almost forgotten that it had rained earlier, but the soaking wet ground was a reminder that life outside had continued on even while all of the lives inside Crenshaw Castle had abruptly ended. Cold and wet, everything seemed a little more sad than it had when they'd first arrived.

Even now, Ash wasn't sure if what he was about to do would ensure his own survival. Nothing he'd done had saved the others, and it wasn't like he knew what he was doing. The plan in his head was built on something he'd seen on *Supernatural* with his brother, for fuck's sake. The longer he stood there, the more he contemplated all of the ways he could royally screw this up. The ways he'd already ruined so many relationships and messed up so many facets of his life. Was there even anything about him that was worth saving?

"*Aaaaaaaash,*" Teddy's melodic voice called in the wind.

It was so quiet that Ash was certain he'd hallucinated it.

But that would've been too easy.

Through gritted teeth, Ash whispered. "Go to hell."

Taking off through the mud, he headed toward the rows of haphazardly placed cemetery plots. Each headstone was vaguely different, a visual reminder of how long this institution had been standing. There were some from the sixties, others from the forties. Some from the turn of the century and even earlier. Each one was named and dated but otherwise devoid of personal details. With the light of the moon to read by, Ash studied each one briefly in search of the one that belonged to Oliver Klein.

Except that none of them did.

There was, however, a row of nameless headstones along the back. Each sported a different birth and death date, but only one shared a birthdate with Oliver Klein. Ash pulled the death certificate out of his pocket and unfolded it to check that that date aligned, as well. It did. That meant that this *was* Oliver's grave and that he'd been right—the boy's body had been buried in plain sight this whole time.

Tossing the paper, Ash jammed the shovel into the soft ground. Each movement became more furious as he continued to dig. Teddy had yet to reappear and that was unnerving. The constant suspicion weighed on his chest as he looked over his shoulder, desperate to dig until he reached the casket. His shoulders, biceps, elbows, forearms —everything ached with a torturous, burning heat. The edges of his vision were starting to fade, feathering out into darkness and tunneling with each passing minute.

As his balance wavered, the end of the shovel hit something dense and rigid. Ash climbed into the hole he'd dug and cleared away a light layer of dirt that revealed a pine box. A huff escaped him at the realization that even the Headmaster's son had been treated like nothing more than an inconvenience. They'd gotten what they needed from their test subject and then thrown him away like unidentified trash.

Maybe that's how Ash would be buried if Luther had his way.

Carefully, Ash wedged his fingers under the lid and pried the box open to reveal the bones of a petite corpse. He'd never seen a child's body in this state before. There were blood stains inside the casket and a dozen handprints on the inside of the lid. Whether the boy had been intentionally buried alive or if the staff had mistaken sedation for death, it was clear that his passing had been even more heartbreaking than Ash could've ever expected.

It was no wonder Oliver wanted revenge.

Reaching into his pocket, Ash felt around for the salt

packets he'd saved from the In-N-Out french fries he'd ordered in Roseburg on their way to Hokisam. He'd saved a few in case the food they were able to find out there in the middle-of-nowhere was bland and tasteless, but now they were going to be his lifesaver. If he could find them, that is. Mid-search, the ground beneath Ash's feet wobbled like an earthquake that only he could feel. Bending over, he carefully climbed out and laid onto the cool ground above. While he waited for the world to stop spinning, it only sped up. His heart rate skyrocketed and both hands became clammy, sticking to the inside of his pocket and all of its contents.

"*There you are,*" Teddy's disembodied voice returned.

Ash tried to look around, but his vision was too blurry and—

Leaning over, he vomited onto the patchy grass as the moonlight began to dim.

"No," Ash protested, bloody vomit running down his chin. "Nonono…"

"*Shhhhh,*" Teddy insisted. "*It'll all be over soon.*"

Tears streaming down his cheeks, Ash shook his head until everything went black.

CHAPTER FORTY-FIVE

R ays of marigold and honey washed over Crenshaw Castle as the sun rose over the eastern mountains. There were no chirping birds in the trees or flying through the sky. The frogs that normally inhabited the area were nowhere to be found. The crickets and cicadas had gone silent. The energy was thick and heavy, like a weighted blanket that had been overfilled and electrified.

Nothing was as it should've been.

A woman's shoes echoed as she stepped through the foyer. Her hair was graying, but perfectly coiffed and pinned. The blue sweater she was wearing sported a vintage brooch with small sapphires. Each step rang out like an alarm beep, pounding at the door of Ash's consciousness.

"You did wonderfully," she purred, patting the walls as if it were a pet.

"Mmm?" His eyes slowly fluttered open as he woke up to find himself on the floor.

When had he fallen asleep?

The last thing he could remember was being outside, the wet grass soaking his back as he laid on it. He remembered seeing a stream of lines above him, or at least he thought he did. Everything was filtered through a throbbing headache that he usually only woke up with after a night of intense drinking. He touched the side of his head and as a sharp pain exploded, he recoiled. Dried blood had flaked onto his fingertips and he remembered the pain. The details were fuzzy, but it was all coming back to him.

The footsteps drew closer and closer until Ash could see her blurry silhouette.

A few more steps and he could see her face.

It was Maura Barton.

"Maura," Ash coughed. "I'm so glad you're here."

A deeper cough transferred bloody phlegm to his palm, which he immediately wiped onto his pants. Glancing around, Ash realized he was not only back inside, but he was surrounded by the bodies of his crewmates. Colt, Embry, Rhett, and Parker all lay sprawled out on the floor in strange positions, haunting him with their grey skin and foggy eyes. Ash forced his eyes shut as he looked away from them, unable to face his failure to save them.

"Oh, Ashton," Maura whispered as she knelt beside him. She reached toward him and her thumb swept across the side of his head, just under the laceration. "I'm so glad to hear you say that."

Ash's relief turned into abject horror as a twisted grin appeared on Maura's face. Before he could react, her thumbnail was being jabbed into his wound as a searing, white-hot agony ripped through his body like a tornado and tore through his esophagus in an excruciating scream. Reaching up for her hand, an unnatural strength kept him from ceasing the torture.

As Maura's laugh grew louder and deeper, it became familiar.

Her soft, elderly features tightened and her jawline sharpened.

Curled grey hair was replaced by straight black tresses.

It wasn't Maura.

It was Teddy.

Horrified, Ash's eyes widened like saucers. Moving backward wasn't an option this time. Not only was he in too much pain to get up, but there was nowhere for him to go. Not now. The bodies of his friends and brother were watching him lose the battle with their cold, dead eyes.

"I told you we'd be here together, forever," Teddy smugly grinned. "That was a nice try, though. Too bad you left these in your jacket." A pair of salt packets appeared between Teddy's fingers as he taunted Ash.

Ash gritted his teeth.

"What?" Teddy prodded. "Nothing to say, hm? Come on, Ash, you know you want to."

The silence between them didn't last long.

Leaning forward, Teddy whispered beside Ash's ear.

"We're one in the same, you and I. Sons of industrious

men who would rather see their own children burn than accept them for who they are." Teddy leaned back, nostrils flaring. "My father was the kind of man who would rather watch the world burn than allow anyone he deemed 'less than' to have the same opportunities that he did. You of all people know what that can do to a person... or people. Don't you?"

A knot in Ash's throat wouldn't go down.

"We both know what really happened to your beloved," Teddy said, motioning to himself. He waited a beat, then did a throat-cutting gesture across his neck and tilted his head with his tongue out.

"Don't you dare." Ash clenched his fists until his nails threatened to slice open the cushiony flesh of his palms. "You took my friends from me. You killed my brother!"

"Everything has a price, Ash," he replied with a solemn face. "This place?" Teddy gestured to the expansive building around them. "It was borne of pain and greed and the evil of humanity. It's alive because of the sacrifices made by hundreds of children over more than a hundred years. There is no revolution without blood."

"Revolution?" Ash scoffed. "Fuck your revolution! You took my only family away from me!"

"Sometimes we have to do unsavory things to get others to see us." Teddy took a deep breath. "It was the only way to get you to see it my way. I had to radicalize you," he shrugged. "The irony—and this is the best part, so pay attention—is that, historically, the marginalized rarely come back with a vengeance. All we've ever asked for is to be treated equally, to be respected. But after years of being treated like trash, that picture has to change. Revenge is the only language that the oppressors understand. You get that, right?" With raised eyebrows, he waited a moment for Ash to nod along. "They see us as bugs to squash under the soles of their shoes, but we're not. We're a bear trap, lying in wait."

As much as Ash wanted to refute Teddy's claims and argue that it wasn't that simple, the anger pent up inside of him couldn't do it. He couldn't defend the people that had experimented on generations of queer people in broad daylight. There were so many examples—the AIDS epidemic, the pink triangles used during the Holocaust, the transgender bathroom bans and attacks on transgender athletes competing on women's sports teams at every level. The despicable, heinous acts done by those in power against those who have faced systemic oppression and the consistent litigation of their rights.

"Use that anger." A smile curled at the corner of Teddy's smirk. "That's why I chose you, to let it consume you. I could see that fire in your eyes. That grief you feel over the life you could've had, the one that you feel you *deserved*? That's the match. And there's enough gasoline to burn them all to ashes for taking it from you."

Teddy held out a hand for Ash to take in his.

"Time's up, Ash, but we're just getting started."

"Five, four, three, two..." The voice behind the camera counted down, entirely out of view in the shadows except for incrementally disappearing fingers on a floating hand.

A woman sits poised on a cushioned chair, her back refusing to rest against its fabric. Like a doll fresh out of its packaging, her perfectly coiffed blonde hair cascades down the front of her blazered shoulders, pin-straight and frizz-free. Her dramatic eye makeup follows the curves of her features, etched there into the marble of her cool flesh just above a rehearsed, plastic smile.

As the cameraman's final finger points directly at her, her eyes narrow at the teleprompter fixed just above its lens.

"Welcome back to STCL-7, your premiere news network serving the Greater St. Cloud area," she introduces. "I'm Tabitha Hunley, and tonight we have a very chilling story on tap." Leaning slightly forward with her shoulder, her tone lowers to entice the viewer before she delivers the goods. Tabitha turns to face her guest and the camera pans to follow her gaze.

Seated across from her is none other than Ash Novak.

Enveloped by an identical chair, a wide smile creeps across his face as he, too, acknowledges the camera. Unlike his interviewer, he's relaxed back in his seat with both hands clasped in his lap. The ends of his hair still fall across his face, but now it barely brushes his eyes. The brunt of it had been chopped, revealing a now cropped, textured style that no longer extends beyond his ears. Several intersecting lines have been tattooed behind his left ear, forming what appears to be an almost-triangle with curved lines and a Roman numeral five.

"Our guest this evening is Ash Novak, Host and Lead Investigator of the renowned television series *Phantom Files* on the TerraX Network. Last fall, Ash and his team visited Oregon's Crenshaw Industrial Reformatory to kickoff filming for their fifth season. Unfortunately, during filming there were a series of incidents that took the lives of four members of the *Phantom Files* crew: Colt Pereira, Embry Van Heerden, Rhett Broussard, and Parker Novak," she says, shifting between speaking to the camera and to Ash. "Thank you for being here, Ash."

"The pleasure is all mine," he croons with a nod, an eerie grin spreading like an oil slick across his face.

"I can only imagine the deep pain of losing your best friend, colleagues, *and* brother in less than twenty-four hours." Tabitha's head tilts with rehearsed sympathy, her lips pressed tightly together while her eyes show no sign of glistening with tears. "How are you holding up?"

Ash sighs, glancing down at his lap for a few calculated seconds before answering.

"It's been the worst pain I've ever dealt with," he says. "I never thought something like this would happen, and to be the sole survivor of it all—" He sniffles. "There's an immense guilt that weighs on me every day, and I can only hope that I bring honor to their memories by continuing the work we started together."

"What a wonderful tribute," Tabitha nods, glancing back toward the camera with a smile. "Can you tell our audience more about how you plan to continue that work?"

"Absolutely," Ash replies, adjusting in his chair. "In collaboration with TerraX Network, we'll be relaunching *Phantom Files* this fall. We'll be bringing a new team to your screens, and a renewed mission for season five: exploring locations tied to the greed and evil of humanity's history. Season five's premiere will start filming next month and will take place at the location that kicked this all into motion— Crenshaw Castle."

"That's incredible," Tabitha says. "Won't that be quite painful for you, though, visiting that place again after everything that's happened?"

Ash's eyes dim as they pierce into hers, hints of a knowing smile tugging at the corner of this mouth.

"Quite, yes," he answers. "But if there's anything I've learned since that fateful day, it's that pain is meant to be felt—in fact, it demands it. It's the consequence for the heinous acts perpetrated daily by those in power against the powerless." Ash sits up and leans forward, closing the gap between himself and Tabitha. "Historically, this has led to so much pain that it's burned itself into the walls of the places we called *haunted*. It's scorched the earth and marred the trees. In comparison to that, my pain feels... manageable."

At a loss for words, Tabitha blinks a couple of times through wide eyes.

"Well, I..." she starts, awkwardly, before fixing her face and correcting her vocal tone. "I'm so impressed by the depth of your thoughts on this, and I am sure that I can speak for our audience when I say that we can't wait to see what season five brings."

Turning to the camera, Ash's eyes flash black and his face—just for a moment—looks eerily like Teddy's. It happens so fast that the few people who see it assume it was some kind of visual hallucination.

"Thank you, Tabitha," he answers, his voice deeper this time with a sinister intonation. "We can't wait for you all to tune in to the premiere. Our new, revolutionized version of *Phantom Files* is guaranteed to *consume you*."

ACKNOWLEDGMENTS

As always, my first round of thanks goes to the people who were by my side cheering me on as I wrote this novel: my parents (all four of you), my fiancée, and every one of my family members who pushed me forward and shared their excitement about this project coming to fruition.

My amazing partner, Giavanna: you have believed in me so much throughout this project, and I will never be able to repay you for it. The unwavering faith and love that you've shared as I've spent hundreds of hours working on this will never be forgotten. I love you so much, Gigi.

Secondly, my friends—who have been equally loud and cheery, and who have shared their enthusiasm about this love letter to the queer community that I poured my heart into. It's been an honor to dive into history and create something that highlights the true horrors that queer people face everyday.

I also want to thank my writing friends that helped me critique this work and improve it immeasurably. My longtime critique partner and dear friend, Jessica Fowler, deserves all the thanks for every unhinged voice message and string of stressed-out texts about this book (and millions of other things). I'd also like to thank my other writing partners/friends: Darelle Cowley, Sophia Plavalaguna, and my fantastic beta reader, Kaylea Stoeltzing. I couldn't have finished this book without you.

To every reader who has ever picked up one of my books, shared it with a friend (or a stranger), talked about it on social media, or written a review—thank you. I appreciate each one of you so much, and it's your support that keeps me going. I hope that you enjoy this one just as much as my last novel, and that you'll be here for the next one, too. I couldn't do all of this without you!

Thank You for the Support & Best Wishes,

J. D. Mills

QUEER HISTORY RESOURCES

Check out the following resources to learn more about queer history:

Websites

- GLBT Historical Society, Museum & Archives External
- Lesbian Herstory Archives
- Digital Transgender Archive
- ONE National Gay & Lesbian Archives
- OutHistory
- History is Gay
- Rainbow History Project
- Actup Oral History Project
- Making Queer History Online Archive
- Invisible Histories Project

- Queer Zine Archive Project External
- The Archives of Lesbian Oral Testimony External
- African American AIDS Activism Oral History Project
- GLAA
- Lambda Literary External– Digital Culture of Metropolitan New York
- The ArQuives (Canada)
- LGBT Materials in the New York Public Library
- LGBTQ Collections University of South Florida
- The Australian Queer Archives (AQuA)
- Wisconsin LGBTQ History Project

Podcasts

- One from the Vaults
- Making Gay History
- History is Gay, Queer Serial
- Queer as Fact
- Closeted History

Books

- We Are Everywhere
- A Queer History of the United States

- Out for Good: The Struggle to Build a Gay Rights
- Movement in America
- Unspeakable: The Rise of the Gay and Lesbian Press in America
- Queering the Color Line: Race and the Invention of Homosexuality in American Culture
- Queer Indigenous Studies: Critical Interventions in Theory, Politics, and Literature
- And the Band Played On: Politics, People, and the AIDS Epidemic
- Queer Images: A History of Gay and Lesbian Film in America
- Odd Girls and Twilight Lovers: A History of Lesbian Life in 20th Century America
- Eating Fire: My Life as a Lesbian Avenger
- When Brooklyn Was Queer
- Stone Butch Blues
- Legendary Children: The First Decade of RuPaul's Drag Race and the Last Century of Queer Life

Open Access Journals

- Independent Voices: An Open Access Collection of an Alternative Press
- Gay and Lesbian Issues and Psychology Review

- Digital Library of Georgia Southern Voice Newspaper
- Lesbian, Gay, Bisexual, and Transgender Studies Commons
- Open Access LGBTQ+ Journals from Harrington Park Press

ABOUT THE AUTHOR

J. D. Mills is a Hard of Hearing, queer, Star Wars loving book nerd who currently resides in the Silver State. They love all things horror and thriller, is a proud supporter of the #DeafShelf.

This is their second novel, and their adult debut. You can learn more about their work by visiting: https://www.jdmillswrites.com/

Check Out Other Books by This Author
SECRETS DON'T STAY BURIED